# THE
# MONEY
# LOVERS

# THE
# MONEY
# LOVERS

## Timothy Watts

Special thanks to J. Mark Montgomery

Copyright © 1994 Timothy Watts
All rights reserved.

Published by
Soho Press, Inc.
853 Broadway
New York, NY 10003

Library of Congress Cataloging-in-Publication Data
Watts, Timothy, 1957–
The money lovers / Timothy Watts.
p.    cm.
ISBN 1–56947–035–9
1. Persian Gulf War, 1991 — Veterans — United States — Fiction.
2. Kidnapping — South Carolina — Beaufort — Fiction.   3. Extortion —
Beaufort — Fiction.   5. Beaufort (S.C.) — Fiction.   I. Title.
PS3573.A88M66   1994
813′.54 — dc20                                        93–41171
                                                          CIP

Manufactured in the United States

10   9   8   7   6   5   4   3   2   1

*For my brother Harvey*

# PROLOGUE

───────────

He was a stone cold killer.

It didn't matter that it had taken him fifty years to figure that one out. Because there it was. Inside of him—the way somebody else might enjoy gardening or cooking gourmet meals. Jesus, a talent. A hobby, maybe you could call it. Something that he didn't even know about until just recently but that already he was comfortable with.

He was sitting in a storage bin, one of those things that are lined up in rows like little garages and have pull-down doors. You could put your own lock on the door and be pretty damn sure nobody was going to ask what you were planning to keep in there. Sitting there, with a twelve-volt drop light hooked up to a brand new Sears Diehard battery—the thing sending just enough light so that he could see the man duct-taped to the chair in the middle of the room.

The whole place smelled like piss and if he wanted to he could walk on over to the bucket in the corner and count how many times the son of a bitch had crapped since he'd been locked up in here.

He'd been there for almost half an hour. Sitting without moving, knowing the taped man was aware of him—seeing him squirm every once in a while and make a few noises that sounded like some kind of animal caught in a trap. The man was wrapped like a goddamned mummy, with duct tape over his eyes and mouth, but all the same he knew he wasn't alone.

Now he got up, started to laugh softly while he walked over to the man in the chair. He began to talk quietly. Saying, "Hey, Larry—*Lawrence*—how you doin', man?" Being nice about it and then reaching down with one quick movement and ripping the duct tape off the man's eyes. Knowing it hurt like hell and getting a kick out of it.

He said, "Hey, whadda you think, you think that wife of yours . . . you think the bitch's gonna be smart? You think she's gonna get that money together—stay quiet about it—and then do what we tell her?" Putting his face down maybe two inches from the man in the chair. "You think she can do *that?*"

He watched Larry start to nod, trying to say yes. The son of a bitch rich motherfucker was begging now. Telling him with his eyes that, YES, the money would be paid. He tore off a new piece of duct tape and put it across Larry's eyes again and then stepped back to make sure the guy couldn't see.

He reached behind him to his belt—to where the .357 Magnum he carried was, pulled the piece out and started to stroke the man's face with it. Saying, "Sure she will, Larry. She's got to." Feeling

4

good all of a sudden because there was a lot of power involved here. Telling Larry, "But the thing is, see, maybe she won't." Nodding like Larry could see him and they were having a friendly discussion. "That's it right there, Lar'—the risk. The gamble. But that's what life is, a gamble. And where are we? We're in Atlantic City. Fucking Atlantic City. You're *supposed* to gamble in this town."

He put his pistol down, pulled out a straight razor, and then spoke into the stillness of the room. "Larry, you got to keep the faith, tell yourself that your wife'll come through. Because, see, think this thing through—ask yourself—what else can she do? You see what I'm saying?"

When he was done he walked back and sat down in the other chair, smiling at the bleeding, sobbing, mummy. He said, "Hey, Larry, you know what, I think you look better like that. I swear to God you do. I think its an improvement.

And then he started to laugh quietly to himself, realizing once again, with a feeling of awe, he *was* a killer. A stone fucking killer. Because no matter how you looked at it, no matter what happened, old Larry, sitting over there, tied up like a goddamned Thanksgiving turkey, old Larry had about three days to live.

# CHAPTER

# ONE

The goddamned pictures changed everything.

Katherine thought she was going to faint. She felt light-headed anyway because she'd had two drinks that morning. No, thinking about it, counting the quick one, the eye opener, it had been three. But it wasn't the alcohol that was doing it now. It was the pictures.

All of a sudden it occurred to her that she was forgetting to pull air into her lungs. Jesus, it was like she had forgotten how to breathe. She gulped at the air, swallowing it, panicking for a second. What if she really couldn't inhale? What if she passed out? Eventually she'd die. And Nicky would come walking in from the pool and find her lying there. With the pictures still in her hand.

She needed another drink.

. . .

She'd been down on the tennis court, practicing, with the ball machine she'd gotten for Christmas set up on the other side of the net. She could remember Christmas morning with Nicky beaming at her while she opened the present. Saying, "So what do you think?" All Katherine could do was smile and nod her head a little bit because otherwise he'd sulk. She had been polite about it, acted like it was okay. But that was all. It wasn't like she was gonna throw her arms around him, tell him what a great guy he was. She wasn't gonna give him that kind of satisfaction—not for a ball machine.

But this morning, before the mail came, she'd put on her tennis whites and lugged the thing down to the court. Put a load of balls into it and stood there, bouncing on her feet. A bit slow-footed maybe, hazy because of the drinks, but still, she gave it a try.

She had a lot of thoughts whipping around her brain while the machine spit balls at her. She stood with her weight on her back foot, moving a little, watching as the ball shot over the net. With her racket going back nice and easy, her wrist relaxed, stepping into it with a smooth motion. Somebody watching her, maybe they'd never seen her play when she was sober, they would have said she was pretty good. An athlete. But she could feel it, the alcohol in her blood, making her a tad slow. She'd try for one down the line, a winner, see it in her head, the way it would be if she was playing a game, but her racket would still be going back when she should have been swinging into the ball. She'd miss the shot by just a little bit, send it a couple of feet outside the line. The thing was, she was on the court, practicing. It wasn't like she was going to let it bother her.

She stepped a couple of feet to her right, so that the ball would come to her backhand and stood ready, waiting for the machine to pop another ball over the net. But it was getting too hot. She hit three more and then took a break, stepping around the balls lying on the court as she made her way to the table over by the gate in the fence.

She sat down facing the pool, saw her husband lounging there. From this far away he seemed like an overgrown kid with his hair messed up and the sun shining on his face. She realized, like she'd just thought of it, that Nicky never really even had to shave, he was that fair, that young looking. She remembered when she'd thought it was kind of cute, his being five years younger than she was. She didn't know what she thought of it now.

He had a phone in the crook of his neck, his hands moving as he talked. Usually he sat pretty still if he was having a conversation. He'd say the same thing a couple of times if he had to, until he was pretty sure the person he was talking to understood. But on the phone he couldn't keep his hands still.

Which, come to think of it, was peculiar, because when she'd met him, up in New York, what she'd first noticed about him was how in control he always seemed. She'd been impressed—not just by that, of course. There he was, a guy on his own, just a year or two out of the Wharton School and pulling down, what, close to half a million dollars that year, doing who knew what on The Street. It had scared the hell out of her at first, how perfect he was. The man she'd been waiting for.

Actually, she never had figured out what he did—could do—to make that much money at his age—except it involved always wearing a yellow Hermès tie, and red suspenders with a Turnbull & Asser striped shirt, and a double-breasted suit to the office when he went there, and an Armani jacket over blue jeans when he didn't.

She didn't know what he used to do when he drove that

pompous Bud Fordyce of Fordyce, Krauss, and Magee down to Atlantic City for some celebration, either. Or later, when Fordyce, Krauss, and Magee had broken up and he was out of a "job," and he went into it on his own.

He'd tried to explain it a couple of times, but what he'd called real estate syndication sounded more like gambling to her than business. So she hadn't been too surprised when Nicky quit that a year or so after they were married and told her they were moving back to Beaufort, where they bought this house.

Now they mostly just hung out here, or at the club, except for the hours Nicky spent on the phone. Or else Nicky would go somewhere by himself. He'd give her a kiss on the cheek, smelling like Scotch and bug spray—she couldn't think of him without thinking she smelled Off! Maybe he'd grab her—playing with her—and then he'd head out to his car, telling her he'd be back. Sometimes it would be hours, sometimes maybe even days. And when he came home he'd get right back on the phone, invite a lot of people over. Light his bug candles and spray the whole goddamn neighborhood with Raid and then have a party and sometimes even forget to tell her about it ahead of time.

Most days she'd sit around the house, work on her tennis, have a couple of cocktails—get a glow going at nine o'clock in the morning that she'd try to maintain throughout the day. And then go over to the club for a while, sit around and chat with the ladies—have a couple more drinks while she wondered what she was doing. The women she played with would tell her how good she looked, smiling at her and saying, Jesus, Kate, seriously, you've got legs I would kill for.

There were always enough women around to get a doubles match going, the women playing pretty well because they all had plenty of time to get good at it. And afterwards, they'd all go upstairs to the bar, drinking gin and tonic mostly, sometimes wine if it was early and there was a party that night. They'd sit there and talk about whoever wasn't around that day. When she was growing up in Beaufort she used to wonder what it was like to be rich—to hang around the club and gossip. Now the routine was starting to kill her, knowing some of these people. Not liking them much but still hanging around with them.

If she didn't go to the club then what she'd do sometimes, she'd call her friend Susie. Spend some time with her because Susie was different. She was funny, for one thing, which was more than Katherine could say about the women at the club. Susie wouldn't fit in there at all. She was younger and she didn't know enough to care one way or another what most people thought of her. She'd wear a skirt that barely covered her ass and four-inch heels, something that the women at the club would make remarks about if they ever saw it. Susie wasn't as polished as Katherine might've liked. She was sort of crude sometimes. But Katherine didn't usually let it bother her. They'd go shopping and Susie would make her laugh and go out of her way to be nice. Katherine thought maybe Susie looked up to her. The two of them would walk through the mall, or else stop for a couple of drinks somewhere. And Susie would point at a guy and make a crack like, "What do you think of that?" Men would look at Susie. Oh, they'd look at Katherine too, but give Susie a little more attention because, a lot of times, Susie would look back. Kidding around, but still, it was kind of fun to see.

Katherine took a sip of her drink and picked up her towel and wiped her face. She wanted to go swimming. The pool was right there. But if she went over she'd have to jump in and try to swim some laps with Nicky acting annoyed because she was breaking his concentration. He hated having her around when he was on the phone and nowadays if she pushed it even a little he'd start yelling. It made Katherine want to scream, walk on over to Nicky and grab him by the arm, ask him, What ever happened to just the two of us? You and me, it used to be fun but it isn't anymore.

And now she saw that Wesley was there by the pool too. Sitting off to one side, in the shade, in a leather jacket that looked like he'd been wearing it for years. He was a lot older than Nicky. She thought he was fifty-five, maybe even more. Sweating probably, with that stupid leather jacket on. She'd seen him the day before when it'd been even hotter and his face had been dripping and still he hadn't taken the coat off. Katherine thought maybe he was sick.

He'd been here all of five days and Katherine had already gotten tired of the sound of his voice. She couldn't figure him out. He'd sit up at the pool with Nicky for hours, or else, if they were eating, and Wesley was staying over for the meal, he'd take a bite of his food and then lean forward to hear what Nicky had to say. Hanging on every word. Smiling and nodding, like he was trying to sell Nicky a used car.

When Nicky had brought him home and introduced them she'd been playing tennis, and Nicky had waved her over, saying, "Katherine, this here is Wes-ley." Drawing the syllables out on purpose and then telling her, "We met up in Atlantic City, you remember me saying somethin' about him? We'll be seeing a lot of him here for a while because he's looking to buy some property."

The man had something wrong with one of his eyes. The left one was all right, but the right one was all screwed up, out of synch with the other one so that it seemed like he was looking past her. He had stared at her for a second and then said, "Hey, you're pretty good."

She didn't know what he was talking about until he told her, "On the tennis court, I saw you. I don't know, I've seen the pros on TV, Chris Evert, Martina—the other ladies, maybe they hit the ball a little harder than you, but the style, you got the same style as them."

It was strange, listening to him say it, because he was being nice. But the whole time, watching his face while he spoke, with that crazy eye, she could sense that something didn't fit. Like the nice tone of voice he was using was just that. He was being polite, making small talk, but watching to see what her reaction was going to be. She felt like turning away at first, walking back down to the court or else going past Wesley and Nicky to go on into the house but then she told herself she was being weird. So she made herself smile back at the man and thank him.

She got up out of her chair and started to pick up the tennis balls. Halfway through, she decided the hell with it, she just couldn't stand it. Out here on the tennis court, with the pool and a beautiful house behind it. Seeing it like she saw it the first time. How perfect it was, with landscapers coming in twice a week to keep everything nice. Somebody else, if they saw a place like this—woke up one morning, got out of bed, and the place was theirs—they'd think they'd gone to heaven. It was the way she felt when they'd first moved in, after they'd left New York.

Except that when she thought about it, realized what it was like, what it made her feel like—going to the club and to parties every other night, drinking way too much because everybody else did and it seemed lately that it was the only way she could get through the day, living here with Nicky day after day, not talking or doing anything else together so she might as well have been alone—she couldn't stand it anymore.

So she made up her mind. She was going to get out. Leave. It didn't matter how. She could get a lawyer of her own. Go through the phone book and just pick one. Wait until she was all ready and then tell Nicky, I want out. If it looked like it would work, if it scared Nicky enough, she'd give him one more chance. Let him find out she was serious and see if he would change. Become the man she thought she had married.

She'd been brooding about it, even raised it with Nicky a couple of times. Testing. He would come home late, maybe smelling of someone else's perfume, drunk and not caring much what she thought. And she'd throw it at him, tell him, "I'm going to divorce you." Watching his face to see if the words had any effect. He'd smile, still drunk, but with a look in his eye. He'd say something like, "Kate, you don't even want to think like that. You got no complaint. Lots of women, they're wishing they were in your shoes." She'd tell him, "Well, if that's the case, why don't you give me a divorce and marry somebody else."

And he'd smile even more. "Why would I want to do that? I got you."

The words sounded all right to her. Hearing them, it was what she thought she wanted him to say, something like that. But the way he said it, grinning, with his eyes sliding past her, thinking about something else already. She wasn't going to settle for that any longer.

She'd tried another tack once. Staring Nicky right in the eye she'd said, "Maybe what I'll do, I'll start talking to some of the people I know, people you're trying to do business with. You think I don't know what's going on? Maybe I'll tell them what you really have in mind with your lousy business deal, your island development. How would that be?"

He had just stood there, with a strange look on his face. Not smiling now at all. Giving it a full minute before he said anything and then telling her, quietly, "Hey, before—you and me—we were only talking. You're a little unhappy, maybe you want to kid around about divorce, play a game. That's one thing." Walking up to her and grabbing her arm hard, he put his face an inch away from hers, saying, "But don't think you can threaten me." Twisting her arm now so that she felt like crying out, it hurt that much. "Don't ever kid around about my business deals. I got the fucking IRS breathing down my neck, I got people I got to deal with. Don't make me have to worry about what you're up to. Don't add to my troubles. You understand?" Walking away before she could say anything else.

It had scared the hell out of her, the look he had given her. Because it was something she'd seen before. His face all scrunched up like that. She'd seen that same expression when somebody Nicky had to do business with or somebody who worked for him screwed up. Nicky'd get that way, not kidding around anymore, with his little-boy personality gone, and you could tell, whoever had pissed him off had better do something quick.

But now, walking inside and picking up the mail, she decided, the hell with *that*. It didn't matter that maybe he scared her sometimes. What she could do, she could do it quietly. Get it all set up. Hire a lawyer, have the papers ready to be served. And then she'd show him. Really get his attention. Let him be the one to be disappointed for once. He'd find out how serious she was. She'd like to hear what he had to say then.

She went through the stack of letters, thinking about it, almost happy. Coming to a big manila envelope finally. With her name on it and no return address. She wasn't even paying much attention as she ran her fingernail down the flap and reached inside. Thinking about divorcing her husband and then pulling the pictures out. No note, nothing but the pictures. Standing there, with her mind blank all of a sudden. Forgetting how to breathe because what were you supposed to do, you open an envelope and inside, what there was, there was a picture of you fucking some guy who didn't look much like your husband at all.

———

Jimmy Decker spent all day on Interstate 95, coming down from Quantico, headed towards Beaufort. He'd started early, driving the rented Ford south, past the battlefields—Fredericksburg and Petersburg—having to slow down a lot while the tourists made up their minds where they were going.

When he crossed the North Carolina state line he gave it some gas because the speed limit was sixty-five. He went past Fayetteville, pulling off at Exit 20, Lumberton, to refill the tank and get something to eat at a Burger King. He got out of the car and stretched, feeling a little uncomfortable because it was the first time in a while that he'd worn civilian clothes for more than a couple of hours at a time.

Getting out of the car and standing motionless for half a minute, he couldn't help it, measuring distances and feeling the wind on his face, knowing how he would compensate if he was there to take a shot—take somebody out from four hundred yards away. He looked down the road at an Econolodge maybe a quarter of a mile away. Letting his training take over. What would he do if it were an objective, if he had a target there? Sighting with his eyes to the office of the motel, the front door just a dot from this far away. But seeing it in his head the way it would look through a scope. A bit of a breeze, and he'd be shooting maybe ten degrees downhill. Smiling because it would be a cakewalk. He had to force it from his mind, try to forget it because it wasn't anything he was gonna have to think about ever again.

Walking up to the restaurant he caught a glimpse of himself in the glass door. A country boy with a T-shirt on, stubble on his cheeks, and his hair still a Marine Corps buzz. The first thing he was gonna do, now that he was out, he was gonna let his hair grow. Walking up to the Burger King and grinning because he wasn't wearing khakis anymore and wasn't going to ever again.

He spent some time looking at the pictures of the food above the counter, feeling his mouth start to water because he still had a craving for fast foods, hadn't been able to get over it in the week that he'd been back. He was accustomed to living on MREs that were maybe better field rations than they used to give you but still tasted like shit after you'd eaten nothing else for months.

The girl who took his order was a cute little thing, eighteen or so. She smiled at Jimmy, flirting, saying, with a nice-sounding accent, "Y'all enjoy it now." She looked at Jimmy a couple more times after he sat down, smiling at him again while he ate his french fries. He glanced out the window every once in a while, at the cars whipping by and at some of the locals driving around on the road that ran under the interstate. Carloads full of teenage boys, with Rebel license plates on the front of their cars and probably a case of beer in the back seat—having some fun on a Sunday afternoon.

When he left he tried to catch the girl's eye, thinking he'd say something just to be nice. But she was taking an order. He went out to his car and sat for a few minutes, lit a cigarette, and leaned back in his seat, grinning because there was nobody around to tell him what to do. He could smell the air, the heat, but not the same as on the Saudi desert. This heat had a different feel, the humidity maybe. It was something that he recognized.

When he pulled back onto 95 he started to fiddle with the radio, finally getting a station that played country music. It didn't interest him a whole lot, but he listened to it anyway, feeling okay about it because it matched the view out the window.

He started to see signs for South of the Border when he was still a hundred miles away. Every couple of miles there'd be one—PEDRO SAYS "CHILI TODAY/HOT TAMALE"—shit like that. It kept him occupied, reading the signs while he listened to the radio and got further away from Quantico with every minute.

When he got to South Carolina he watched the trees for Spanish moss, knowing it meant he was getting nearer, seeing more and more of it and some palmettos—the state tree—as he got closer to Beaufort. He saw a sign for Savannah, pointing south, drove through Wilson to Yemassee, and got off 95 and onto 17. He went a couple of miles down the road and then made the left onto 21, thinking that things looked a lot different the closer he got to town. He'd been away for a long time and there'd been quite a bit of building going on.

He drove through Beaufort slowly. The whole town was bigger, with a couple of car dealerships and some motels on the north end. And some mobile trailer parks where there used to be nothing but salt marsh. It wasn't just a Marine town now, with the air station to the north, Parris Island on the other side, and the naval hospital in between. It bothered him a little, gave him a feeling that he'd been away for longer than he had. But driving by the places that he remembered from growing up felt good. It was still his town. With some luck, he could relax and get his head together. He was back home.

Passing the big mall, where the Winn-Dixie and the movie theater were, he was trying to read the sign to see what movies were playing when a jeep coming up from his right ran the light and caught the rear panel of his rented Ford. He had a quick glimpse in the mirror of a woman behind the wheel, wearing sunglasses with long brown hair blowing in front of her face. And then he felt her car plow into his, the force of it knocking his hands off the wheel so that all he could do was sit there while the two cars slid to a halt.

He made sure he was all right and then opened his door and stepped onto the pavement. He could feel the impact still running through his body. Like when he'd been in Iraq, occasionally a shell would land close by—either the Iraqi gunners or someone from the Coalition forces screwing up. There'd be a tremendous *whoosh,* you could feel it coming, and then it would hit the ground—shake your teeth if it was close. And for a minute afterwards, with everybody checking themselves, making sure they were okay, you wouldn't move. You had to wait, come back to reality, before you took the next step.

He could see the woman in her jeep, looking around like she didn't know where she was. He walked over, leaned down next to her window, and said, "You okay?"

It took him a couple of seconds to realize she was swearing, shaking her head and saying, "Shit, shit . . ."

He reached down and touched her. "Hey . . ."

When she did look at him he didn't recognize her. Half-hidden behind beautiful long brown hair and sunglasses, she could've been anyone. Jimmy thought she was probably attractive, but had no hint that he might have seen her anywhere before.

Her eyes moved past him to his car and then she asked, "Are the cars all right?"

He stepped back and looked at the two vehicles, flung together like somebody had welded them like that. He shrugged. "They need some work but I guess they're drivable."

"Good." She started to dig in her purse.

He didn't know what she was doing until she pulled a wallet out and fished through it, saying, "Damn" a couple of times. And then she handed him her insurance card.

She told him, "Look, I know I ran the light, I know it wasn't your fault, but I'm late, I've got to be on Lady's Island"—she looked at her watch—"Jesus—ten minutes ago." She pointed at the cards in his hands. "I'll leave these with you, you call my insurance company, whatever you want to do. But I've got to get going."

She started her car and began to back away without waiting for him to answer. He had to step out of her way, saying, "Hey," as the two cars screeched apart.

He said it again. "Hey, wait a minute." Thinking, damn crazy woman—has an accident and takes off.

She said, "Just call my insurance company. I've really got to go. Please."

He saw her reach down and shift gears, heard the clunk of the transmission as she put it in drive, and then she was gone.

It wasn't until he was back in his own car, starting it up and turning in his seat to see what was behind him, that it struck him. There was something familiar about her. He didn't know what it was until he looked at the card in his hand. He saw the name and remembered. Katherine. A different last name, though—Kramer. Hell, she was probably married by now. But still, it had to be the same girl. Get rid of the sunglasses and he could see it. The same face. Like it had been only ten days since he'd seen her, but it had been, what, ten years. He looked back to the place where she'd been.

Katherine. Son of a bitch.

# CHAPTER

# TWO

===

Nicky said, "Watch this." Holding the shotgun like it was too heavy and then waiting for the pigeon to shoot up into the air. Yelling, "*Pull.*"

They were at Edgewater, Nicky's club, out past the golf course, where the skeet range was. There was a teenager, a kid named Eddie, working the skeet machine. He let the piece of clay go, and Nicky, already too late—aiming *at* the thing instead of in front of it—missed it by a fair amount. He shouted at Eddie, "Wait 'til I tell you, goddamn it."

Eddie said, "Maybe it's the gun, Mr. Kramer."

Nicky just looked at him like he was retarded. He said, "It ain't the goddamn gun. You know what this is"—holding the shotgun out while Eddie started to blush—"it's an Ithaca. That's what it is.

It's not something, you go to K Mart when they're having a special and you pick one up for a hundred bucks."

He looked at Wesley. "This is a custom-made gun—it fits my shoulder almost better than my arm."

Wesley thought Nicky looked like a fat little kid, bragging about his toys. His belly was hanging over his belt and he was wearing a T-shirt with a collar—a bear on it instead of an alligator. Like one of those college kids that Wesley used to serve drinks to back in Atlantic City. And every time Nicky took a shot at a clay pigeon he'd hand the shotgun to Eddie afterwards and then pick his drink up from where it sat on the ground. Stand there, an American sportsman, guzzling Scotch and bullshitting with Wesley.

Wesley wanted to tell Nicky, "Hey, man, you keep drinking like that, it ain't like your aim's gonna get any better." But he didn't really give a shit. Long as Nicky didn't point that Ithaca anywhere near him he could be kind of patient.

He'd been down here for five days now. He'd flown down from Atlantic City and rented a house out on St. Helena Island because he thought maybe this was gonna take a little while. Wesley had only met Nicky once before, about six months ago up in AC, both of them playing blackjack at Resorts International. Nicky would double down on twelves and thirteens even if the dealer had a strong up card. Wesley thought it was a dumb way to play until Nicky won ten grand in just under six hours. Wesley couldn't believe the man's luck and had stuck around to watch. Nicky had bought Wesley a drink afterwards, acting really calm about the money, which Wesley had to admit was as impressive as hell. Ten grand in a short afternoon and the man acted like it was no big deal.

So Wesley had gone with Nicky across the casino floor to the bar by the front of the building. The two of them, sipping Cuttys and watching the ocean and the people walking back and forth on the Boardwalk. Hearing the constant ringing of the slot machine bells behind them while Wesley thought about Nicky's luck and kissed the man's ass.

He kept calling him "Mr. Kramer" because Nicky seemed to like it even though it felt stupid, being twenty years older and calling this smooth-faced kid *Mr.* Kramer.

Nicky asked Wesley a lot of questions. He'd taken a sip of his Cutty and said, "Wesley, what kinda name is that?" So Wesley had to make a joke about it, saying, "It's mine. Wesley Hops, the name I was born with." Remembering how for the first ten years of his life he hadda take a lot of crap because of his name. Kids asking him, Hey, how far can Wesley hop? Until he got tired of it, and bigger too, and beat the hell out of some little fucker who said it once too often.

Nicky asked him about his eye too, which was rude as hell but which Wesley let him get away with. Nicky was like a little kid who couldn't control his curiosity. Coming right out with it: "Man, what the fuck is wrong with your eyes?" So Wesley had to explain that too. Keep his temper and tell Nicky that he'd been poked in the eye by his sister when he was a kid. Which was only half-true. He got poked in the eye, all right, but he wasn't a kid and he didn't have a sister. What'd happened was he had borrowed some money. Bet the Eagles in the '81 Super Bowl because who ever heard of a Wild Card team—which is what the Raiders were— going all the way. Watching it on TV, he'd seen the Eagles coming out, the looks on their faces tighter than a drum. And the Raiders—Jimmy Plunkett running onto the field looking like it was a warm-up game. Spring training. He could still picture it, seeing how loose the Raiders were and knowing it was over before it began.

He'd bet five thousand bucks against the point spread and afterwards he couldn't pay back the loan. He could still remember what it felt like, the needle going in while two guys held his arms. And afterwards, wanting to get a gun and do something, walking downtown every week to pay his loan. Cause the thing was, they take your eye, that was one thing. But you still had to pay the money.

They had sat in the casino lounge for over an hour, bullshitting, with Nicky acting like they were best friends and telling Wesley, "Hey, you ever come south—come on down to my stretch of the country—you-all look me up."

Wesley had thought maybe he was full of shit. Thought all Nicky was doing was bragging, trying to impress Wesley and maybe the waitress too, because Nicky would talk a little bit louder every time she came over to their table. Nicky told Wesley how he could take some money, say that ten grand he had just won, for instance, invest it, pull some kind of scam, and turn it into a lot more, while Wesley wondered if there was any way he could separate Nicky from his cash—maybe take him for a walk someplace quiet and hit him on the back of the head. But then he started to wonder, what if . . . just what if the guy wasn't full of shit?

So Wesley had kept Nicky in mind. Running football pools during the day and then tending bar at some dive until two in the morning. Playing blackjack at the casinos and hearing Nicky's voice every once in a while in his head while he waited for his chance to make some kind of score. Not knowing for sure what it was gonna be until the thing fell in his lap practically. Watching TV one night, some stupid movie, a miniseries that was supposed to be true about some jerk who had kidnapped a guy. And gotten caught. Wesley had looked at the screen while he drank a six-pack of Budweiser and wondered how come the guy, if he was gonna go to all that trouble, how come he'd been so stupid about it? The man kidnaps somebody—gets away with it basically—and then goes out and spends all that money when he hadda figure it was marked. Wesley went to work the next day with the idea still in his head, mulling it over and realizing that he probably could do it better.

Looking at Nicky now, Wesley was thinking, what the fuck kind of businessman is this? Out here at the country club, on a day when maybe they could be getting some things done, playing with his shotgun. Nicky had said, right when Wesley had arrived and told him about the big score he wanted to invest—giving him the same smile that Wesley remembered from the casino—"See, it's going to seem like we aren't doing anything at first, like all we're doing is sitting around. But what you got to do, if you're gonna put a business deal together, you got to be patient about it. Give it a little time."

But it had been nearly a week now. So Wesley was gonna give Nicky a quick peek at all that money in the gym bag he was carrying, see if that wouldn't get Nicky's mind back on what they were supposed to be doing. He was tired of standing here holding it while Nicky made all that fucking noise with his gun, so he opened the bag and held it where Nicky could see it, almost smiling because the man leaned so far forward to get a better view that he almost fell over. And then Wesley zipped the bag shut.

Nicky licked his lips and said, "So you had, what, a good night at the tables?"

"I got lucky I guess, Mr. Kramer." He was waiting for Nicky to say something else but Nicky didn't ask any questions so he went on. "See, I could walk around all the time, keep this bag by my side, but it starts to be a pain in the ass after a while."

"And you don't want to put it in the bank?"

"No, see, you do that, first of all, what're you gonna get nowadays, three and a half percent, something like that?"

"And besides, somebody's gonna want to know where you got it," Nicky added.

"Uh-huh."

"You'd have to think about taxes, whatever?"

"Yeah, what I had in mind was different. I figured, this money's here, why give any of it away? I can just use it, maybe turn it into more money, like you were talking about before back up in Atlantic City."

And then Nicky, looking serious all of a sudden, said, "I think I know just what we're gonna do with that bag of yours. We're going to buy an island. And then we'll develop it and get rich."

And Wesley put an expression on his face like he thought Nicky was a fucking genius. "Hey, see that, Mr. Kramer, that's why I came down."

Nicky held the shotgun out, asking Wesley did he want to give it a try. The man acted like it was some kind of big deal to let Wesley have the gun. He said, "It's not hard. All you got to do is point and shoot."

Wesley was tempted. Take that pump gun away from Mr. Nicky Kramer and show him how to do it. The guy was getting drunk enough now so that the weight of the shotgun was making him sway. But he shook his head. "I don't think so, Mr. Kramer. I think what we should do, maybe we should give this a rest. You can drive me past this island. Or, hey, you could show me the plans, let me see what this thing looks like on paper."

"Shit . . . we can do this anytime. You want to do something else, we can do that instead."

"You wanna explain this deal to me? How the whole thing is gonna work?"

"Yeah, we could do that. You want to do that? We'll go back to the house. I got all the paperwork up there. Plus, we could swing by the island on the way. Take a look at our investment."

Wesley said, "Why don't we do that, man. You got this great idea, a way to take money and make more money. Why don't you show me what it is?"

Nicky told him, "Hey, that makes sense."

Wesley nodded. "I'll tell you, it beats shooting pieces of clay."

———

Jimmy Decker went out to Katherine's house about six hours after the accident. It was a nice feeling, driving through Beaufort again after all these years. He passed a lot of places where he'd spent time as a kid. And it felt like he had all the time in the world, time to get reacquainted with the town.

He figured Katherine was in such a rush to get wherever she had to go—maybe she was running errands—that she was probably through by now. He had to ask once, stop at an Exxon station to get directions, but after that it was easy. Go back out 21, past Gardens Corner to where 21 ran into 17. Take the left and then a right onto Cotton Hall Road. Past the big plantation on the right, maybe a quarter of a mile further on and there it was.

It was hotter than hell out. He could smell the ocean, the salt marsh at least. The tide was all the way out and as he drove over the salt creeks he could see tons of fiddler crabs scurrying across the mud. He used to go out there and catch bucketfuls of them and then take them out to the docks and fish the pilings for sheepshead.

He drove through stone pillars and then up a long driveway, thinking, Jesus, if he had the correct address then Katherine had to be doing all right. Married to a rich man. A doctor, lawyer, somebody like that.

The place was huge. One of those old southern mansions with white pillars out front and hundred-year-old oak trees draped with Spanish moss lining the driveway that made you think you were driving through a tunnel.

It crossed his mind, what was he doing? Returning her card and if it turned out that he became friends with her and her husband, maybe that was all right too. Telling himself it didn't have anything to do with just wanting to see her again.

He parked the car next to the banged-up Jeep Cherokee that Katherine had been driving that morning and then walked to the front door and rang the bell, looking around the front lawn until he heard the door open.

When he turned and saw Wesley just inside the door, he grinned and said, "I know you're not the butler." He was thinking what he should've done, he should've mailed the card back.

Wesley said, "I was walking by, I hear the doorbell ring, and I figured I'd see who was there." Then he just stood there.

An older guy. Almost as tall as Jimmy, like he'd go five eleven in his bare feet. But not too good looking. Not healthy. Something wrong with one of his eyes. Wearing a leather jacket over his shirt. Jimmy was wondering, was this Katherine's husband? They wouldn't make a very likely couple. This man wasn't the kind of guy that you'd figure to own a place like this.

Jimmy finally said, "I got in an accident today."

"Everybody all right?" The man acted concerned but, still, he was checking Jimmy out. Jimmy could feel it.

He said, "Yeah, everybody's fine. Only, the person involved, the other person besides me, she was in a rush and only gave me her insurance card. Told me to contact her later."

Wesley said, "Uh-huh." He stepped out onto the front step and looked past Jimmy. "See, the wagon there, what is that, a Jeep?"

"A Jeep Cherokee," Jimmy said.

"Yeah, well, that thing there, it looks like maybe it hit something recently."

"That's the one."

"Yeah?"

Jimmy told him, "Hey, you know what—I'm getting the feeling you don't give a fuck what happened to the car."

"Ain't my car."

"No, I didn't think so."

Wesley held the door open so Jimmy could enter. "Ain't my house either, man. What you want to do, you want to see Mrs. Kramer."

Wesley led Jimmy through the house. "She's playing tennis," he said. "Got her husband out on the court and is whippin' his ass."

Jimmy said, "Yeah?" Picturing Katherine on the court, coming up with a vague idea of what she would look like, the image a little confused because he could see her face as it had been earlier that day, but the rest of her was kind of hazy, mixed up with what he remembered of her from ten years before.

The house opened up, once you got inside the door, into a big front room, with the ceiling going up two stories above Jimmy's head and a wide staircase, carpeted, on one side. Wesley led Jimmy into what looked like a living room. There was a big Oriental rug on the floor and a piano in one corner against a wall lined with bookcases.

Jimmy said, "This place reminds me of my own house. It needs a little work, of course. But if you sunk a few grand into it, maybe got the piano tuned, it would come close."

"Well, you know how it is, some people, they don't keep up appearances."

They walked on through the living room and out a pair of French doors onto a flagstone terrace. Jimmy could hear the sound of someone hitting a tennis ball. Below the terrace, maybe fifty feet away, was a pool, and beyond that, the tennis court. The other man walked over to a table and sat down. Jimmy stood there for a minute. Looking around, seeing some gardens on the side of the terrace, with a guy bending over to pull weeds. There was a hedge that ran the length of the terrace on the other side and over towards the driveway, where there was a clear space, someone had trimmed the bushes to look like animals—a lion and something that looked like a horse. He looked over at Wesley and said, "Jesus."

"Yeah, I know." He waited a second and then said, "That's them."

Jimmy could see a man and a woman playing. The man, in his late twenties, had curly blond hair. A little heavy, with a potbelly. He was wearing a white outfit. The woman had on a short white skirt and a white polo shirt with a collar. Same woman. Katherine. But she looked different in the tennis outfit, younger than she had that afternoon.

Jimmy watched her husband serve. He threw the ball up, stepped into it, and sent it weakly over the net. The woman hit it cleanly, with a lot of topspin. Put it low over the net to the other side of the court for a winner. The man swore.

Jimmy turned to Wesley and said, "He footfaults."

"Yeah, everybody knows that. But nobody ever says anything to him."

"Why not?"

"Man, it's his court."

Katherine was serving now. Jimmy stared at her legs as she stretched to reach the ball—seeing a hint of ass cheek, white bloomers under her skirt. He decided she looked terrific in a tennis outfit. Relaxed. Like she was concentrating pretty hard but having fun with it too. Every time she hit the ball he could hear her grunt. He liked the sound of it, liked the way she put a lot into it.

The man on the other side of the table asked him, "You like a beer, something like that?"

"A beer would be fine."

Wesley got up and Jimmy turned back to watch Katherine and her husband. Katherine said something, leaned towards her husband and smiled—kidding him maybe because she'd won. But then her husband made some kind of remark—Jimmy couldn't hear what it was—and the smile left her face. She stood there, with her shoulders slumped, not having fun anymore. Staring at her husband as he put a towel around his shoulders and started to walk slowly up the hill towards Jimmy.

Wesley came back, put a glass and a bottle of Heineken's in front of Jimmy, and sat down. "He lose?"

Jimmy nodded and Wesley said, "He always does."

Jimmy asked, "What about you?"

"What do you mean?"

"You work for him?"

"No, I don't *work* for him. I'm down here for a visit."

"Social thing?"

"I got some business interests around here. So what I do, instead of coming down, maybe get a place at a motel, which would drive me nuts after a couple of days, I rent a place out on one of the islands."

"Yeah, I can see where that would be better."

"Uh-huh. What about you?"

"What do you mean?"

Wesley said, "It ain't any of my business, but I get the feeling you just made it into town."

"I was overseas."

"Yeah? I'd say, what, Marines?"

Jimmy smiled. "See, I thought I was hiding it."

"You in the Gulf?"

"Uh-huh." He was waiting for the man to say something else but instead Wesley's gaze slid past him. Jimmy turned in his seat and saw Katherine's husband about ten feet away, still sweating from the tennis, staring at them.

Nicky said, "Hey, Wesley, you invite a friend?"

Wesley stood up and said, "Mr. Kramer . . . ," surprising Jimmy because his whole attitude changed. He spoke to Katherine's husband like he was afraid of offending him. Pointing back to Jimmy, he said, "This is . . ." He nodded at Jimmy.

"Jimmy Decker." He walked over to shake Nicky's sweaty hand. Seeing him from close up, hearing him breathe, Jimmy was surprised again because the man looked a lot younger than he would've expected. Shorter too.

Nicky was looking at Jimmy, his eyes pinched halfway shut from looking into the sunlight. "I know you?"

"I met your wife. We had an accident. . . ." He didn't know what else to say because Nicky was already shouting down the hill, "Kate, you have company. You want to come on over and tell me who he is?"

He was being an asshole about it. Jimmy thought he already knew what kind of guy Nicky was. The kind of guy who didn't like losing at tennis, had to say something shitty to his wife about it and then go ahead and be rude if somebody dropped by that he didn't know. A real young guy to own a place like this too. Unless he'd inherited it.

Wesley was still behind them, sitting at the table again. Jimmy stepped away from Kramer so that he was a little closer to Katherine. She was only about ten feet away now. He couldn't help staring at her. Thinking, Jesus, she's all grown up.

She was a year younger than he was but not just out of high school any longer. Mature now, with a woman's body. He thought she looked beautiful, standing there, in her tennis whites, with the sun beaming down on her and the pool in the background. She was looking at him, ignoring her husband. He thought that she was going to say something. Give him a smile, step forward and say, Jesus, it *is* you. But there was nothing in her face except vague curiosity.

Finally she said, "The accident. God, I almost forgot."

He felt kind of stupid, because he thought she was at least gonna recognize him. Coming here after ten years and what did he expect? She was gonna run into his arms, maybe right in front of her husband, and say, what, I've been waiting for you? Shit.

"I've brought your insurance card back," he told her.

She said to her husband, "This is the man I told you about. I hit his car." She looked at Jimmy. "You didn't have to do that."

Nicky said, "You could've mailed it. It would have saved you a trip out here." But not saying it to be nice. More like it was a pain in the ass that Jimmy had come by.

Katherine added, "You didn't have to go to all that trouble. But I appreciate it."

"Yeah, well, it's a rented car so it's already insured. I may as well just use that, save you the trouble."

Nicky said, "Now that's all right then. You want to do that, it's probably best."

Katherine said, "You're sure? I mean it *was* my fault."

"Bullshit." Nicky took a step forward, reached out to the table, and grabbed Jimmy's beer. He took a big gulp and then said, "Nobody's at fault. That's why they have no-fault insurance. You're better off handling it through your own insurance company."

Remembering what kind of girl Katherine used to be and now seeing her, married to this prick and having to stand there while the guy acted like a jerk, Jimmy wanted to tell the guy to go fuck himself. But all he said was, "Yeah, that's what I thought. I figured, hell, it's not even my car, you know, so why get worked up."

Nobody else acted like they wanted the conversation to continue. Nicky had begun to walk away. Jimmy felt foolish. So he told Katherine, "Well, I was out this way anyway," not sure why he was lying.

He reached into his shirt pocket for her insurance card and set it on the table. And then he said, "Well, I guess maybe we'll both be a little more careful on the road." Wanting to say more, maybe yell at her, ask her, How come you don't know who I am?

# CHAPTER

# THREE

N icky came back to the pool half an hour later wearing a navy
linen jacket, a tattersall shirt with an ascot, white slacks, and
loafers with no socks. He walked up to where Katherine was
lying on a beach chair by the side of the pool. He was breathing
deeply, his face turning a little red. He reached into his jacket
pocket and pulled out some suntan lotion. She could see the label.
It was level 45. God. It was getting cloudy, not even that bright out,
and he was putting level 45 on. She watched him.

He folded his jacket, tucked his ascot in the pocket, removed his
shirt and hung it on the side of the chair next to him. Then he
started smearing the cream all over his shoulders and chest. He
put some on his belly too, having to use a lot because he'd put on
weight since they got married. Looking at him, sometimes she
couldn't believe it, because when they'd met he'd been one of the

best-looking guys she'd ever seen. Younger than she was, which had seemed like a nice change because she'd dated a lot of older guys and he seemed somehow more alive. More fun to be with back then. He'd looked almost like a male model—the blond, preppy kind from a J. Crew catalog. Somebody you'd turn around and watch walk by. Always grinning, being friendly to everybody. And what had happened? He'd sat around, drinking up all his money, spending all his time cooking up deals on the phone, and he'd ended up carrying around a bowling ball for a stomach. Sometimes she wanted to grab him by the ears and ask him, "What happened? What'd you do to the man I married?"

He was putting too much sunblock on so that there were white streaks of lotion all over his face and neck. And who wore an ascot anymore? She wanted to ask him, Is somebody having a contest? Best-dressed poolside lounger? You in the top ten?

He hated the sun, never went anywhere without his sunblock. He said it gave him a rash, sitting out in the sun for too long. It sure as hell didn't make him tan. Or sunburned either. He'd spend a little while in the sun, playing golf, whatever, and if he didn't put sunblock on he'd come to her later and show her a patch on his neck or shoulders, point to it and say, See, I should've worn sunblock.

At first she used to look, trying to find the spot on his skin that was bothering him. But she never could. She thought maybe it was the mix. He kept putting the lotion on and then spraying himself with bug spray. Maybe when the two combined it bothered his skin. But it wasn't as if it would do any good to tell him that.

She'd tell him, I don't see it, thinking, Come on, Nicky, because she wanted him to do more than act like a kid who had stepped on a bee. But all he'd do, he'd get mad and point to it again, the skin no different from anywhere else on his body. Point and say, Jesus,

35

you don't see it, right there, it's all red. I got a rash. And then he'd scratch it and tell her, It's driving me crazy.

It had never made sense to her. In private he'd get hurt or angry and he'd pout, get a look on his face like he couldn't believe how unfair the world was. But if you watched him with other people— doing business—you'd see a different side to him. A guy who would do anything—it didn't matter who got in the way—to make a buck.

He sat down, getting sunblock all over the chair so that she'd have to remember to wipe it off next time she came out or else she'd end up with white marks all over *her*. He sighed and then reached over and touched her, saying, "You wanna tell me what that was all about?"

She didn't look at him. She was reading *Cosmopolitan,* an article titled, "How to Avoid Men Who Are Creeps." She wondered, if she turned the page, was she going to see a picture of Nicky? What she wanted to do was keep on reading and ignore him. But finally she put it down and glanced over at him. "What was all what about?"

She could hear a bird, a mockingbird, she thought, going crazy in the bushes over by the tennis court. She listened to it until Nicky said, "That bullshit, the thing with the car. You get in an accident and the next thing you know, a guy's coming out here. *'I came to see Katherine.'* Sitting there, drinking my beer, and he thinks he's gonna visit my wife."

"He was being nice. That's all."

Nicky picked up the magazine and said, "Uh-huh?" He flipped through the magazine, coming to a picture of a woman in skimpy underwear, an advertisement. He showed it to her and said, "You see that?" his voice changing. He was going to give her a hard time. Holding the magazine in front of her face so she had to look at it. "This picture, they get some woman, pay her money to sit around in her panties. They put the picture in a magazine. Maybe a bunch of magazines. Someday, her husband, he's sitting around the house and he picks one up. Maybe his wife's got a copy of this lying around so she can read it, read one of those stupid articles that'll tell her what's wrong with her husband. He's looking through it, checking out the broads. What happens? He sees the picture of his wife, there she is, smiling into the camera, she ain't got nothing on except her undies. What's he supposed to think?"

She wasn't sure why he was bothering to pick a fight. It made her forget what he was talking about for a second because all she could think was how much she wanted to shut him up and shake him up. Starting a fantasy of walking out on him but then letting go of it because she remembered the photos that had come in the mail the day before. She forced herself to sound nice, looking at him and saying, "Nicky, *I* used to do underwear ads."

"Yeah, I know. You did underwear ads and shampoo ads. See, that's what I'm saying." Grinning now because he knew she didn't like being reminded.

"Nicky, when I met you I was a model. I posed in underwear, it was what I did. Later I specialized in shampoo ads because I have beautiful hair. But when I first started out, if they wanted an underwear ad . . . well . . . it's not as if it's some kind of pornography."

"You think so? Let me tell you something, which I think is true of most men. I see a good-looking woman in her underwear, it's not like she's wearing a bathing suit. Uh-un. I'll tell you, you get a broad in her undies, maybe a bra, with a little peek of her boobs hanging out, one of those Victoria's Secret things. I swear to God it's sexier than anything. Somebody posing naked, maybe her legs

37

are spread, it isn't the same. But show me a woman posing like you used to, it's better. Makes you use your imagination. You see a girl like that, you can picture it, walking in and tearing her clothes off."

Katherine said, "God, Nicky, you're disgusting. You know that?" She stood up and started to walk away.

He yelled out, "Hey, what the fuck, I was only talking. It's what married people are supposed to do. Communicate." He got up out of the chair and trotted after her. Caught up to her as she was about to step onto the terrace. He grabbed her arm. "Hey, don't you like to talk?"

"Nicky, let me go."

"All I was doing was letting you know how I think."

She wrenched her arm away, "I don't give a damn how you think."

"Sure you do. Hon, we're having fun."

"It's not fun anymore. Ever."

He said, "Sure it is." Stepping closer to her and grabbing her face with his hand. "It's fun as long as you don't go wrecking any more of my cars. Meeting men by driving into them with my Cherokee."

She looked at him until he let go of her face. And then she asked, "What would you do if you figured out you couldn't stand the sight of somebody? If when they walked into a room you felt like you had to throw up?"

He managed to look surprised. "Hon, I can't think of anyone who makes me feel like that."

She said, "Jesus, Nicky."

He waited until she was almost to the house and then shouted, "Hey, you gonna go upstairs and lock yourself in your room, have a couple of drinks? Is that it? You gonna go up there and try to forget how rotten your life is?"

"No, I'm going shopping."

He stared at the house for a second and then yelled, "What the fuck is the matter with you?"

———

Driving along Carteret Street, through Beaufort itself, Katherine was thinking about the day before. Jimmy Decker coming over. She hadn't realized when she ran into his car who he was. Even after she'd given him her card and driven away it hadn't occurred to her. She'd never really looked at him. There had been too much on her mind. She'd been going way over the speed limit, with a million things running through her head because she'd been on her way to give some guy money so he wouldn't show Nicky the pictures. You're doing something like that, with your brain on overdrive because you're so scared, was it strange that you might not recognize somebody if the last time you saw them was ten or eleven years before?

But later she'd known. Even with Nicky and Wesley standing right there she had wanted to shout his name. She was in the middle of something—married to Nicky, and now some sleaze had pictures of her—and all she'd been able to think after she saw Jimmy was that he looked so normal. So good. But she hadn't said anything. Hadn't been able to with Nicky right there. She'd made herself act like she didn't recognize him.

But when she got out of bed that morning she decided to go see him. And when she thought of how mean Nicky had been it gave her the push she needed. It bothered her that maybe Jimmy thought she'd been rude the day before. Or maybe he didn't remember. Maybe what he'd done—coming out to her house—he was just being nice. Didn't remember her but was nice enough to return her insurance card anyway.

She was crossing the bridge over the Beaufort River and wondering, what was she supposed to do? Walk up and ask him, So how's it going? If you don't see somebody for that long—ten years—somebody who at one time you were very close to, what were you supposed to talk about? She didn't want to do anything silly. Tell Jimmy how messed up her life was. Come right out and tell him, I hate my husband and now I'm being blackmailed. She didn't want to do *that*.

She had told herself, waking up that morning and having coffee, that she would go see him sober. Maybe she'd go the entire day without a drink. Sitting on the edge of the bed in her panties and a little camisole—trying to read the paper but not having much success because she kept thinking about Jimmy—she decided it would be ridiculous to go on over to his house smelling like gin. He'd take one look at her, get a whiff of Beefeater's, and he'd know something was wrong.

But she couldn't do it. She got dressed, with her mind made up, and then went downstairs and told Nicky, "I'm going into town." She didn't even wait for a reply, just grabbed her keys and left. She almost made it but then she had to run back upstairs and get her sunglasses. She saw her glasses and next to them, on the night table where she'd left it the night before, the bottle of gin. She wondered, did she forget her sunglasses on purpose? Was it as easy to figure out as that? Had she given herself a reason to come on back up here so she'd have to take another look at the booze?

Because the truth was, looking at the gin, she decided she could maybe use just one quick drink. What it would do was wake her up.

Get her ready for the day. She sat on the bed for a couple of minutes, holding the opened bottle and then figured, to hell with it. She took a drink right from the bottle, pouring it down her throat. Her mouth filled up with spit at first because the stuff was awful. She did it two more times, though. Each time was a little easier because already she was feeling a glow. She pictured it down there in her stomach, sloshing around with her coffee. A nice combination.

She saw herself in the mirror when she looked across the room. A woman all dressed up to go out and see some man. With her hair done and a nice outfit on. Something conservative that she'd picked out carefully. She could hear her friend Susie's voice in her head, telling her, You're going to see some man, why'd you want to be dressed up like you're going to a business meeting?

She was dressed up, ready to go see an old friend, and what was she doing? Guzzling gin. But it didn't matter. She was feeling better already. Thinking, go see Jimmy, it will be fun. She saw herself in the mirror again. She looked a little silly, holding the bottle to her mouth like that. It wasn't something they taught in charm school. But she didn't let it bother her.


What she finally decided—driving slowly so that she didn't miss the turn onto Meridian Road—was that she'd just act like she was glad to see him. Find out what he'd been doing and pretend everything was all right with her. Be friendly but not get involved in telling him her problems.

She saw the house, his parents' place that she used to visit all the time when they were still alive and she and Jimmy were back in high school. She wasn't sure if he was still living there. He'd gone into the Marine Corps, she knew that much. But had he held on to the house or was she about to knock on the door of somebody who she'd never met before?

It didn't seem to matter because when she got out of the car—remembering the fun they used to have there—nobody answered when she rang the bell. She almost gave up. But then she walked around to the side of the house and saw his car parked under some palmettos.

She was going to go back up and ring the bell again when she heard the sound of shoes hitting the pavement. Jimmy came jogging up the driveway towards her wearing sneakers, shorts, and a red T-shirt that said USMC on the front. He looked at her and began to grin. She remembered the way he used to look at her back when they were going out. He'd be real happy about something, feeling good, and he'd get a grin on his face. He had that look on his face now, like he was glad she was there.

When he was a couple of feet away he stopped running. He was breathing just a little bit heavily. She had it in her head she was just there to say hello. Maybe talk about old times. And then she was going to leave. She opened her mouth to say something, tell him, I was driving by and I thought I'd stop in. But all of a sudden she couldn't talk. Looking at Jimmy, and Jesus, she had tears in her eyes. She took a step towards him, confused, because it wasn't what she had planned. He moved closer and then she was crying. Leaning into his arms and telling him, "I'm in trouble."

When she started to cry, he made her tell him the whole thing. After the first bit of surprise was over, he felt kind of sorry because maybe he could see why she'd done it. Gone out one night and slept with some guy she met in a bar. She told him, "I thought it was something I should do. Maybe, I don't know, maybe I thought it would help. Maybe I just wanted to meet somebody. Somebody who would make me feel good."

"There's that possibility." But he smiled at her, making a joke out of it, so that she smiled too.

"The thing is, I don't even remember it. I got so drunk, I don't remember what happened."

"You by yourself?"

"You mean before?"

"Uh-huh."

"I went there with a friend. Nicky was out of town. I don't remember where he went. This was like a month ago. But there I was, alone. I'm talking to my girlfriend Susie. Susie's telling me, Come on. Telling me to lighten up and have some fun. You have to understand Susie—she's different. She can be a little . . . tacky." She took a deep breath and told him, "I don't think, when I first agreed to go, I don't think I had that on my mind. Meeting someone. I think I just figured, you know, go on out and have a good time."

"What happened?"

"I remember up until a while after we got there. I had a couple of drinks. Somebody asked me to dance and I didn't want to. And Susie, she's telling me I ought to be more friendly. Later, somebody asked me to dance, somebody else. And I think I did."

"So you're dancing with some guy, and you don't remember after that?"

"No."

"Same guy as sent you the pictures?"

"I think so."

Jimmy said, "So now he's got pictures of you."

"Uh-huh. His name is Ellis. Ellis Bowers. He told me his name—introduced himself like he's not worried do I know who he is or not. If I wanted to I could go to the police. Turn him in for blackmail."

"But you can't."

"I guess he knows that. Yesterday, when I paid him, I looked at him. There I was, handing him an envelope with five hundred dollars in it, trying to decide if I remembered him. I didn't."

"He's the one in the pictures?"

"Uh-huh."

"What are they?"

"They're just . . . pictures. Me with my clothes off. That kind of thing."

"Uh-huh."

"I'm doing things. With him." She started to cry again.

Jimmy told her, "Hey, there's no one here, nobody's looking at you and thinking anything bad about you."


Katherine felt better. It was a big relief, telling Jimmy about it. Letting him know what had happened and then answering his questions while he gave it some thought. It felt good, his telling her, Let me decide what the best thing to do is.

It was a little windy out now. Hot, but the wind made it seem cooler.

They went inside finally. Had coffee while she explained how she'd gotten into the mess in the first place. It sounded strange, coming from her mouth. Telling somebody else how stupid she had been but not quite believing it herself because it wasn't like she had a clear recollection of the night the pictures had been taken.

She kept waiting for him to make some kind of remark—be snotty about it—until she realized that it was the kind of thing Nicky would do. And Jimmy wasn't like Nicky at all.

He finished his coffee and stood up. "You're supposed to see this guy again?"

"He called, told me to meet him again later on at the Huddle House. I don't know, maybe he expects me to buy him breakfast too."

Jimmy told her, "Why don't we do this—why don't we go see this guy. Go to the restaurant. Maybe talk to him, see if we can't get him to be reasonable about it."

# CHAPTER
# FOUR

J immy'd been sitting at the restaurant with a cup of coffee in front of him for about half an hour before the guy showed. The place was air-conditioned, fighting the morning heat, and it felt good to just sit there. The waitress kept coming over, asking did he want to order yet? Letting him know the table could probably be used if he finished his coffee and left. But he didn't let it bother him.

Now Jimmy watched the way the man walked past the cash register, looking around for a minute and then seeing Katherine. Moving slowly over toward the table with a grin on his face. Wearing leather pants and a leather jacket, with a body that looked like he lifted weights. He wasn't even real tall. But it was almost unnatural, how bulked out he was, walking stiffly like the leather pants were way too tight. Jimmy'd seen it before, somebody starts lifting too much, gets obsessed with it—maybe starts taking steroids—next thing you know they're *too* muscular. They can't move well at all.

The man was wearing a white shirt to go with the pants and jacket. Black on white. With big shit-kicker boots on and a lot of old acne scars on his neck. And something weird about his skin. Jimmy didn't get it at first, seeing that something wasn't right but taking a minute to realize that the guy was wearing makeup. Not a lot, not like a woman would wear. But some kind of skin coloring. Like one of those fake tanning gels they used to sell that'd turn your skin orange if you used even a little too much. Jesus, what did the guy see when he looked in a mirror—did he have friends who told him it looked okay? When the guy slid into the booth and sat directly under one of the fluorescent lights it looked even worse.

It looked like the man was getting ready to pose for the cover of a Bruce Springsteen album. Except that he had real close-cut brown hair that had a blond streak in it—something that you couldn't help but see from even this far away. The haircut made Jimmy think of the corps. But the guy had a different feel to him, a feeling that he gave off as he passed right by Jimmy's table on his way to where Katherine was sitting. Jimmy saw Katherine stiffen, her face frozen in a grimace, and then he heard the guy in the leather suit say something, call her Sugar. There was a look on Katherine's face, like maybe she was gonna throw up. Either that or she was gonna toss her coffee in the guy's face.

Katherine slid an envelope out of her purse and handed it across the table.

Jimmy started to wonder, now that he'd had a little time to think about it, where the hell had this come from? When he and Katherine had been going out, spending all their time together and saying what they'd do was someday get married, have a bunch of kids, and grow old together, she had asked him one summer day, "What would you do if I ever got in trouble—if I ever really needed help?" And Jimmy, being serious because it made him feel good, made him feel like an eighteen-year-old bigshot had told her, "Katy, I'd kill somebody for you." Seeing her now, across the restaurant, he asked himself if that eighteen-year-old kid was still around someplace.

Because all he had wanted, coming back here, was to see if he could get some peace of mind. He'd felt burnt out from the war and from being in the Marine Corps—taking orders from hard-asses for ten years. He hadn't even had time to decide—with Katherine bursting into tears—if this was something he wanted to get involved in.

It hadn't worked out, him and Katherine. They hadn't gotten married, hadn't had any kids. Things had changed. He and Katherine had argued about everything they could think of. There had been nothing left to say because they were out of high school and staring at real life. It had probably scared the shit out of them. So they'd stopped seeing each other. He'd enlisted, gone into the corps, and managed after a while to stop wondering what she was up to.

Right now, though, he didn't feel like he had a lot of choice. It was already happening. What if he got up and wandered over? Grabbed the guy by the back of the neck. Maybe shook him up a little bit and then told him it wasn't gonna happen again, he was gonna leave Katherine alone.

But instead of walking over there and maybe busting the guy one, starting a fight, he sat there, drinking his coffee, until Ellis Bowers got up and started heading in his direction. Jimmy, trying not to be conspicuous, looked at Ellis so he would know him later but then wanted to kick himself because Ellis noticed Jimmy staring. He stopped right there with a little grin on his face that didn't have anything to do with being friendly. Jimmy tried to make it look like maybe he was just glancing out at the room—a guy having a cup of coffee with a lot on his mind, he can't help it if he makes a little eye contact with somebody standing right in front of him.

But it didn't work. Ellis said, "Hey, you don't got enough to do? Sitting there with your coffee, you got to stare at people?"

Jimmy gave him a look like was the guy talking to *him?* Seeing his face from up this close, his complexion all fucked up. Old acne scars that he'd tried to cover with the makeup. And something darker, rouge maybe, on his cheeks. Not much, but if you looked for it, or if the guy stood in the light a certain way—there it was.

He finally said, "See, if I knew . . . if I had an idea what you were talking about—that would be one thing."

Katherine was twenty feet behind them, frozen in the act of picking up her purse. The guy had an envelope sticking halfway out the side pocket of his leather jacket. The money Katherine had given him. He makes five hundred dollars that easy and he can't even walk out of a place without picking a fight.

The guy told him, "I'm talking about you staring at me. You some kind of faggot? Like to watch men walk?"

Jimmy figured if it was gonna happen he'd as soon make it happen outside. Get out in the parking lot where he had some room to move. Use the other man's bulk against him. He stood up and brushed past him, doing it quickly enough so that the guy didn't have time to react, laying a couple of bills on the counter while Ellis started to say something else. And then he said, "Hey, maybe you didn't get enough sleep last night. Maybe all you got to do is get out of here and go back home. Take a nap." And then he walked out. Knowing the guy was gonna follow him but still thinking, don't do anything that'll make the situation worse.

When Jimmy got outside he made a big deal out of looking for his car keys, fishing through his pockets like he couldn't find them. Wanting to avoid trouble but making sure that Katherine got out of there all right too. He was turned sideways towards the restaurant, like he had forgotten about Ellis, but still he could see what was happening over by the front of the building out of the corner of his eye. The guy was starting to move in his direction.

An anole ran across the parking lot right in front of him, one of those little lizards that could turn from brown to green in half a minute. It cocked its head and peered up at Jimmy. He moved his foot and said, "Scoot," watched the thing streak across the parking lot. And then he looked back at Ellis.

Jimmy waited until Ellis was about two feet away. As if he'd already forgotten what had happened in the restaurant, he said, "Listen, it's a nice day. Maybe you got something on your mind that I'm not aware of. Something bothering you."

But the guy was still pissed off. "Yeah, you're the one that's bothering me." He stood there posing, like the bodybuilders Jimmy'd seen on ESPN. He had a look on his face, teeth clenched a little bit, that made Jimmy think he was straining to make his muscles look even bigger. Reaching down to his pocket, he pulled out a knife. The thing flicked open in his hand, reflecting the sunlight, looking deadly all of a sudden.

Jimmy couldn't believe it. The man was what, gonna try to kill him because he'd looked at him in a restaurant? He got a different idea of what the guy was like. A few hours earlier all Jimmy had had on his mind was going for a quick run. Then Katherine showed up at the end of his driveway, told him she was in trouble, and two hours later some nut was pulling a knife on him.

But he was also feeling a little bit of rage. Getting pissed off.

Recognizing the feeling because it was how he'd learned to cope when he was over in the Gulf. He'd taught himself to get mad because it kept him from getting scared.

The man started to move towards him. Jimmy was no longer concerned about was he gonna do anything to screw up Katherine's chances to get out of her fix, was it something that he wanted to get involved in. Because he was looking at staying alive now.

He tried to come up with something that might calm the man down, drew a blank, and then decided, Fuck it.

An instructor he'd had on Parris Island maybe ten years before had lined them up and told them, "Hey, you fuckers, you want to talk about a fight, that's one thing. You find somebody that wants to talk, it means they don't want to fight. They're gonna try to bore you to death with bullshit." The same guy had looked at Jimmy one day and asked, "What would you do, you know all this hotshot training, hand-to-hand combat. What would you do if you found yourself in a situation"—always calling things *situations*—"and you're up against some guy who's bigger than you or he's got a weapon. What are you gonna do?" Jimmy had looked at the instructor. If he had wanted to, the guy could kill people with his bare hands. Jimmy thought about it, and then said, "I guess I'd kick him in the balls."

So that was what he did—he stepped towards Ellis and kicked him, as hard as he could, in the balls.


Ellis Bowers rolled on the ground. What he wanted to do was puke, maybe get to his knees and throw up right there. But he was afraid if he moved it would hurt even more. Or else, if he moved, the guy leaning over him might kick him again. He didn't think he could take that.

He couldn't believe it. You pull a knife on somebody, you're gonna fuck with them, maybe cut them up a little bit. You do something like that and most people would act scared. Not this son of a bitch. The guy hadn't wasted any time. Jesus, Ellis probably should've been able to see something in his expression, the way the guy was relaxed back there in the restaurant, not getting upset when Ellis said something. Not intimidated.

Ellis had thought at first maybe he was a fag. It happened sometimes and there wasn't a lot you could do about it. You spend time, lifting weights, eating the right things to keep yourself in shape, and what'd happen was you'd get a lot of women staring at you. But sometimes, if there was a queer around, he'd look at you too. Which was what Ellis had thought when he saw the guy in the restaurant. But then it'd crossed his mind that maybe the guy was just a hard-ass, a person who thought it was all right to stare at somebody while they went about their own business. Which pissed Ellis off even more and made him want to come out and teach the son of a bitch a lesson. Except it hadn't worked out at all.

The guy rolled him over and took the envelope out of his pocket. He took Ellis's compact out too, his favorite one, with the little mirror. The one he used to check his face in when he thought nobody was looking. The guy grunted in surprise and said, "I don't know, pal, but if this is yours you maybe want to talk to somebody, a shrink, somebody like that."

Ellis saw him pick the knife up off the pavement and then the guy was behind him, digging in Ellis's pants for his wallet. Taking it out and then leaning down to put his head next to Ellis's ear and saying, "See, now I know who I'm dealing with. I got a South

Carolina driver's license right here in my hand that says your name is Ellis Bowers and tells me where you live." Ellis wanted to tell the guy, You want the wallet, you want the envelope and the little makeup kit, go ahead and take 'em. Still trying hard not to puke. Thinking the guy was robbing him.

But the guy kept talking. "See, that woman in there, the one you ate breakfast with, you know who I mean?"

"Mrs. Kramer?"

"That's the one. From now on, I don't even want you to say her name. You're gonna return the pictures. Get them all together with the negatives, and then I'm gonna come on over"—the guy looked at Ellis's license again—"to 14 Pigeon Point Road. And we're gonna burn them. What do you think, Ellis, that something you and I can do?"

Ellis nodded and the guy said, "This is gonna be the end of it, Ellis. I think maybe you better find yourself some other line of work."

Ellis felt the pressure in his stomach ease as the guy stood up. Then he was alone, lying there on the asphalt while the guy stepped right over him to get in the car. He heard the motor start up and had to roll to one side, away from the car, because the guy didn't even seem to care whether he ran Ellis over or not—he just started the thing up and put it in gear and went. Ellis, feeling like shit, managed to lift himself up on his elbows and get a look at the car. He watched it roll to a stop by the front of the diner where the Kramer bitch climbed in.

It wasn't much, seeing the car like that, from kind of a sideways angle. It didn't make the pain go away, knowing that sooner or later he'd figure out who the fuck the guy was. But it didn't make it hurt any worse either.

Katherine told Jimmy, "I used to model. You know, pose for magazines. Mostly hair ads. Shampoos, conditioners, that kind of thing. After I got out of school."

Jimmy said, "I didn't know that."

"I made pretty good money at it, got to the point where people would pay a lot."

Jimmy smiled. "You've got the looks for it."

She said, "Well, what they really loved was my hair. The Farrah Fawcett look, but brown." There was a pause and then she continued. "My friend Susie, she's said a couple of times why don't I get back to it?" Waiting to see if he was going to say anything else, maybe compliment her again. When he didn't she told him, "But what happens, it can be such a sleazy business. And a lot of work. People see a picture of you, in *Cosmo, Mademoiselle,* or just one of those circulars the department stores put out every Sunday. You look happy, smiling, wearing those nice clothes and maybe some jewelry that looks like it's worth thousands of dollars. They turn a fan on to make your hair look a little wild. And what do people think? They see the ad, and they're thinking, What an easy way to make a living. Like all I ever had to do was go to a studio and stand there for maybe five minutes and get paid a ton of money."

Jimmy told her, "Yeah, well, I guess the people who do it, the advertisers, they want it to look like that. A pretty girl and we just happened to catch a picture of her."

"Right. But what a lot of people, most people, what they don't think about is how maybe you had to pose for hours to get that one shot. They don't see you practically starving yourself to stay skinny. You go into a shoot, maybe you couldn't sleep the night before and the photographer's looking at you, asking, What the hell happened?"

She was leaning against the fender of his rented car back at his house. She'd turned to look out at his backyard, at the marsh grass at the far end and the bay behind it, noticing that the tide had gone out. There was a Sunfish out in the bay, a couple of people on it, skimming over the surface of the water. She watched them for a while because it looked like fun. She turned back to him when he spoke, seeing the way his mouth moved and the little lines in the corners of his eyes that weren't there when she knew him before. Remembering what he'd done to Ellis Bowers back there in the parking lot, seeing it again in her head, and realizing that he hadn't even been breathing hard when he'd come back to pick her up.

What had she done? She'd seen him for the first time in ten years the day before, spent a couple of hours with him, and picked up a piece of the past like it had never been gone. It felt like they were back in high school again. For the first time in a while, she was with a man who acted like he cared about what she was thinking. Maybe it was just that Jimmy still seemed like a nice guy. Until he'd taken care of Ellis Bowers. Then she had to look at him and realize that he was different. That it had been a long time since high school.

She couldn't make up her mind if it was something she liked. She saw him almost like some kind of white knight, coming to her rescue. It made her feel pretty good. Not that she liked to see people fight. But the idea of it, that a man would do something like that for her, it was kind of nice. She wondered, was it something Nicky would do? She couldn't picture it. Not even before he'd gotten a little heavy. She almost felt like telling Nicky what had happened. Knowing she couldn't—because of why it had happened—but still liking the idea of it. Letting Nicky know that other men appreciated her. That had a nice feel to it.

Now she asked Jimmy, "That stuff you did, in the parking lot. That the kind of thing they taught you in the Marines?"

He wondered what he should say. What could he tell her? He could tell her that all it was was him trying not to get hurt. Do something to the other person because you were pretty sure they were gonna try to do something to you. A guy pulls a knife on you, it wasn't like you had a whole lot of choices. Thinking back to what it had been like in the Corps. And what it had been like over in the Gulf.

The first time Jimmy had killed a man he didn't have time to think about it—everything happened so fast that he only had time to put his rifle to his shoulder and pull the trigger. He was scared to death because there was all kinds of shit going on, artillery rounds coming in, people shouting all around him, and a lot of small arms fire.

It was a place he'd never heard of before, probably no one he knew had either—Khafji—a hellhole in the Saudi desert about six miles below Iraq. They'd been flown in quickly, the helicopters streaking across the desert only seventy-five feet above the ground, because the Iraqis had decided to cross the border and attack a ghost town, a place that had already been evacuated.

When they got there, the Iraqis already controlled the town, what was left of it, and Jimmy and his men had deployed along the southern edge, supposedly to help the Saudi infantry—get them out of a jam and help them retake the town. Jimmy's unit, all six of them long-shot experts—snipers—had orders to find a high spot. Get close enough to the Iraqis to take them out one at a time without making a big stink over it. Everyone wanted to be as low key as possible at this point. They wanted the Iraqis to get the fuck back home but nobody wanted to start the ground war by accident. They told Jimmy to take his time, get his men set up, and then make his move. Told him, Don't rush into anything.

But the place was out of control—street-to-street gun battles and no one knew who controlled what. Jimmy's unit took fire five minutes after they got there, Iraqi gunners from the building across the street pinning them down behind a cement wall next to an open-air market. Jimmy told his guys to lie low—return fire if they could but just stay there while he took a look around. He took one guy, the radio operator, and ran around the back of the market, following an alley until he got behind the Iraqis.

There were two of them and Jimmy crawled through the rubble until he was a hundred and twenty feet behind them. They were sitting ducks from that distance. He was close enough that he thought at first what he'd do was yell to them, tell them to drop their rifles and put their hands up. Because it wasn't anything like the kind of shots he'd been trained for back at Parris Island, where they run you through the woods or else make you climb a goddamn tree and then point at a target—you're so far away you can barely see it—and then watch you try to hit the thing.

But as he sat in the rubble and watched, they opened up at his men again, the one lying low while the other one raked the cement wall where Jimmy's unit was. He figured they were pretty confident, firing like that without ever looking behind them. By the time the radio man got up to where he was, Jimmy had made up his mind. He lifted his rifle, looked at them through the sight, and then thought, The hell with it, and took them out with two shots.

Later, back at the base, he thought about it again. Maybe if it was a couple of guys—the Iraqis—trying to give themselves up, which he'd heard was happening in other places, he'd have acted differently. But these guys had been serious, trying to kill people, and he'd done the right thing.

But with Katherine asking him now was that the kind of thing he'd learned to do in the Marine Corps, what was he gonna tell her? He could say that Ellis Bowers was lucky—that Jimmy knew guys that given the choice of getting kicked in the balls or getting shot, would have been helping you put your boots on before you finished asking. Only they didn't get the choice.

So all he said was, "I don't know. You learn things, how to react in a certain situation, and sometimes you don't even realize you're learning it."

She wasn't sure what he meant, but he was acting like he didn't want to go into it. She let it go. Leaning on the car next to him and feeling the heat from the metal on her hips, she wondered what should she do now? She could go home. Thank him for his help and then say maybe she'd see him sometime. But she didn't want to leave yet.

She asked him, "What do you think will happen?"

"With Bowers? The pictures?"

"Uh-huh."

He shrugged. "There's no way to tell. The guy could be smart. Maybe realize that it's not worth it. If he's someone, say, he does this kind of thing a lot, he's a pro, then what he might do, he might find somebody else that's an easier target."

"Because of what you did?"

"He might."

She smiled. "I guess I owe you."

He looked away. She could see he was nervous, could tell it the same way that she'd been able to when they were both eighteen years old.

"Kate, there's nothing to owe," he said quietly.

A little shy—Jesus, she couldn't believe it. She liked it because it wasn't something she was used to, living with Nicky. And calling her Kate. It made her feel like a model again, like when she used to pose for pictures and the photographer would say, "Kate, you look *great* today."

She reached out and put a hand on his arm. She wanted to do more. She could picture leaning over and kissing him. She'd shake her head to get her hair behind her and then lean down and kiss him. Almost doing it but then holding back, because it wouldn't be the right thing to do. She decided that maybe there *would* be a time when it would be all right to kiss him.

She felt pretty good. Surprised, because for the first time in a while she hadn't thought about having a drink. It was something that hadn't even crossed her mind since she told him about Ellis Bowers. Jesus, *that* was pretty amazing.

She tried to imagine what it would have been like if she'd never met Nicky. If she'd stayed here, in Beaufort, and never gone up to New York, never gotten involved in modeling. She could've stayed with Jimmy. Traveled with him when he joined the Marine Corps. At the time she probably would have been bored with it. When she was younger and wanted to get away from this town, it might have seemed like a drag. But now, looking back, maybe it was something she should've tried harder to do.

She almost said something, told him what she was thinking about, but didn't because it would sound ridiculous and besides, he was starting to tell her something. Saying, "There's one other thing. Another way he could be."

She asked, "What's that?"

"He could get mad."

# CHAPTER

# FIVE

W esley had rented a nice little ranch house out on St. Helena Island. A white frame house, freshly painted, on stilts and set back from the highway a ways. It had a couple of big shade trees out front—live oaks dripping Spanish moss—a brick wall running out the front to the driveway, and a dock out back with a deep-water channel that had ten feet of bottom at high tide. You stand at the back door, look out over the tidal flats past the bay, and you could see the lighthouse in the state park maybe three miles away.

Every once in a while traffic'd back up. The drawbridge between Harbor and St. Helena Islands would swing open for the shrimp boats and then take about twenty minutes to close. It was all right if you were going to the beach, had all day to kill. But if you were trying to get home, sitting in the car with the temperature inside rising to over a hundred degrees, it got to be a pain in the ass. Sometimes, people headed out to Fripp to stay in a fancy beach cottage would slow down passing Wesley's place. Guy driving from someplace like Philadelphia or New York—where it got cold—would turn to his wife and say, That place, when I retire, that's the kinda place I'm gonna get.

He sat there now, in the kitchen, with the gym bag open on the table in front of him—all those little Andy Jacksons peeking up at him. Wesley told himself he was being smart, being patient. Because a lot of people, they pull a score like this, what'd happen is they would rush things. Get impatient, greedy, whatever, and the next thing they knew they'd be talking to some stuck-up public defender in a room with a guard behind the door and bars on the windows.

It almost made him laugh. Down here, with all this cash. And he couldn't spend a dime of it. Sure—walk into town, go into a drugstore and buy a pack of Marlboros, maybe he'd get away with it the first couple of times. But if he kept it up, started to spread that marked money around, eventually he'd get the goddamn FBI on his ass. Be hanging out somewhere, maybe this place even, and all of a sudden the door would come crashing in and some douche bag in a leisure suit would be sticking a .357 Magnum in his face.

Because, the truth was, the money was the only thing that tied him to the kidnapping. Nothing else. He remembered what had happened to the guy on TV—the miniseries—the thing that had given Wesley the idea in the first place. The idiot went through with it, with not a bad plan, and then what'd he do? Went all over the place spending that goddamn money is what he did. So Wesley had spent weeks, running it over in his head, what to do with the money after he got it. Because that was the big thing. If he didn't get the money in the first place then he was gonna have other worries.

Outside he saw a boat, a nice big Bayliner, going through the channel. About five people in it, looked like they were having a good time—he could hear their voices from inside the house. He kept waiting for the boat to slow down. He stood up to watch the boat cut through the water. It was going too fast because the channel was pretty narrow, and if they hit the side, ran the boat into the bottom where it hadn't been dredged, they were gonna get a pretty big surprise. Wesley couldn't believe it. Fucking tourists. Guy probably had the boat out a couple of times a year, if that. Bring it down here, throw it in the water, and act like the ocean was a friendly fucking place.

What he would do, when he converted his money, maybe he'd get a boat like that. When he was through dealing with Mr. Nicky Kramer. Get whatever the hell he wanted—that's what he'd do.

Fifty-three years—that's how long he'd waited for this kind of deal. Back up in Atlantic City, the cruds that owned the bar he worked at, they paid him eight dollars an hour plus tips to serve beer to a bunch of college snots. You think they tipped? The hardest thing they ever had to do was talk their parents into buying that BMW for their graduation present, because, Jesus, Mom and Dad, everybody else is getting one. They wanted to come into Wesley's bar—the place he worked—act like life was one big goddamn party, try to pay for their booze with a MasterCard. Come to think of it, they reminded him of Nicky Kramer, you get rid of the potbelly and add a little more hair.

He'd gone to work the day after he'd collected his score. For a couple days after that too. For one thing, he wanted to make it seem like nothing was different. Gotten the money—the ransom—and still he'd shown up for work. Say the cops come around. There he was—See, what are you talking about? I'm working is all.

He let a little time go by and then when he was ready to leave, the money safe in a locker at the Greyhound station, he waited until a fight broke out at work. A couple of jocks trading punches over some slut that'd probably banged her first guy when she was twelve. He'd seen the thing happen from behind the bar, known it was gonna happen five minutes before it did, and hadn't moved to break it up. Didn't even pick up the phone to call the cops. He waited until Morrie, the little Jewish guy who was part owner of the place and who Wesley was pretty sure was queer, came over and yelled at him. Morrie, wearing some kind of fag jacket and little trousers that hugged his ass and were tucked into cowboy boots. Drove a Mercedes 450 SL that he'd had repainted a fucked-up orange color. He'd come over to where Wesley stood behind the bar, wringing his hands and screaming, "Wesley, come on, DO SOMETHING." Like a goddamn broad. Wesley, thinking of all those twenty-dollar bills sitting in that Greyhound locker, smiled nicely at the little fag Hebe. He spoke slowly, so he could enjoy the sound of the words, telling Morrie, "Hey, I got an idea, why don't *you* do something?"

Outside the boat was beginning to slow down. Wesley saw that the people on board had quieted down, no more yelling and carrying on. They were all looking at the front of the boat. The man at the wheel kept turning his head, looking in front of him and to both sides. It made him look like something was wrong, like he had some kind of nervous disorder.

Wesley took his pistol out from under his arm. A six-shot Dakota .357 Magnum with a 4⅝-inch barrel. He broke it and took the shells out and then walked over to the kitchen window and pointed it at the boat outside. Just playing around because it made it easier to think.

He had shown Nicky the money and now it was up to Nicky. The man could talk, Wesley had to give him that. Sitting beside that pool of his, or else at that stupid club, lounging around and drinking Scotches, trying to impress Wesley. It didn't seem to bother him that he had a wife, all she did, she hit green balls on the tennis court all day long and then seemed half-drunk the rest of the time. Nicky, with his goddamned landscaped lawn and the bushes trimmed to look like animals, telling Wesley, "With your money—we show that around, let some people hear about this deal we're putting together. They get greedy, they show us some of their own money." Wesley, trying to follow, not quite sure it would be as easy as that. Listening to Nicky and then asking, "And then what happens?" Nicky, grinning: "We take *their* damn money is what happens."

Wesley saw that the boat had run aground. Everybody in it had moved towards the front and was looking at the back. He walked to the table and picked up the bullets, started to put them back into the gun, taking his time about it. Wondering for about the thousandth time, was Nicky really gonna be able to do it? Cause he didn't want to waste his time down here.

He slid his hands through his hair and then walked out onto the deck. He heard a roar from the water and looked up in time to see the Bayliner lurch backwards, free from the marsh mud. The people in the boat all started to clap, and the man at the wheel took a bow as he turned the boat back into the channel and headed away from Wesley's house.

With nothing better to do, Wesley raised the pistol until he was sighting with his good eye at the receding boat, watching it for a second but then seeing Nicky Kramer, his stupid little-boy face and his big mouth. Loudmouth spoiled brat wanted to get some money together. That was one thing. He wanted to split it with Wesley, take something that Wesley had worked pretty goddamn hard for?

That was something else.

# CHAPTER

# SIX

Nicky decided he was horny. He was sitting out by the pool trying to decide if it was worth getting up out of his chair to walk on over and stick his legs in the water, sit on the side and let them soak while he finished his drink. He decided to stay where he was. But he smiled because he liked it when he felt this way. He wasn't gonna play golf today. He'd go on out tomorrow, play eighteen holes and then hang around the club for a little while.

Today he was going to call Susie. But he knew that it wasn't a thing he had to do right away. He could have another drink. Call her up in a while and tell her he was coming over. Get rid of the pressure. Quit worrying, was he gonna be able to take Wesley Hops's money and use it for a stake, as bait, to give him the score he needed before the IRS came crashing down on his head?

He'd call Susie up, tell her what to wear and know that when he got there, it would be what she had on. Sometimes, if he was out shopping, maybe in the mall or else if he was down in Savannah, looking through the stores, he'd see something he liked. Something sexy. And he'd buy it for her. Or else, every once in a while, he'd order something in the mail. Get a catalogue from Frederick's and order a bunch of stuff. He'd bring them over to Susie's apartment and make her try it all on. And then maybe, if he felt like it, he'd rip them right off of her.

He was having maybe his fourth Scotch of the day, thinking about getting laid. He looked at his watch. One o'clock. He could be over at Susie's place and back by three, three-thirty at the latest. He picked up the phone and dialed her number, finishing off his Scotch as he waited for her to answer. Sitting up, after he put the glass down on the cement, and hearing her voice. Saying, "Hey, sugar, guess what time it is?"


Susie was trying to talk to Ellis Bowers. He was sitting on her couch while she stood in the middle of her living room by the fireplace, with her hand touching the wall right next to the Hockney print that she'd talked Nicky into getting. That was before he'd told her about Wesley Hops and his gym bag full of money. Looking at Ellis and thinking of her mother, Susie said to herself, Oh, Momma, you should see who I have to deal with these days. Maybe you didn't tell me near enough about men. She watched Ellis gulp his drink—some kind of juice—and listened to him tell her he was gonna kill the son of a bitch who had kicked him in the nuts.

He looked terrible. His jacket was torn and he had a scratch on the side of his face. It must've killed him to get his face scratched up like that. Already, since he'd arrived, he'd gone into her bathroom four times to look at himself in the mirror—to check the damage. Trying to hide what he was doing but coming out the last time with the scratch a lot less noticeable because he'd borrowed some of her makeup. Used a little foundation to cover it up. She felt like telling him, Hey, it's only your head, it isn't like there was a lot there to begin with.

He couldn't stand still. "What the hell happened? I'm there, I'm talking to the Kramer woman. Everything's cool. And this guy shows up outta nowhere." It seemed as if he was gonna start crying any second—big, tough Ellis Bowers. He asked her, "You wanna tell me who he is?"

"Ellis, how do I know? I look like I've got ESP?" She was wondering the same thing herself: Who was this guy who'd showed up out of nowhere to help Katherine? But it was something she'd have to figure out for herself.

She was also wondering how long was *this* going to go on? Ellis was complaining that his crotch hurt him. She wanted to laugh because it had to have been a pretty good shot. With what Ellis had down there—pretty small change—the guy must've taken his time, gotten his aim just right. But what'd he expect *her* to do about it?

Now he told her, "I'll tell you how. You're the one set this thing up. Everything's working out and then this smart-ass shows up. If you don't know who he is then you'd better find out. Cause I'm gonna kill the motherfucker is what I'm gonna do, soon's I find out who he is."

He was still pacing back and forth in front of her. He was being so dramatic about the whole thing, Susie thought he probably watched too much TV. He said, "The son of a bitch took my money. He took my wallet." He looked away from her. "He took my compact for Christ's sake. What's he gotta take that for?"

Susie put a sincere tone in her voice instead of laughing, which was pretty hard to do because the man was talking about a compact. "Hey, it's okay to worry about your appearance. But your face will be fine in no time." She had a sudden idea. "Hey, before . . . before I came up here, you want to know what I did? I worked in a hospital. As a nurse's aide. We'd see people, they'd be all banged up. Got in a car wreck. They'd look a lot worse than you and they'd be all right."

He gave her a look. "You think that's all it is, my face?"

"You're afraid he kicked you so hard down there, you're afraid he injured it *permanently?*"

He shook his head. "Don't even say it. You got no idea what it feels like. Something like this, a bruise in a spot like that, it can really do some damage."

"Ruin your sex life, huh?"

He was pissed off now. "The fuck're you saying? You think that because I like it a little differently, like to have fun when I'm with a girl, play some games, you think this isn't serious?"

She was thinking, Ellis, he liked it *differently?* It was like saying elephants were big. You look at Ellis casually, maybe you pass him on the street, you see a guy who's pretty good looking except for a few acne scars so maybe you think he's normal. Until you get to know him better. You find out he wears makeup and carries a little mirror around all the time. That he stays up late at night worrying about his complexion, was his blood sugar all right and his cholesterol level low enough. Not knowing what the hell they were but losing sleep over it anyway. And *then* you realized how messed up his head was when it came to sex.

She'd asked him one time, a couple of months before—the first time in bed with him—when he was trying so hard and not a lot was happening. Whispering, "Ellis, you ever look at other men?"

Saying it quietly because she didn't want to upset him but she wanted to know. Moving out from under him and leaning on one elbow. "I mean, you're down at that club, lifting weights, taking a shower after. You ever take a peek at any of the other guys? See what they look like in their birthday suits?"

He was already in a bad mood because he couldn't get hard and he got pissed off. He'd told her, "I ain't no goddamn homo-sex-u-al." He'd tried even harder after that. Like a kid trying to put a square peg into a round hole while she lay there and thought about what she was gonna do the next day. Made up a grocery list. Ellis got a strange look in his eyes after a while, with his face turning a little red because he hadn't known her for that long yet and it must have embarrassed him to ask her, "Don't you have a wig or something—something you can put on to make yourself look different?" And there it was—an idea and also a weapon—something she could use on Ellis, really keep him in line. Susie shook her head. "Ellis, honey, I don't have any wigs."

She had made herself wait while he sulked, timing it just right, and then told him, "Wait, we could go out, pick something up. A wig, or maybe some kind of costume. Something like that." His expression changing almost immediately—getting happy again—but for all she knew he was picturing her as Marie Antoinette. Maybe Minnie Mouse. She wondered how long could she put up with *that?* But she was relieved that it had been this easy, thinking back to what her momma used to say: "Hey, you got to do something to get ahead, go ahead and do it. Don't be ashamed, honey. You got to make the best of what you have."

Now she told him, "Ellis, I don't think we want to discuss your sex life right this minute." She heard the phone ring and stood up to get it. Looking at Ellis one more time she said, "We're going to go ahead and do it like I said. Stick to what I originally planned and that's the way it's going to be."

She moved into the kitchen and picked up the phone. Saying hello and then smiling. Putting on her sweetest tone, letting the South creep into her voice a little more, trailing the cord as she looked in at Ellis.

She said, "Nicky. See that, I was just thinking about you-all and look at this." Listening for a second. "No . . . no, my cousin stopped by. Ellis here, he came over for a visit. But he's about to leave."

She waited and then laughed. "Honey, you-all want to come over now, that'd be fine."

She hung up, walked back into the living room, and said, "Why don't you go on home. Take it easy and rest."

"While Nicky and you are gonna have a good time?"

She wanted to tell him to shut up. She was tired of his complaining all of a sudden, but she made herself smile. "Jesus, you know what he thinks is a good time. I sit here, maybe walk around in my underwear. He comes on over and tells me what a great guy he is."

"Uh-huh?"

She put her hands on her hips and looked at Ellis. "Hey, what is this? You knew, going into this thing, you knew what it was going to be like. We want to do this thing and come out with some serious money, then we got to do it the right way."

"We're gonna make a lot of money? Tell me again," Ellis said, "how're we gonna make any money when all we're doing, we're blackmailing some bitch, five hundred dollars at a time. How're we gonna get rich doing that? And what are we gonna do about the son of a bitch that kicked me in the balls?"

"We aren't gonna do anything until I figure out who he is and what he's up to."

Ellis said, "Well, maybe I'll go on out and find him myself. Take care of the situation on my own."

Even though she'd gotten to know him pretty well it surprised her sometimes how dumb he could be. She took a deep breath and said, "Ellis, I want you to know something here. Something I think maybe you should know about me."

"What?"

She sat down on the couch and took his hand in hers. "You know what I did before I came up to Beaufort?" He started to interrupt her. "Ellis honey, this is important. You just listen to me for a minute, all right? Before I came up here I worked in a day-care center. You believe that? *Me* . . . taking care of kids? This was a couple of years ago. What I did, I helped out, made sure all the kids had a good time while their folks were off working. You know what I mean?"

Ellis said, "I thought you worked in a hospital?"

"That was before."

"You took care of a bunch of brats?"

"No, see that wasn't the case at all." She began to talk a little slower so that he'd get the point. "Most of them—a lot of them at least—they were real cute. Nice kids. But, hey, you have any idea what kind of work that is? You chase kids around all day. Make sure their undies aren't wet and they eat their food and they aren't killing each other."

She waited for him to nod. "But my point, the one I want you to think about, is this—I did this for three years, and every year, it didn't matter how many kids you were taking care of, you'd always have one or two—I don't know, maybe they were having trouble at home—anyway, these kids would go out of their way to be a pain in the ass. You'd be feeding these kids, giving them a treat, and every day, it didn't matter what you'd do, one of them would be putting his Jell-O down the shirt of one of the others. Or pulling some girl's ponytail, punching her, until she started to cry. Something like that."

Ellis was smiling, now. "Little fuckers gave you a hard time, huh?"

"Uh-huh. And see, maybe you see that happen once or twice, you might even think it's amusing. Little girl standing there with Jell-O in her dress. With a silly expression on her face. But let me ask you something—how do you think it would make you feel if it happened every day? Every day you tell some smart-ass not to do it, and as soon as you turn your back, there he goes."

Ellis shrugged. "Pissed off, I guess."

"That's right. Eventually, somebody, it could be anybody, if they keep causing trouble, they won't do what you say, it gets under your skin a little bit."

"Wait a minute. What the fuck you telling me this for?"

She took her hand out of his and touched his cheek. "I just want you to think about it. Not start causing trouble by wondering what are we doing and thinking maybe you have a better way. Don't start thinking, acting like one of those kids back at that day-care center, playing around with your Jell-O."

"I seem like a kid to you?"

She let him see the look on her face and then made herself kiss him full on the lips. She said, "Hey, it came to mind, is all."

Nicky, wearing powder blue boxer shorts, was walking up and down in front of the fireplace, telling Susie, "All you have to do is make them believe. You give them an idea, but you present it to them like you're not sure you even want them to know about it. Like it's too good. A secret. Let them think maybe you *don't* want them in on it almost." He laughed. "Don't forget, these fellows, they came to me. Looked me up because they know I got the contacts and asked me, Nicky, can you find us a property on the QT?" Shrugging his shoulders and giving her a wink. "See, now I can show them I've got some money too. Show them what Wesley has and get them to up the ante."

He'd shown up at her place after Ellis Bowers left. Wearing khaki shorts, white socks and sneakers, and a button-down brown shirt. Susie thought he looked like an overgrown Boy Scout.

He grabbed his glass from the mantelpiece and then told Susie, "They see all that cash and they hear something in your voice like you're trying to hide how good it is and they can't think straight. Next thing you know they're begging you to take their money."

He had a leather eyeglass case in his shirt pocket. He'd told her once, "See, my vision is fine. I don't need the glasses. But I like to carry them. If you're talking to somebody, maybe working a deal, you take the glasses out—do it real slow. A guy sees you do that, put glasses on, it makes it look like you're giving the thing a lot of thought. Makes you look smarter."

Susie, listening to him, had wondered, where did the man come up with his ideas? Now she asked him, "That's what you do? Make it sound too good to be true? Put together a deal for a piece of land and then make it look like it'll be worth buying?"

She was lying on the floor with nothing but a negligee on, trying hard to look like a Playmate of the Month. Feeling ridiculous but not letting herself think about it. Making herself concentrate on being slutty instead, picturing it in her head. What was Nicky used to seeing, old copies of *Hustler* with the pages stuck together? Or *Playboy*, because the articles were so good? She told herself it was all right—what she was putting herself through—because she was going to be rich when it was over.

What would Nicky say if she told him, Hey, I got an idea, why don't you take *your* clothes off and I can stand over you like some kind of idiot while *you* lie around like you're in the middle of a porn flick. See how it feels.

She had a sudden thought—what would happen if somebody walked in, somebody she knew from back home. If they saw her like this, maybe they'd get embarrassed and tell her, "Excuse me." And she'd have to say, "Hey, no, it's all right, all I'm doing here, I'm working. It's a job." Because that was what it was, the only way she could look at it and still pose half-naked for Nicky Kramer. Look at it like it was a job she was gonna eventually get paid for.

She turned her body, catching the light and watching him stare at her. With a little peek of the hair between her legs dyed red to match the hair on her head. She could tell he was wondering could he do it again? Give himself enough time and maybe he could give her one more shot before he had to go home to Katherine. She moved on the carpet, let her legs open up a little bit more, seeing the sweat start to trickle down the side of his face. She felt like laughing at him, standing there in his boxers, with his gut hanging out and a stupid look on his face because no matter how many times she let him see it—flashed it at him—he still forgot what he was talking about when she showed him.

She had to ask him again, "Is that all you do? You make it seem too good to be true?"

"No, that's the thing. If you make it *too* good, if it sounds *too* easy, then they won't go for it." He came on over to where she was lying on the carpet and squatted down next to her. "The thing is . . . the thing you got to do . . . you got to make it sound *just* right. Tell them up front, say, Hey, there's gonna be some risks. Talk it down a little.

Act like you don't want to be responsible if they lose their money. Make sure they know it was their idea to do it in the first place."

"So they won't blame you?"

"Yeah, there's that. Plus—and this is something you got to understand—if they think that there's a risk it sounds more real to them. They can tell themselves, Yeah, maybe there's a risk, but I'll be lucky."

"And then what, they just give you their money?"

"Well, they're already looking to give me money. They're the ones that got in touch with me. All I have to do is find them a property. And I already lined one up. They give me their cash and I swear to God my tax problems'll be over."

"And that's it?"

He said, "Look, they see that money of Wesley's, it shows that I'm serious. It's like a demonstration of good faith. And that's what blinds them. They can't wait to put up money of their own. Otherwise they feel like they're gonna miss out."

"It's as simple as that?"

"No. It gets complicated. You have your lawyers, your accountants, people you've got to use to make it look good. You have to pretend a lot. You got to put a lot of shit on paper—hire people to make it look legitimate. Make it look like you're actually gonna go through with the thing, pass a lot of documents around for everyone to initial. But once you start dealing in cash, cash that someone else wants to hide and use at the same time, you can really clean up."

She could see that he was making an effort to explain it to her. Give it to her in language that he thought she would understand because he thought she was pretty dumb and he wanted to get laid again. It was a game Susie played. She'd act like she couldn't even tell time, and Nicky, what he'd do, he'd try to show her things, explain things *slowly* so that she could see how smart he was.

He told her, "These are some greedy sons of bitches we're talking about. What you do is act like you're gonna split expenses. You know, show them that you're putting up a half mil too."

"And then what, you just take their money?"

He grinned. "What are they gonna do? They think they're doing something illegal in the first place, which is what it would be if we went through with it. I got them talking bribes, kickbacks. I got it on tape. They make a fuss . . ." He made a face and held his hands up in the air. "Are they gonna call the cops? I take their money and then a couple of days later I tell them, Hey, we're all set. The people we paid, they did what they were supposed to do. Paved the way. And then I convince them that with their money in there I'm gonna be able to get the loans for the rest of it. Get more investors. See, it's the money that starts it all, the money they put up. It's all cash. Nobody knows where it goes. If you can convince them, really get them going, then what you do, you ask for a *lot* of money. Enough so that if you pull some kind of scam it'll be worth it. Worth the risk."

She stared at his face like she couldn't believe it. "You know how to do that?"

"It's the kind of thing, you do it a couple times, it's easy. I've been doing small things. But you got to take the plunge sometime. Make a big score." He sounded a little like he was talking himself into something, Susie thought.

She wanted to ask him, What's a big score? Find out from him how much money they were talking about. It sounded fine, hearing him mention a figure like half a million dollars, but she wasn't sure if he was exaggerating to make himself look good.

She asked him, "What about Wesley?"

"What about him?"

"Well, you going to take his money too?"

"What if I did?"

She let a concerned tone creep into her voice. "Aren't you worried? What's he gonna do when he realizes?"

He got up off his knees and looked down at her. Not answering. She could see, underneath his boxers, his pecker starting to come to life, poking at the fly of the undershorts. She wasn't gonna get anything more out of him—not information. Already he was starting to pull the boxers off, ripping clumsily at them and almost falling over because they were stuck on his hips.

She had to raise her voice, stop him for a second by saying. *"Nicky . . ."*

"What?"

She turned her head sideways, giving him her cheerleader look, like she was too fascinated to let it drop, and asked, "What's he going to do?"

He shook his head as if he thought she was slower than usual today. "What the fuck can he do? You see that jerk, what is he? He's fifty-five, maybe sixty years old. All his life, you wanna know what he does? He pisses his time away tending bar, playing the slots and a little bullshit blackjack up in Atlantic City. Finally he wins a little money. The man ran football pools for Christ's sake. I don't have time to worry about what some loser is gonna think if I take his money."

She let what he had told her settle and then smiled, the cheerleader in her taking over. Clapping her hands, thinking about all that money but then thinking, Shit, watch it. Putting a blank look on her face again and acting impressed. "Nicky, you're gonna do *all* this."

He wasn't paying a lot of attention to what she was saying, but he nodded. "See, you don't have to *do* anything. You just make it *look* like you're going to. Keep everything looking good until you have the cash. After that, if you got the balls, you can do anything you want. I already explained that."

She said, "That's right, you did." Storing it all away and then looking up into his face. Leaning back and spreading her legs even wider on the carpet, smiling at him like a half-witted whore. Wondering which was worse—Ellis, who couldn't do it at all, or Nicky, trying to prove how many times he *could?* Wanting to slam her legs shut, tell him, Sorry, no vacancy. But then thinking that sooner or later Nicky was gonna have a whole lot of cash lying around. Counting dollar bills in her head and looking over his shoulder at the Hockney print, making herself concentrate on it so she wouldn't have to think too hard about Nicky.

# CHAPTER
# SEVEN

Jimmy Decker didn't know what to do. Katherine was standing there at the end of his driveway, next to her car, looking different than he'd ever seen her before, than he'd ever even imagined she could look. She wasn't posing for a magazine layout now. Only her hair looked all right. Her face was distorted and red and she was out of breath from yelling at him. He felt like saying, Hey, come on, what is this? He'd done the best he could, trying to get her out of a jam.

But she wouldn't stop yelling, smelling a little bit like gin, swearing and asking at the top of her lungs, "What the hell are you gonna do? The guy—you beat him up—and what happens? One day later he's calling me back. I thought it was gonna be over. And now he's calling me again. But this time he wants a *thousand* dollars. Now what the hell are you gonna do?"

Jimmy asked, "You want me to go see him?"

"You think if you go see him, maybe beat him up again, it's gonna end?" She laughed. "That's all you can do. Strong-arm him. That's not going to work. Jesus."

"Kate, I didn't plan it like that. He came after me." He was feeling a little pissed off himself because he could hear that he sounded like he was making excuses.

She staggered and almost fell. He could see how drunk she was, catching herself on the edge of her car and then struggling to stand up. "You didn't plan anything? It just happened?" She took a deep breath and said, "I was a goddamn idiot for ever telling you. For thinking you could fix it. You just made it worse."

Jimmy said quietly, "Maybe you're drunk."

"I'm *drunk?* Why the hell shouldn't I be drunk? I got a husband who's a total jerk. I got some guy, the one time in my life I ever did something really stupid, he's got pictures of it. And I got *you.*"

"Kate . . ."

"You know what I think? I think you never should've gotten out of the Marines. I think you belong there. Your only solution is to punch somebody." She opened the door of her car, slid into the seat.

He leaned into the car and said, "Kate . . . don't go. You shouldn't be driving."

Maybe she'd have an accident and get hurt. And then how would he feel? But when he reached into the car and tried to take the keys out of the ignition she grabbed his hand and tried to bite him.

He pulled his hand away. Jesus, what did he *really* want to do? Help her? Okay, but what did *that* mean? Go on over to Pigeon Point Road and kill the guy? Take his .45, the one they issued to him in the Marine Corps, and go looking for Ellis Bowers?

When she spoke it was like she was reading his mind. "He told me, on the phone, he said, 'Tell your boyfriend that it's not just me. I'm not the only one.' He said, 'Your boyfriend comes after me again and I'll make sure your husband gets the pictures.'"

He could hear the sarcasm. "Is that what you are, Jimmy? You my boyfriend?" Squinting at him. "Maybe—maybe all it is—you thought you could get into my pants too. Is that it?" She gunned the car back down the driveway without waiting for an answer.

He stared after her car as it whipped down the road. What should he do? She was pretty lit. Should he call, make sure she got home all right? He almost laughed because he could picture it— he'd call her house, maybe get Nicky on the phone. Then what? He could maybe tell Nicky, Your wife just left my place and she was pretty drunk. Where would that get him?

He went back inside, feeling bad because it had been nice, seeing her again. Spending some time with her, getting used to the sound of her voice after so many years. And now where was he? Ellis Bowers, the little shit, was gonna try to make Katherine pay for what Jimmy had done. And Jimmy didn't know if there was anything he could do to help her. And the thing was, he wasn't sure he even wanted to try.


Nicky was listening to the radio, Frank Sinatra singing "My Way," Nicky yelling along with it. Standing naked in front of his mirror, looking at his body and singing at the top of his voice. Laughing because he was feeling great. A little hungry because he hadn't eaten anything since that morning. But he could put that off. Get dressed, go on downstairs and have a couple of Scotches. Figure out what he wanted to do next.

He heard a door slam and he walked over to the door of his

bedroom in time to see Katherine navigating the hall to her room. He was gonna say something, ask her did she want to try some of it? It killed him. What would she say if he told her, Hey, I already did it twice but maybe if you tried hard I could do it again.

He saw Katherine stumble and almost fall. She knocked into a lamp table in the hallway just outside her room but didn't even stop. He realized that she was drunk again. Jesus, his own wife, in the middle of the day and she's having trouble walking. He could still hear the sound of Frank Sinatra's voice from the radio. He started to laugh as he left his room and walked down the hallway to Katherine's bedroom.

He went in without knocking and saw her sprawled on the bed, her skirt hiked up over her thighs. He wanted to say something to her, maybe give her hell for drinking too much again. Turn her over on the bed and tell her, Hey, you can't hold your liquor, you shouldn't drink. It was why he had come in. But now, looking at her—maybe she was already asleep—staring at the backs of her thighs, he was getting a different idea in his head.

He walked over to the bed and looked down at her with his pecker sticking straight out now because he liked the idea of it, giving it to her when she didn't have a choice. It would teach her to look down her nose at him, threaten to tell about his business deals. He reached down and grabbed her hair, her precious hair, and felt her start to spin away from him but he pushed her down again.

He said, "Hey, you're a little drunk. That's okay, cause I know what'll help." He told her, "Don't talk." She was squirming down there with her face pushed into the pillow. He said, "Hey, it's all right." He lifted her skirt up over her butt and climbed on top of her. Telling her again, "Don't talk." And getting more excited because he could hear her start to cry.

. . .

Katherine got up about ten minutes later. Not crying anymore because it had dawned on her, what the hell good was that gonna do her? She could hear, outside by the pool, the stereo going full blast and Nicky singing along. She was almost sober now because that's what happens, your husband comes in and rapes you—it's the kind of thing that'll help straighten you out if you're drunk. She didn't even know if that was what it had been. Was it her fault? What would happen if she did quit drinking? Would that change things? Wondering, was it something she could do?

She was sitting on the edge of the bed with her skirt up around her waist and her panties on the floor. Saying Jesus Christ to herself because what was she doing, coming home to this house and having to deal with somebody like Nicky?

She remembered when she had first met him, he was so cute. He seemed so different from the other guys who used to come on to her when she was modeling. She'd liked him when she'd first met him. He seemed almost shy. She had to make the first move. She'd been the one to act interested first, take Nicky by the hand, almost, and show him that it was true, she did like him. And then, since he'd seemed like a nice guy, and she was able to tell herself that she loved him, she had married him and quit modeling, because at the time he had enough money for both of them.

She took a shower, standing under the water for a long time because she wanted to get rid of the feel of Nicky. Taking the soap and washing between her legs carefully. After she got out she dressed and spent some time putting a few things into a suitcase. She closed the case and looked around the room one more time, telling herself, No way, she wasn't ever gonna come back here.

She grabbed the bottle from the side of the bed and took a big drink, starting to feel drunk again even though she'd taken the shower. But not the way she usually did—like everything would be okay if she just stayed a little drunk.

She went along the hall to Nicky's room, carrying the gin bottle, still hearing the stereo blasting from the pool. She went in, banging her shin on the bed, and then limped around to the table where he put his Scotch glass every night and opened the top drawer. She had to pull some stuff out, get rid of some of the papers he had crammed in there, to get to the gun. She got it, though, a .38. She remembered when Nicky had shown it to her, looking at her with a glass in one hand and the gun in the other. Saying, "Hey, somebody ever comes in here at night—gets cute—I got this here to stop 'em." She'd thought it was kind of sexy back then, exciting, that he kept a gun nearby.

She held the pistol in her hands for a second and then picked up her suitcase. Then, carrying the gun in one hand and the suitcase in the other, she made her way downstairs and out the French doors to the patio above the pool. She stood there, with Frank Sinatra singing to her from the CD player and Nicky and Wesley sitting about fifteen feet away at a table next to the water. She didn't know when Wesley had gotten there. Had he been there the whole time? Jesus, had Nicky been upstairs holding her down on the bed while Wesley was making himself at home by the pool?

If she had the guts, she'd walk on down and shoot Nicky. Be polite about it, walk right by Wesley—maybe smile—ask him, How's it going? And then put a bullet in Nicky's face. But it wasn't something she thought she could do.

She left the suitcase on the patio and walked down the flagstone steps. There were insects in the air all around her, little gnats that she had to brush away from her face. And up in the trees, the cicadas were going crazy, buzzing away so loudly that it was almost hard to think. But she didn't let it bother her. She walked by Nicky and Wesley and went directly over to the CD player, pausing for a second when she got there to take a deep breath and lift the gun. She let her breath out slowly and then squeezed the trigger. She put a bullet into the middle of the CD player—killed the damn thing on the first shot.

Nicky had a look on his face like he couldn't believe it, like maybe he wanted to do something about it but wasn't sure what, because she still had that .38 in her hand. She looked at him for a long time and then said, trying hard not to slur the words, "Fuck you and fuck Frank Sinatra."

Wesley was looking right at her with a weird expression on his face—his one eye going crazy. Not quite smiling. But he looked like he had enjoyed it, like the sound of the gunshot had done something to him. Woken him up. Staring at her face, he said, "Nice shot."

She was ready to say something to him, but he had dropped his gaze and was staring at the pistol in her hands. Something seemed wrong. It took her a second until she figured it out: He seemed *excited.* She almost told him to go to hell, but all she wanted, now that she'd done it, was to get out of there.

By the time she reached the house, Nicky had found his voice. She could hear him down at the pool, screaming, "What the fuck is the matter with you?" But he didn't make any move to come after her.

She didn't stop until she had gotten into her car, started it up, and set the .38 down on the seat next to her. Then she sat there for a second to think it through. Because now that she'd made a move, decided to walk out—thinking it was way past time she did it—the thing was, she didn't have the slightest idea where to go.

Jimmy had spent the night thinking things over, coming up with an idea he thought might work—something that might get Kate out of the situation with no complications. But it wasn't a thing he could do on his own.

That morning he thought maybe he'd go on out and see about getting some kind of job. What he could do was apply for something with the sheriff's department. Use his military experience to get started in a career as a cop. He didn't know if it was something he wanted, or if there were even any openings. But it was a place to start.

Then, driving by, he saw Wesley walking into a bar. A place called Steamer's that had a little parking lot just off Highway 21 near the shopping center with the Winn-Dixie and the liquor store. He pulled in and parked his car and then got out, feeling the heat and smelling the salt from the bay. He walked over to Steamer's, not at all positive that he really wanted to speak to the guy, but then decided, Fuck it, he'd have a beer, say hello, and then leave. He stepped inside, felt the air-conditioning start to cool him off, and then saw Wesley at the bar.

Jimmy walked past the fish tank in the middle of the room. There were about twenty tables, with galvanized buckets set in the middle of them—you ate your dinner and threw the clam shells and crab claws in the buckets when you were done. They had little brass plaques embedded in all the tables with people's names on them. Maybe if you ate there often enough and got lucky you got your name stuck on a table.

There was nobody else at the bar so he slid onto the stool next to Wesley, who asked, "You driving or did you walk here?"

Jimmy said, "I got my car parked out front." He ordered a beer from the bartender and then asked Wesley, "Why?"

Deadpan, Wesley said, "See, I didn't hear a crash. I thought, knowing how you drive, you might've had a little trouble parking."

Jimmy smiled. "Well, I guess I got lucky." He took a drink and then looked at Wesley. "Ever since I got back, you know what I've been doing?"

Wesley shook his head and Jimmy said, "I've been going in Burger King, McDonald's, places like that. Ordering food. Or else I'll go into a bar and have a couple of beers, just to taste them. Since I got back from the Gulf, I can't get enough of fast foods. And beer—beer tastes better than I remembered it."

"How long were you over there?"

"About ten months. It's funny, because when I was over there, what do you figure I'd be thinking about? You know, getting laid, or coming home in one piece. Un-uh. Mostly, what I thought about was food."

Wesley said, "Yeah, well, see, man, you got to eat, build up energy before you can fuck."

"Uh-huh. That's all I had over there was energy. They work your ass off, getting you ready for it. I guess they figure it'll take your mind off of it. Off of what might happen. But there's no such thing as too busy to think about getting shot."

"Well, I guess it could be pretty hairy." Wesley sounded like he was trying to be nice, but Jimmy sensed that the man wasn't all there. He'd make a crack about Jimmy driving poorly, or about getting laid, and it would sound like a joke. But there wasn't any humor in the man's face. He'd sound sympathetic, tell Jimmy that being scared was understandable, but that was as far as it went. Like he was just going through the motions.

Jimmy tried not to let it bother him. "You know what the worst of it was? It wasn't getting shot, or even worrying if they were gonna use chemical weapons. I mean, some guys were terrified of gas." He thought about it and then said, "They had what they called Selective Unmasking."

"What the hell was that?"

"It's where, say you had an alert, the sensors picked up a trace of gas, or indicated that they did. See, everybody'd get into their chemical suits so fast, stand around and try not to act like they were terrified. And then word would come down, the fucking brass—some colonel down the line—would pick one platoon, or one tank unit. And they'd take their masks off first."

"No shit. Like a guinea pig?"

"Yeah. I never had to do it. But I can imagine what it would feel like, somebody orders you to be the first ones." He took a drink of his beer and then said, "For me it wasn't that—it was all the stories you heard, you know, about Moslem fanatics. The Republican Guard. I'd go to sleep at night and have these nightmares— millions of guys running at me, all they wanted to do was die, get to heaven."

"Like that truck bomb?"

"Yeah, I knew a couple of guys that were there. Guys I went to boot with that were in Lebanon when that happened."

Wesley said, "Ain't nothin' you can do about it, somebody wants to die that bad."

"Yeah, well, that's what I finally told myself."


Wesley wasn't sure what was going on. The guy shows up out of nowhere, he guessed that was okay. They could sit here for a little while and talk about things. But Wesley had a lot on his mind.

It would be all right to have a beer with the guy. Maybe he could ask Jimmy, "Hey you ever kill anybody over there?" Thinking it and saying the words almost at the same time. The Marine's expression changed. The man put his beer back on the table and said, "Yeah, two that I know of."

Wesley wanted to laugh. The guy all serious now. What he could do, he could say, Hey, don't let it bother you. Tell the Marine that he, Wesley, knew what it felt like too. Knew what it was like to squeeze a trigger. He felt like asking, Hey, you ever had some guy, over in that war of yours . . . you ever had some guy, he's down on his knees begging—got piss running down his leg he's so scared. Thinking back to it. Back up in New Jersey. The jerk-off he'd kidnapped. The guy had *watched* Wesley count the money. Still duct-taped to the chair but he must have been thinking Wesley was gonna let him go. And then Wesley had blown the man's brains all over the back wall of the storage garage. Wesley was wondering, what would the Marine say if he told him that one?

But Jimmy changed the subject. "Hey, how's it going, your business thing. Everything working out?"

Wesley paused with his hand outstretched towards his glass of beer and then said finally, "Well, it looks like it'll be all right."

"Uh-huh. Everything all right with Nicky?"

"Nicky. There's one for you." But he didn't add anything else.

Jimmy got two more beers, one for Wesley, and then asked, "You know him pretty well?"

"Nicky?"

"Yeah."

"I just met him . . . maybe six months ago." Taking a sip and then smiling. "How 'bout you?"

"Me? I just met the man the one time."

"Uh-huh." Wesley leaned back and turned a little on the stool so that he was facing Jimmy. He asked, "How about the wife?" And watched the Marine think about it, how much to say.

Jimmy was trying to be nonchalant about it, telling Wesley, "We knew each other from before. It's not a big thing."

Wesley leaned over on his stool so that his face was only about ten inches away from Jimmy's. Jimmy started to pull back— maybe because of Wesley's crazy eye.

It wouldn't be the first time somebody had backed away from Wesley and he wasn't gonna let it bother him now. He was getting a kick out of it, killing some time, playing around with the Marine. "Hey, I saw her on the tennis court, hitting those green balls all over the place—she's got that little white skirt on. That's a *good-looking* woman. If I used to know her, come back to town and found out she still looks that good, hell, I wouldn't think it was a little thing."

Jimmy stood and put a couple of bills on the bar. "I didn't give it a lot of thought. She's a married woman now." Turning to walk out.

Wesley waited until Jimmy was right next to the saltwater tank. He cleared his throat and said, very quietly, "Hey, I don't know, maybe yesterday—the day before that—maybe she was married then. But I don't know if she's still married today."

He watched Jimmy walk back. Wesley was enjoying himself now. Telling Jimmy about Katherine coming down to the pool and blowing a hole in the stereo. Seeing Jimmy's face, like he couldn't understand it at first. Then, when Wesley kept talking about it, he could see the Marine believed him. Jimmy waited until Wesley was done and then asked, "You know where she went?"

Wesley stored it away in his brain. The Marine *did* have a thing for Nicky's wife. "No idea, man," he said.

He waited until Jimmy left and then turned back to his beer, smiling and asking himself, "What ain't no big thing?"

# CHAPTER
# EIGHT

Nicky called Susie that afternoon. She had to hold the phone away from her head because Nicky was yelling. She was gonna have to wait for him to calm down before she could talk to him. She looked at the kitchen clock and wondered how long was it going to take before they could have an intelligent conversation. Every once in a while she'd say "I know," or maybe "Uh-huh," listening to him bitch about his wife.

She'd been getting ready to take a shower because Ellis was coming over and she wanted to look good, keep Ellis happy for the time being. Show him what a nice girlfriend he had.

Nicky was still furious. "She took a fucking gun. You know what I'm saying? Took a goddamn gun and shot it at my stereo. You know how much I paid for that thing?" And Susie knew that if she asked how much, he'd be able to tell her—show her the receipt. It didn't matter what it was, if he bought something, say he got a new car, he'd tell her, bragging about it, You wouldn't believe the deal I got on it. Wholesale. Act like he'd broken the salesman's heart. But the same car, if something happened to it, say it got in an accident—he'd be out in the driveway, looking at it and wringing his hands, telling her, Jesus, I paid a fortune for the thing.

When he finally calmed down she said, "What'd she do? She take off?"

"Yeah, she got in her car and left. She's been gone since yesterday. I don't know where she went, which is the reason I'm calling."

"Cause you think, what, maybe she came over here?"

She could picture Nicky throwing his hands up in the air like he always did on the phone, even though he knew she couldn't see him. Being dramatic about it and telling her, "Where else is she gonna go? You're supposed to be her friend."

Susie was surprised. She thought she had Katherine figured out but now she had to reconsider. She tried to picture it—Katherine, shooting a stereo—but had trouble with the image. Seeing instead the way the woman usually seemed to be, half-drunk most of the time. With her country-club clothes and the way she talked to Susie sometimes—like Susie was lucky to hang around with her.

Susie said, "What are you worried about? So she ran off mad. You going to tell me it's the first time that happened?"

"It's the first goddamn time she shot a gun at my stereo and then left for twenty-four hours."

"So?"

"What do you mean, 'so'?"

She had to slow down so he would listen. "Look, she wants to run away. Let her. If she comes back later, then you can see what you want to do. Give yourself a little time and maybe you won't even *want* her back. Meanwhile, go out and get yourself another stereo."

"That's not the point."

"Nicky, hon, maybe what you should do, you should tell me what the point is." She was going to have to get off in a minute and get ready for Ellis.

He hesitated. "Wesley was there. It was embarrassing."

"That's it?"

"It's not something I'm in a position . . . I can't let her do something like that."

"Why don't you wait? She'll be back. Or else, what'll happen, she'll call me. I'll get her to come on over and then I'll give you a call."

"You think so?" And then, "I told her what I got in mind, what I'm trying to do with this island thing. She looked at me like I'm some kind of criminal. Went into her room and had a couple of drinks and then came on out and talked to me like I'm some kind of slime." Susie heard him take a breath. "Hey, she doesn't seem to have trouble *spending* my money. Now, all of a sudden, she's wondering where it comes from?"

"Nicky, we've been over this, what, a couple of hundred times?"

"Yeah, but I don't want anything to happen. She's mad and she could screw everything up."

She said, "You have the whole thing under control. She got a little upset is all. But it's not like she's gonna do anything drastic."

"How do you know? Do you know what's at stake here?"

"Jesus, Nicky, she can't afford to. You know it, I know it, and she knows it. That's all—she's got to realize what'll happen if she does say anything. That's all there is to it." When he didn't argue she said, "Look, I've got to go. You sit there, or go out for dinner or something. Don't worry so much."

"What are you gonna do?"

"I'm gonna take a shower, make some dinner, cause my cousin Ellis is gonna come over."

Nicky asked, "Why's he comin' over?"

"Nicky, the man is family. Every once in a while he comes on over and I feed him some shrimp or something. Ellis is useful. Besides, I can't go out. If Katherine calls then I've got to be here."

"Yeah, all right."

"You-all sit there, have a nice evening. Think about what you've got to do next, what you're gonna say to Wesley. Keep this thing rolling."

"Yeah, but it pisses me off."

She told him, "Nicky, business first and then you can deal with your wife."

———

Susie thought Ellis Bowers looked like some kind of fish the way he was gulping down shrimp. She watched him. He'd pick one up off the pile on his plate and hold it up into the air. Look at it like he wanted to make sure it was really dead and then run it through the sauce on his plate. He didn't seem to chew it either. He'd let it sit in his mouth for a couple of seconds, sucking on it, and then he'd throw his head back and swallow the whole thing. Making a big deal out of it because he knew she was watching. All he had was maybe forty-five shrimp on his plate, some cut-up carrots, and some kind of goo in a glass next to it—a protein supplement milkshake.

He only ate fish. No red meat or even poultry. With a lot of steamed vegetables. Or else sometimes he'd just have a salad. With a big hunk of cheese and maybe some bread to chew on. A roll or something like that. Stuffing it in his mouth and trying to talk to her at the same time.

The first time he'd ever eaten with her she'd been trying to figure him out, get to know him and at the same time start telling him what she wanted to do with Nicky and Katherine, find out if Ellis was gonna be able to help her or not. So she'd made dinner for him. A first date. Asked him what he wanted and then, when he said fish, she'd gone out to Gay's Seafood and picked up a couple of flounder. Fried them up.

Ellis had complained, telling her, "You don't want to fry them, all that oil is bad for you." But he ate it anyway and then poured out his protein shake. Seeing the look on her face when he drank it, he told her, "It's healthy—one glass of this has all the vitamins you need, plus extra protein." Being serious with her.

She'd tried to kid around with him, humor him a little by saying, "Hey, maybe you should make a commercial."

He'd started to act like he *was* making a commercial, lifting the glass up so she could see it better—with a little protein mustache above his lip the same color as the blond streak in his hair.

Tonight she had a pile of tails on her plate. Not many, because she wasn't hungry. Watching Ellis eat was starting to make her feel a little queasy.

She only heard half of what he said because while she wanted to stay on top of whatever he was thinking, she also was wondering, where was Katherine? Knowing that the thing to do was find her—at least find out where she'd gone and then try to get her to talk to Nicky. Try to figure out a way to keep Katherine from doing anything stupid, something that might mess up Susie's plans. She'd told Ellis about Nicky calling. Let him think that she was keeping him informed.

Ellis asked her, "So what'd Nicky say? He misses his wife?" Tossing another shrimp into his mouth. "He's afraid maybe his old lady is gonna leave him for good this time?"

"I don't think Nicky knows what he wants. He tells me one day I can't stand my wife. Tells me she's such a priss, he can't stand it. Then she walks out and he wants her right back."

She was trying not to look at his face now because he'd gotten a piece of shrimp shell stuck above his lip, and it was catching the light and looking like some kind of fish scale.

She told him, "The thing is, with Nicky, you can't tell, you got to be careful. He'll tell you he hates his wife, and the next thing you know, he's on the phone trying to find out where she is."

"You think he misses her?"

Susie shrugged. "I don't know. He's supposed to be concentrating on business. Now all he's thinking about is his wife. He's got this idea in his head that she's gonna screw up his deal. Leave him, and then tell the investors—some of whom she knows—that he's trying to cheat them."

Ellis asked her, "What do you think?"

"You've got something on your face."

"What?"

"Right there." Pointing and then watching him wipe his mouth with his sleeve, grinning at her like a country boy, a hick. "I think, from listening to her talk about Nicky, I think she was getting ready to do it. I think she was getting her nerve up."

"Except, all of a sudden, she gets a package in the mail. Pictures of her doing something she probably should've thought twice about, huh?"

"Uh-huh. All of a sudden somebody starts to squeeze her."

97

He picked up another shrimp. "Well, hon, why don't you explain to Nicky, tell him not to worry about it. She ain't gonna say anything."

She picked up her plate and stood up. Acting mad. "See, I don't need you to tell me that. It's what I just finished telling Nicky."

"Hey, don't go getting angry. I'm talking to you about it is all." He followed her into the kitchen. "So Nicky, he's upset because his wife has gone off. And he thinks she's a risk."

"And that's what we want him to think. But, see, with Nicky, you got to keep reminding him of things like that. So, when this thing works out, whatever it is Nicky's working on, when it works out and he looks around, gets curious as to who it was that helped him out so much, there *I* am. Standing at his side with a pretty smile on my face."

He touched her arm. "Hun-bun, you can dance, you know that? You take ol' Ellis here. You been takin' him dancing. Cookin' up your schemes and you expect, what, he ain't gonna catch on? I know what you got in mind. Give Nicky over there all the encouragement in the world, keep him calm. Maybe every once in a while you wave your titties in his face. Then, when things look good, he gets rid of his old lady, it stops bothering him that she's run off because, hey, he's got you."

She got angry for real this time, because she couldn't stand it when Ellis actually started to think for himself.

Then he said, "I guess not. A smart girl like you, you'd figure out I wouldn't be happy about something like that."

"Ellis, honey, I don't know what you're getting at. The important thing here is to find Katherine. Find out where she is, but make it look like we don't know anything about the problems between her and Nicky."

She made herself talk nicely to him. "See . . . you find out where she is and I get in touch with her. She's probably sitting in some motel room, doesn't know what to do. What she needs now, she needs someone to talk to."

"You her *friend?* Is that it?"

"Hell, Ellis, that girl has told me more things about herself. Every time she's got some kind of problem—Nicky does something she doesn't like—where's she go?"

"To her buddy Susie."

She smiled. "See?"

She saw him stop looking at her face and slide his gaze down to her chest, maybe getting it in his head to try for it. She had to give him credit—if nothing else, the man was determined. She moved a little further away from him and said, "Ellis, if we got to find her, that means we don't have time to fool around."

"What're you talking about?"

She shook her head. "Jesus, Ellis, you been listenin' to anything I'm telling you?" A confused look appeared on his face because, she could tell, he wasn't sure what she was talking about.

He said, "Yeah, I'm hearing you."

"Ellis, I got this feeling, maybe you don't take this thing seriously enough. I want you to ask yourself something—you want to go back to what you were doing before? Which was, what, holding up gas stations and back-country liquor stores? Is that what you want to do?"

He said, "Hey . . ."

"Don't 'hey' me, Ellis."

It surprised her sometimes, how easy it was. Like pulling strings, watching the way he reacted to her. It crossed her mind that what she could do, someday when they had more time, she could run him through his paces. Like you would if you were training a dog. Get him to do tricks. Maybe feed him little pieces of shrimp if he did them correctly. She could get a hoop, tell him, Come on, Ellis, jump. If he got it right, she'd pop the shrimp into his mouth.

"You want to sit around and waste time, or you want to keep this thing going, so you and I have a chance to make some real money?" She stared at him for almost a full minute before asking him, "You know what my momma used to say?"

Ellis shook his head and asked, "No, what'd your *momma* used to say?"

"She said anybody that just sits around when there're things that have to be done, they aren't ever gonna get ahead."

"Hell, we're only having a little fun. Relaxing."

"You want to have fun, we can do that. After you find out where Katherine is. We get this thing worked out and you and I can do whatever you want."

Now *he* was getting a little irritated. "You keep saying that. You know that? You keep telling me . . . we do this . . . or do that—and *then* we're gonna have fun."

"Ellis, this is important. We *have* to find her."

"How the fuck am I supposed to do that?" He was still looking at her chest.

She held her hand up in the air, snapped her fingers until he looked up into her face. When he was staring right at her she said, "Ellis, I *told* you, most likely she's going to be in a motel somewhere."

"So?"

She said, "God. If she's in a motel in town, what do you think you should do?"

It took him another couple of seconds. And then he said, "You think I should drive around, look at all the motels?"

"I think that would be a good idea."

"Shit, hun-bun, why'n't you say so?"

Jimmy got the call that night. He thought maybe it was a wrong number, or a prank, because at first he couldn't hear anybody on the other end. Holding the phone, he said hello twice. He almost hung up before he heard a faint voice saying, "I don't know what to do."

He said, "Katherine . . . ?" Having to say it again before she answered, hearing her better but still having trouble making out her words. He said, "Hey . . . ," trying to be calm about it because she sounded a little drunk and he didn't want her to hang up. "Tell me where you are."

It sounded like she dropped the phone, or maybe knocked something over, Jimmy couldn't tell. He waited, thinking maybe he should shout her name, maybe she fell asleep or something. But then she said, "I'm in a motel. I ran away," sounding like a kid, talking to him in a thin, scared voice.

She told him, "I'm drunk."

"I know." He didn't know what else to say so he added, "That's okay," which sounded kind of stupid to him.

He asked her again, "Where are you?" And then had to listen to her tell him again that she was at a motel. Trying to be patient with her and saying, "I know, Kate, but tell me which one."

"I don't know . . . I forget."

He said, slower and louder than he normally would, "Kate, are you in town? You at a motel in town?" Feeling a little foolish because it was how he would've talked to a four-year-old.

After about a minute, while Jimmy chewed his fingernails, he heard her voice again, saying, "Best Western. On Bay Street."

He almost hung up because he wasn't thinking about anything

but going out and getting her. But he caught himself in time to tell her, "Don't go anywhere. Just stay there."

"Why?"

"Cause I'm gonna come get you, okay? Is that all right?"

Again he had to wait before she told him, "All right."

"What room?"

"Wait." He heard the phone being put down and a minute later she picked it up. "Room one-oh-five."

He said again, "Kate, I'm gonna come down and get you." Waiting for a reply. Not getting one. He said her name and then realized that she had hung up.

He stood in his kitchen, looking at the phone, thinking about her, seeing her in his head, pretty drunk, stuck in some motel room. Saying, "Shit" out loud and then going to get his car keys.

---

Ellis was getting pretty bored with it, driving around town to every motel he could think of. He'd started at the edge of town, right at the Beaufort River on Carteret Street, driving away from the bridge down 21, hitting the Lord Carteret Motel first and then stopping at every other motel on the way. He thought at first that it was gonna be something he could do pretty quickly. Cause how long could it take?

But it was more of a pain in the ass than he'd figured. He had to drive down the road, come to a motel and pull in, cruise around the parking lot, looking for Katherine's car, going around back too, because it occurred to him that she might have tried to be sneaky about it.

After he'd been to four or five motels he suddenly thought what if she was even sneakier than that? What if she parked down the block? Her car could be a couple of hundred feet away, or on another street, and he'd never see it. What he decided to do was start all over. Go on back to the Lord Carteret and check with the manager. Walk in the office and act like he was lost. Smile at whoever was behind the desk and tell them, embarrassed about it, Hey, I'm supposed to be picking somebody up, a date, you know? Thing is, I can't remember where she's staying.

Everybody was real nice—polite—liking the way Ellis acted. They'd check their books, look through them carefully, but come up shaking their heads. Tell him, Sorry, nobody by that name staying here.

It was starting to piss him off. He'd figured it was gonna take an hour, tops, and here he was, he'd been driving around for almost two and a half already. He was heading back from the Marine Corps Air Station. Still on Highway 21 because he'd decided to try one more time, go on back through town, take the right onto Bay Street, and see if maybe he'd get lucky. He pulled into the Best Western and didn't see Katherine's Cherokee. He didn't pay any attention to any of the other cars. So at first he didn't even notice the Ford—he drove right by and saw the dinged-up fender but it didn't register. Not until he put his car in reverse and started to back up so he could go to the office to ask whether or not she had gotten a room. He saw the Ford again, the fender, the way it was crumpled up a little bit, and it hit him, Hell now, I've seen that car before. Smiling because it came back to him. Lying on the pavement, with his nuts killing him and watching the guy out of the corner of his eye, getting into that same car and driving over to pick up Katherine.

Ellis pulled into the corner of the lot and killed the engine. He was grinning in the darkness, saying to himself, See, you go out, you're trying to do one thing, and what do you know, you end up doing something even better. What would you call that, when it happened, something unexpected, bigger than you thought? Escalation? Maybe that was it. He'd heard a newscaster on TV say that about some war one time—it had escalated. Yeah, running the word over in his head, because he was gonna fuckingescalate the owner of the banged-up Ford, was what he was gonna do.

He reached over to the glove compartment, opened it, and took out his gun. A Colt All American, Model 2000. A 9mm semiautomatic pistol that had fifteen fucking rounds in the magazine. He held it in his hand, looking over at the Ford and pointing it. He stared down the barrel and said, "Pow." Thinking, Hey, you want to kick somebody, make them feel like puking, come on out here and see what I got for you.

Maybe what he'd do, he'd wait for the guy to come out, wait for him to get in his car, and then, right when he was ready to pull out, Ellis would drive on over, block him and smile. Say something. Ask the dude, How's it going? And then pull that 9mm out and let him look at it. Let him see what was happening. See if he looked like one of those kids Susie'd told him about. The ones always getting Jell-O put in their clothes. Yeah, point the Colt at the guy. See what kind of look he got on his face. And then put a couple into his chest.

Ellis was trying out different lines—drive over and smile, say, Nice night, huh, and then pull the gun into view. He shook his head, wanting to get it just right so the guy would be totally shocked. Trying it again, saying, Surprise, asshole, but not liking that much either. Maybe he could just ask the guy, You ever been *escalated?* He wasn't sure though if the guy would get it. He decided what he'd do, he'd just wait until it happened, say whatever came into his head because it wasn't like it mattered. The guy wasn't gonna have a whole lot of time to appreciate the humor of the situation.

He was still thinking about it when a door opened and he saw Jimmy step into the light. He tried to get a better look, make sure. He reached for the ignition switch so that he'd be ready. He was thinking, Give the man just enough time to get to his car—wait until he closes the door and then drive over and pull in front of him. He was drumming his fingers on the seat, waiting, when he saw Katherine step into the light. It took him by surprise, because he'd forgotten about her. He'd put her out of his head because he'd just assumed that it was the guy who had the motel room.

Ellis wasn't sure what to do now. Because now he wasn't gonna be able to use the gun. He watched Jimmy walk Katherine across the parking lot, holding onto her with one hand and carrying a suitcase with the other. Katherine didn't look too steady to Ellis. She was half-asleep or else she was drunk. Wearing a T-shirt and a pair of jeans, with her hair falling down in front of her face. Ellis thought it didn't matter if she was drunk, she looked pretty good to him. Get a nice-looking woman like that, she's had too much to drink, hell, you can make her do anything you want. Ellis got a little excited and almost forgot that he should follow them. They drove away before he even reached for his own keys. He had to gun his car, screech the wheels when he started up, to make it out onto the road before they disappeared.

When it got to the Beaufort River the Ford kept going and Ellis followed it across the bridge, slowing down when they got across. The Ford signaled for a turn and then took the right onto Meridian Road. He gave it a couple of seconds before he made the turn. He wasn't worried anymore was he gonna lose the Ford, and he didn't want the guy to see that he was being followed.

He got to Jimmy's house just in time to see the car lights go off on the Ford. He coasted to a stop a couple of hundred feet up the road. He sat there, with a clear view of the house and the driveway. The dome light came on and two figures got out. Ellis got out of his car after a couple of seconds, taking the 9mm with him, telling himself he was only gonna go over and check things out—see if he could find out what the guy's name was.

He heard the door to the house slam as he stood by the mailbox trying to make out the name on it. He read "Decker" and then wasn't sure what to do next. He figured he'd go on up to the house, maybe peek in the window. He was moving up the driveway when the side door of the house opened and Jimmy stepped out into the light. At first Ellis thought Jimmy might've seen him, because he looked out towards the road. But he was only looking around in the night, the way anybody would if they stepped outside. Ellis told himself that there was no way the man could've seen him.

Jimmy went over to the Ford and opened the door. The man leaned into the car like he'd forgotten something while Ellis watched, hating the guy, picturing the way he'd kicked him and wanting to do something back. Thinking, Hey, maybe I can't kill you but I can see what you're up to. See where you fit into things with the Kramer bitch. And maybe I can put a scare into you, make you poop your pants.

Ellis raised the Colt All American. Liking the way it felt, pointing a gun at some motherfucker, some cracker that'd been a jerk. He enjoyed it. Thinking about it, in the second before he actually pulled the trigger, he decided it was the right thing to do.

Jimmy stood up with the suitcase in his hands. All of a sudden he turned towards Ellis. Ellis didn't understand it, he hadn't made a sound, hadn't moved. There was no way the guy could've known he was there, but somehow he did. He turned and looked at him, stared right at the spot where Ellis was standing and then dove to the ground just as Ellis fired.

Ellis felt the gun kick, heard the sound of glass breaking, and then fired again. He felt great. It was like getting laid almost. He fired one more time, grinning like a maniac, and then realized that he had no idea where the motherfucker was. With all the noise, the guy could've made it through the bushes and Ellis wouldn't've known it. Hell, he could be ten feet away right now.

He started to walk back down the driveway towards the road, not remembering until he was pretty far down the drive that he had wanted to say something, yell something at the guy. Trying to think of something good, remember what he'd practiced back there at the motel, remember the word he'd thought of. But all he could come up with was, "See . . . see that." Staring down at the Ford, with its rear window gone now, he yelled, "See that, asshole."

He raised the pistol one more time and fired towards the house, heard the bullet ricochet, and then turned and started to trot back to his car, hurrying a little bit, so that by the time he got there he was almost running. Not scared. He told himself it wasn't that, it was just that he'd better get out of there. Maybe somebody had called the cops. He started the car up and made a U-turn. Driving back towards Beaufort he was smiling, thinking he'd done the right thing. Somebody fucks with Ellis Bowers and what would happen, Ellis Bowers would fuck with them right back.

It was amazing to Jimmy how fast the reactions returned. The feeling of combat rushed back into his head so that it wasn't like he had to think at all. He had stood up with the suitcase in his hands and all of a sudden he could feel it. It was something that he knew, without being able to explain it. Something inside his head that made him look down the driveway to where the man with the gun was. He saw the man's silhouette and it wasn't like he had to think about it. He just got it in his head suddenly that he'd better move, get out of the light.

He hit the ground just as the rear window of the Ford exploded. He lay next to the car as pieces of glass rained down on him and then crawled quickly to the front of the car, away from the gunman. He heard two more shots, one of which slammed into the Ford.

He knew he had to get away from the car, playing all the old movie scenes over in his head where somebody shot a gas tank and the whole car went up in flames. He had a gun, his Marine .45, sitting upstairs in his bedroom, and his old 30.06 up in the attic, but that wasn't gonna do him a whole lot of good now. Another bullet thudded into the car and it occurred to him that whoever it was out there wasn't being very patient about things. It sounded like somebody was out by the end of the driveway and just plunking away at the Ford. Like he didn't really have any idea where Jimmy was. Not aiming at all. An amateur.

He was hoping that Katherine wouldn't come wandering out. She was pretty drunk, and the last time he'd seen her, a couple of minutes before, she'd been lying down on the couch like she was gonna pass out. But if she did come out she'd be standing right in the pool of light from the house.

He heard somebody yelling, "See that . . . asshole." And then one more shot followed by the sound of running feet and a car door slamming. A second later the car roared down the road.

He climbed slowly out from behind the car, not taking any chances. He hurried over to the house and went inside, past where

Katherine, still awake, sat on the couch looking at him with wide eyes, and up the stairs to his bedroom. He got his .45 and went back downstairs.

By the time he got outside it was like it had never happened. The insects had started up again, the cicadas, and he could hear the sound of traffic out on 21. He made his way to the end of the driveway, keeping to the shadows, being careful but not really worried about it. He was pretty sure that it was over. It had sounded like one person, maybe somebody who had never done anything like that before. Somebody fairly pissed off, standing at the end of the driveway and taking a couple of shots at him.

Now who the hell would want to do a thing like that?

# CHAPTER

# NINE

Nicky said to Wesley, "This guy coming out, he's Tom Neff, our ace in the hole." And then he lowered his voice. "He's going to bring two potential investors with him. Tom knows what the score is. He doesn't know about you, that you know what's happening too. But I want to keep it that way. See, he's out to make a couple of bucks just like you and me. But that's it."

Wesley said, "Okay."

And Nicky told him, "What we're trying to do—you and I— we're trying to convince a couple of people that they'd be crazy not to come in on this deal. We want them to think that buying this land is the best idea they've ever heard."

Wesley said, "I know that."

Nicky nodded. "The thing is, these guys, they're a little nervous but they know me, know my wife. Which is the reason they're willing to consider it."

Wesley heard a little syrup slipping into Nicky's voice and said, "You want me to be quiet mostly, huh?"

Nicky grinned, slapping Wesley on the back. "You don't mind? All you got to do . . . you're just another interested party. Another investor. That way, when you act like you think it's a good thing, something to jump at—hell, they're gonna feel the same way."

"You're gonna scam 'em."

Nicky frowned. "Hey, we're talking about grown-up fellows here. They got their eyes open."

Wesley said, "Uh-huh." Thinking he was gonna keep *his* eyes open too. "Long as we remember whose money you and I are using to make it look good."

"Hey, you don't have to worry about *that*."

When Nicky introduced Wesley to Tom Neff, he made a joke out of it, saying, "This is Tom, he comes with the pool." There were two other guys with Neff, two men dressed in golf clothes who'd come out to talk about buying an island. Wesley heard their names, Garner and somebody else, a doctor. He didn't give a fuck who they were.

Wesley took time to study Neff. The man acted nervous, asking did Nicky have any iced tea when everyone else said Scotch would be fine.

The other two men were older than Neff, maybe late fifties. Both of them were pretty tan, but Wesley noticed that their tans ended right where their shirtsleeves did, like they either spent a lot of time on the golf course or maybe they went boating without taking their shirts off.

Neff perked up when they got down to business. He opened his attaché case when Nicky started to talk about the land deal. When Nicky got to the part about putting up condos on the island he looked at Wesley to let him know he was supposed to go into his act, pretend he was just another investor.

Nicky walked over to the liquor cart by the gate to the pool. Acting a little different now, not fooling around. Doing business, with a look on his face like he knew what he was talking about. Wesley could see it, thinking maybe it was the reason Nicky could win ten grand at the casino and act cool about it. Because maybe, underneath the bullshit, a part of Nicky knew what he was doing.

Nicky said to Neff, "Why don't you tell everyone where we stand?"

Neff cleared his throat and nodded. He was just getting a word out when Susie walked through the French doors and looked down at them. She stood there with a pair of shorts on and a little halter top—a T-shirt that she'd cut the arms out of and then cut high along the waist—grinning at everyone, and then she walked down the steps to stand near Nicky. She waited maybe half a minute, with everybody looking at her quietly, and then said, "Nicky, I come all the way over and you're not even going to *introduce* me?"

Nicky seemed pissed off at first. Wesley, looking at the two of them, thought Nicky looked like a kid who'd just got caught stealing something.

Nicky got up out of his chair and took Susie by the arm, walking her over to the cabana. Neff said to Wesley, "I didn't expect this."

Nicky, holding Susie's arm, asked her, "The fuck're you doing?"

"Nicky, I got to thinking—you're over here; your wife, you don't even know where she is; and I thought, why not come on over and see how you were doing?"

"Jesus, I got a meeting going on."

"I know." She was frowning, acting stupid. Looking at the men in the chairs and asking Nicky, "What's the matter with his eye?"

"What?" He was off balance, still worried about her being there.

"His eye, the one guy, what's wrong with it?"

He shook his head, impatient, glancing at Wesley and saying, "He got poked with a stick or something." Taking a step closer to her and saying, "Look, I got people here, they don't want to have to talk about things in front of you. They don't know who you are."

She grinned at him. "But you do."

"So?"

She reached over and took his hand off her arm. "Nicky, what you have to do is relax. Act like you want me here, is all. Guys like that, it makes them feel important to talk about money in front of a woman."

He didn't say anything until she touched him and said, "You have that guy there." She pointed at Neff. "That one. He's looking at me like he's never seen a woman before."

"So. Everyone else is too."

"Not like him. He can't take his eyes off of me."

"So?"

"So, let me ask you this, is he someone important to you?"

"You mean, do I need his help?"

She nodded.

"Yeah, sure." He looked at Neff. "I need him to make the thing look good. Convince the other investors."

Susie reached up and grabbed Nicky's chin, turning his face back to her. "Hey, you got a guy over there, he's staring at me, can't take his eyes off of me. If you need him you'd be crazy to send me away."

She had to wait for a minute, while he thought it over, the idea going through his head until he decided he liked it. Nodding finally, saying, "Okay."

She smiled. "Jeez, of course it's okay." Putting her arm through his and turning him back to the pool.

They came back from the cabana, with Susie linking her arm through Nicky's and Nicky trying to smile. He walked Susie over to the four men and said, "Hey, this here is my friend Susie."

And Susie, standing there like she belonged with the house and the pool and everything else, smiled at everybody and said, "Hey," exaggerating her southern drawl. She said, "You-all gonna buy an island?"

She took her halter top off and then dropped her shorts to reveal a tiny bathing suit, the top barely covering her boobs. Wesley saw Tom Neff staring at her, his eyes looking like they were gonna fall out of his head, and he wanted to say something, ask the man was he okay? But he didn't. The other two men were staring too. He wasn't sure what was going on. Was this something Nicky had planned?

Susie folded her clothes carefully and then sat down on the chair between Wesley and Neff. She said, "Don't go letting me interrupt anything."

Nicky cleared his throat. "We're talking about buying this island."

Susie said, "I know *that*." But then she smiled at the other two men, including them in some kind of joke, her teeth flashing they were so white. She said to everyone there, "I've heard a lot about this. So I figured, why not come on over and meet all of you." She touched Wesley on the knee and said, "You don't mind, do you?"

Wesley thought maybe somebody should smack this little girl— put her over their knee and give her a couple of whacks on her bottom. But it wasn't like he was gonna let her know that now. He thought maybe it was something Nicky *had* planned. "Make yourself comfortable," he said to Susie.

The doctor said, "There's room for everybody."

Neff nodded finally, looked at Nicky, and said, "Well, the property we're looking at is virtually undeveloped. We're talking about an island that has remained almost untouched for fifty years. No electricity, no water, except from one small well. A couple of cabins—shacks, really. And what they are, they're grandfathered in. You can't change them."

Susie said, "What's that mean?"

Neff said, "All it means is that they were built before there was any zoning, probably thirty or forty years ago. And then passed down from the original owners." He spoke to the whole group. "The thing is, you have a property like that, right now the state has it zoned as a wilderness preservation area. They've declared parts of the island a wetlands. That means you can't build anything on it."

Wesley said, "I can understand that."

Nicky spoke up. "Gentlemen, what we're talking about is an island that hasn't changed in fifty, maybe a hundred years. It's just sitting out there."

Neff cleared his throat and Wesley glanced at his face. He could see the man was into it, talking faster now. He seemed to know what he was talking about. The other two men were listening intently. They looked like overgrown school kids, listening to the teacher because they thought maybe there was gonna be a test later.

Neff said, "Right now, realistically, the island is almost worthless."

Wesley had to ask, "All that land?"

Neff smiled. "Uh-huh. Virtually worthless. Think about it. It's zoned as a wilderness preservation area. But the titles aren't owned by the state or the county. All the state—or in this case, the county—controls is the zoning. The cabins and the land are privately owned."

Nicky said, "If the zoning stays the same, you can't build. And if you can't build on it, then the land is useless, not worth a thing." He laughed. "What are you going to do, rent out a couple of fifty-year-old cabins? That ain't gonna make you a lot of money."

Wesley said, "So you change the zoning? Get it changed to residential?"

Nicky said, "No. First you buy the fucking thing. That's the beautiful part."

Susie interupted. "Wait a minute, you buy something that you know is worthless?"

Neff nodded. "Yes. Since, at this point, the island has no developmental potential, you can buy it for a song."

Nicky said, "A song means around a thousand dollars an acre. The three families that own it are desperate to get rid of it."

The doctor asked, "Why?"

Nicky smiled. "Because the nearest one, the only owner currently on the East Coast, lives in Pittsburgh. So every year, what are they doing, the three families? They're paying taxes on something they can't even get to."

Neff told the group, "We've already approached the owners with an offer. We get an option to purchase the land at a thousand dollars an acre—it'll cost us forty thousand dollars a year to hold the option. We option it for two years, say eighty grand, by then we're ready to start construction. We're all set. We do that, we're talking eight hundred acres, three-quarters of it usable land.

Maybe an eighth of it is beachfront—quarter and half-acre lots. Minus enough for the marina, stores, and the golf course. You're talking around five hundred acres. That's fifteen hundred mixed-use lots."

Garner said, "Wait a minute . . ."

Nicky laughed. "How're we gonna start construction if nobody can build on the island, is that what you're thinking?"

"And you've got an answer."

"Uh-huh. But why don't I have Tom tell you a little more about the island first."

Neff pulled out a map from his briefcase and spread it on the concrete. "What this is, it's called an illustrative master plan. You can see exactly what the island'll look like when we're through." He pointed to a spot on the map. "See, here you got the entrance, the gate house. It's the only way on or off the island except by boat."

Nicky said, "By the way, that gate house will be manned by the island's private security force."

Neff said, "Sure, we'll have patrols, make sure everything is all right. Make sure nobody's there that isn't supposed to be."

He went back to the map. "You can see here, this road, it's Bayshore Drive. It's where the single-family dwellings will be. They all face the ocean. You got a shopping center, a minimall with small strip-shopping areas—your convenience stores—and around that we put up high-density, multifamily units, four floors.

Nicky grinned. "He means condos."

Neff smiled too. "Yes, condos."

Nicky took a step closer. "Up here, you got the golf course and next to it, the driving range. You got two pools, one here and one over there by the clubhouse. You got tennis courts, a marina, and next to it, a small boat ramp. You set it up so that you can get charter fishing out of the marina, take folks out to the Gulf and have 'em fish for marlin."

Neff smiled. "I'll go out myself."

Nicky said, "Fifteen hundred units, the back lots, maybe you can't even *see* water from them, *they're* gonna be going for ninety-five grand."

Neff pulled another paper from his attaché case. "Listen to this, this is what's known as a current market activity survey." He started to read. "'Population and household formations in South-eastern South Carolina, specifically Beaufort and Jasper counties, was modest in the 1970s, with an annual gain of only 1.1 percent in terms of population and only 2.0 percent in terms of house-holds.'" He flipped through the pages and then started to read again. "'The above table shows that during the 1980s, specifically the late 1980s, the population increased more than 3.7 percent annually.'" He put the paper back into his case and said, "That may not sound like a lot but it is."

Nicky said, "It's more than three times what it was fifteen years ago. And all those people're going to need a place to live. And they're going to want to be close to the water."

Wesley heard Susie say, "Jesus," but he ignored her. When he looked at Nicky, the man actually winked at him. Wesley wished he could take Nicky aside for a couple of seconds and tell him not to be *too* much of an actor. Grab him by the arm and say, Hey, don't overdo it. Wesley asked Neff, acting like he wasn't sure it sounded so good, "Tell me—all this money we're gonna make—tell me how much it's gonna cost."

Nicky spoke right up. "I can answer that. But before I do, let me tell you something else, the beauty of the thing. You got your lots, you're selling them, starting at quarter-acre density, in the neighborhood of ninety-five thousand. Then you get prospective buyers, they buy the land. Who're they gonna get to build? We've already got it set up where they're gonna have a choice between one of three construction firms. We put a tag on it, call 'em preferred builders, some shit like that. Get the builders to offer incentive packages to the buyers and then, since we got these builders in there to start with, they kick back ten percent of their gross to us."

The doctor said, "Yes, get that money rolling back in." Everybody looked at him and Nicky grinned.

He said, "We're gonna get that money rolling in from every direction. It's the way you do it."

Wesley cleared his throat. "You didn't answer my question. How much?"

Nicky looked like he was gonna have to give them some bad news. He took a swallow of his Scotch and then said to Wesley, "See, that's where it gets a little heavy. We're talking about a gold mine here. We're talking about taking useless land and turning it into something that's worth a fortune. But it involves a lot of time and expense to get going. Just to get started is going to cost a lot. You got to get sewers and electricity in there. You have to build roads, an access bridge. You have to have plans for subdividing the land, a plan you can take to the county and say, Lookit here, this is what we're thinking of doing." He waited a few seconds and then sighed. "All that costs money."

"You got other investors. What do they think?" Wesley asked.

Neff answered, "Are you kidding me? They can't wait for us to get going."

Nicky said, "As soon as we get the okay, we have a sewage treatment plant built. Seven hundred thousand gallons, which is more than enough for us to start to sell the properties. See, you can start construction as soon as the basics are in place. We expect to get okays for the treatment plant within the month. We got two deep-water wells ready to be built. The sites are already selected." He got out of his seat and started to walk back and forth in front of the group, acting excited. "You start construction, get the okays, and the thing is, you can start to sell right away. You don't have to wait." He looked at Neff. "Am I right?"

Neff nodded. "You get brochures made up, get a couple of townhouses built. They don't even have to be finished, just put up the basic shells and you can start to sell. Start to get money back on your investment."

Nicky said, "Hell, there're people all over—up north, Ohio, Pennsylvania, wherever—who'll be fighting to get a place on an island like this."

There was silence for about a minute. And then Garner asked, "The bottom line, all you have to do is get the zoning?"

Nicky nodded. "See, that's not a problem, though." He pointed at Neff and said, "What Tom does, when he's not out here enjoying my pool, what he does is, he works for the county commissioners. They control county land use." Waiting and then telling everyone, like it was the punchline to a joke, "Zoning."

Wesley wondered how much Neff was thinking to make? Was he gonna do it for a flat fee or was he in for a percentage? He asked, "That's your job?"

"Uh-huh."

Nicky said, "But there's a catch. See, Tom, he's on our team. He knows what a beautiful thing this is going to be. He's got the vision to see it. We buy that land, change the zoning, and bingo, it's worth twenty times what it is now." He walked over to where Neff sat and put a hand on the man's shoulder. "That's not a problem. But the members of the board, they see it differently." Nicky paused, making sure they were all following him. "We got the investors, the people with the money, ready to move. And I mean the big money for construction. But the county commissioners, the board members, they only see it as what's in it for them."

Wesley said, "Uh-huh." Still acting like he wasn't too impressed. Pretending he was an investor who wasn't too sure. "You wanna tell me something?"

"What?"

"What *is* in it for them?"

Neff started to reply but Nicky interrupted him. "One point five million dollars. Spread out among all five members of the board." He took a breath and then said, "Cash."

The sound of his words floated in the air for a minute. He could hear Susie take a deep breath and then let it out slowly.

Wesley looked back at Neff. "That much, huh?"

The man nodded and said, "Then it's guaranteed."

Wesley thought, Ain't nothing guaranteed, man. He told Nicky, "I'll think it over and let you know."

Nicky said, "Hey, I can't ask for anything more than that."

Wesley said good-bye to everybody and then got up and started to walk back into the house. Nicky caught up with him by the French doors, reached out and touched his shoulder.

Nicky said, "Hey, you did all right back there."

"It's not a big thing, scam guys like that. And Neff, he can't take his eyes off your girlfriend."

"Yeah, well, that's all right. It doesn't hurt. And you need guys like Neff to get a thing like this going."

"Yeah, I can see, you got to have people in a position to help you out."

Nicky bobbed his head. "Right. You gotta have people like that. Convince the others. I got people lined up, friends of my wife, they want in on this so bad they can taste it. Not just those two. I'm talking respectable men of the community. They got cash lying around they don't know what to do with."

Wesley said, "Yeah? They're such good friends of your wife? Lemme ask you something, what're they gonna say, since, when they come out here, you got your girlfriend walking around with a bathing suit on, it's not any bigger than my thumb practically?"

"No, that's all right, I got her out here just for Neff. Let him stare at her a little bit. Make him feel important."

Wesley made a show of looking around, turning his head to look back at the tennis court. "And your wife? She around? Cause last time I saw her, she had a pistol in her hand and was making a statement about the kinda music you listen to."

"Hey, let me worry about that. My wife knows what she's gotta do." He put a smile on his face. "Just relax. It's going over very well. We got it practically sewed up. Garner is the biggest talker in the club. He and Hills, the doctor, are already half-convinced. And they got all kinds of connections. They spread the word and then we get them to put up half the bribe money. I'm talking cash. And then . . . BANG. You and me, we walk with it, we smile at those snotty sons of bitches and tell them to get fucked."

Wesley didn't say anything until Nicky and he had reached Wesley's car. He looked up at Nicky's house and then at Nicky, nodding finally and saying, "So, you use people your wife knows . . ."

"Hey, I know them too."

". . . and then you fuck 'em?"

Nicky grinned. "Sure, why not?"

Wesley shrugged finally. "See, if that's the way to do it . . . if that's the way it is, then okay, man."

"Sure."

"But here's the thing. You want to fuck somebody, make somebody come out on the bottom end of this thing." Looking at Nicky pretty hard. "You want to make sure it's somebody else, make sure it isn't me."

Nicky said, "Hey, what is this? We're friends here."

# CHAPTER

# TEN

Jimmy was out back on the dock, sitting there with a fishing rod in his hands. He'd cast his line out into the bay, with a piece of shrimp on the hook, and let it sit there. Nothing was biting. A couple of times he thought he felt something, a quick tug. He'd reel the line in and the bait would be gone but he knew it wasn't a fish, at least not a fish big enough to hook. Maybe it was crabs. Blue claws. They'd be down there in the muck on the bottom of the bay, get to the bait, and start to eat it off the hook. Not jerking on it but maybe moving with it a couple of inches so that Jimmy would feel the line tighten a little bit.

There was a lot of glare on the water. It made it difficult to see. But if he looked further out into the bay, a couple of hundred feet away, he could see some porpoises. It looked like there were two or three of them, chasing a school of mullet probably. And above them were a bunch of seagulls, scavengers, waiting for any piece of mullet that might float to the top.

He was watching the porpoises and thinking about his bait down there in the water because he didn't want to think about Katherine. He didn't know what to think about her.

She'd come out of the house about ten minutes earlier puffy-eyed and squinting against the sun. He figured she had to be hung over. She was moving slowly, holding her head very carefully, and not taking the chance of doing anything quickly, making the pain in her head even worse.

He wondered, when had she started to drink so much? And why? Back in high school, they'd get a six-pack, or maybe a couple of bottles of beer that they stole from their folks. And they'd go out to the beach and have a couple of drinks. But nothing much, nobody getting out of hand, getting sick or passing out. And now all of a sudden it looked like she was a lush. He didn't know if it was something she did regularly or if it was something she just started because she was upset.

He'd seen her coming across the lawn, carrying two mugs and wearing jeans, sneakers, and one of his shirts. Not making a sound except for the creak of her shoes on the wooden dock. She handed him a mug and sat down, held her cup to her lips, and looked out at the water. She had on sunglasses, the same ones he'd seen her wearing when they'd had the accident.

He didn't know what to say to her. She didn't look too hot. He thought she would always be pretty, but she looked run-down. Sick. Which was understandable.

But what was he supposed to say? There was a lot going on. He didn't even know what most of it meant. Or what to do about it.

Had he even thought of Katherine before she ran into him with her car? Maybe every once in a while, in the past ten years, he'd be somewhere, or something would remind him of her and he'd get a picture of her in his head. But it wasn't like he'd spent his nights dreaming of her. And now what? He'd come back here and all of a sudden she was staying in his house.

From spending just a little time with her, just a couple of hours in the last two days, he realized that he still liked her. But it wasn't like he'd planned the thing. Jesus, if somebody had asked him what do you want to do when you get back from the Gulf, first from a war and then from eight months of sitting in Saudi Arabia, he wouldn't have told them that he wanted to get involved in this mess.

She was sitting sideways a couple of feet away from him. With her legs crossed and the coffee mug between her hands. Not looking at him either. Staring out over the water. A little hung over and embarrassed. Maybe she too was thinking it hadn't been such a smart idea to call him. When she woke up that morning and realized where she was, what if the first thing she'd wanted to do was get out of there?

She startled him by saying, "You think I drink too much?"

He didn't say anything. He was listening but otherwise he didn't do anything to stop her from talking.

She smiled weakly. "Maybe I do. I even had a couple of drinks the day I first came over here. Like it was something I couldn't do sober." She pulled her hair away from her face, ran her fingers through it, and shook her head slowly. "I guess that's a shitty way to be. You do something, anything, go to the grocery store or go visit an old friend and you're at the point in your life where it seems impossible unless you have a couple of drinks first."

He said carefully, "Well, a lot of people feel like that. You go somewhere, a party, there're people you don't know. You feel awkward. You have a couple of drinks."

"Uh-huh. Yeah, everybody does that. Most people, I guess. But what I'm saying, I'm not talking about that"—she took a sip of her coffee—"I don't know—I can't even really remember because it's not something you can look back on and say, That's what happened. But I suppose that's how it started, you know, drinking like that, and then maybe it became a problem. You can't seem sometimes to get through the day without making everything a little blurry."

"Is that what you do?"

"I think, if I hadn't been drinking, taking the edge off, for something like the last two years, I think I wouldn't be here."

"What do you mean?"

"See, I know it's not a way to be. Not a good thing if you believe that the only way you can cope is if you're drunk. It's no way to live."

"No."

"But what if . . . what if the alternative seems worse?"

"I don't know."

She stared at the sky for a minute and then told him, talking a little too loudly, "See, I can quit. Anytime. I just don't see any reason to. That's all. It's easier this way."

He asked, "Is that what happened to you, you just started drinking?"

She looked out at the water again. She was quiet for a minute and then said, so softly now that Jimmy had to lean forward to hear her, "I don't know what happened to me."

He put the fishing rod away and walked with her back into the house, feeling the sun on his back. He remembered when he was a kid, he'd come out here with his old man, fish for croakers or flounder until his mom called them in for dinner. The same smells and sounds. The feel of the bay breeze coming in and the sound of cars whizzing by out on Highway 21.

A few minutes later he was sitting at the kitchen table and watching Katherine do the dishes. He didn't say anything at first because he couldn't help it, he liked the way she looked. More wide awake now. Maybe the coffee had helped. Standing there, with her back to him, she was washing dishes. And what he was doing—sitting at the table—he was staring at her.

Did she know he was looking at her? Know what he was thinking? Looking at her fanny right now and trying to compare it to what he remembered when they were back in high school together. She was a little heavier back then. Not fat, but she would've filled the jeans out more. You get a teenage girl, she could be beautiful but she'd have a different kind of a figure than a woman in her thirties. Even back when he was dating Katherine, every once in a while he'd see an older woman. A woman who seemed a lot older to him because she was maybe twice his age. And he'd take a look at her. Even back then, he thought it was better, sexier, the way an older woman looked.

He wondered what Katherine looked like now with her clothes off. Was she a lot different than she'd been twelve years before, when he used to watch her undress? They'd be in his house, maybe his parents were out for a couple of hours and they'd sneak up to his room and do it. He'd sit there on the bed, feeling stupid because he'd be down to his socks in about seven seconds. But she'd take her time about it. Smile at him and maybe giggle because she knew he was dying for it, knew he wanted her to get in the bed right then. But she'd tease him. Take her time getting naked and then she'd crawl into bed with him and they'd fuck. Except she always made him call it "making love." She'd look at him back then and say, "I don't like the sound of it—the 'F' word. I don't like the way it sounds at all."

Had she ever thought about the two of them, back in high school, finding out about sex together? He was still looking at her, not even realizing that the water had stopped running, that she was done with the dishes, until she turned towards him. He knew he'd been caught staring and wondered should he say something, try to make a joke out of it? Smile and say, Hey, I'm kidding around here.

She stepped away from the sink. He was locked on to her face now, not able to take his eyes from it because there was something new in the room, something that hadn't been there five minutes before, and he knew, without even really putting it into thought, that it was important to both of them.

She reached down slowly now, to the waist of her pants, and grabbed her shirt. He could see her hands trembling, thinking, Jesus, she was nervous too. She peeled the shirt up and over her head, getting it caught in her hair and having to twist her neck to get free. She wasn't wearing a bra. Her breasts were smaller than he remembered. But beautiful. With a little row of freckles across the top of them. Still not saying anything, she unbuttoned her Levi's. Pulled them down over her legs and then stepped out of them and moved towards the table.

He couldn't believe it, looking at her from two feet away, in nothing but her underwear. White, with lace along the top and along the edge of the crotch. She was gorgeous, standing in his kitchen, trembling a little bit, like she was about to start crying.

He stood up and touched her face. "Hey, you don't have to . . ." But not finishing it because she leaned into him. Pressed her face into his shoulder and said, "Don't say anything."

He could feel her breasts, pressed into his arms. Felt her hand go down to his belt and then she was tugging at him. Having trouble with it so that he had to step back and help her. Both of them pulling at his clothes and then he was naked too. He took her by the hand and led her into the living room. Over to the couch. They lay down with her underneath him and he kissed her. Still nervous, but then getting used to it, remembering the way it had been before and thinking maybe it was still gonna be the same.

She must have been thinking the same thing because she said, "Do you remember how it used to be?"

He nodded, stroking her cheek. "It was good back then. Everything was good." And then she moved back into his arms again. Pressing against him and starting to moan, then saying, right into his ear, "Fuck me." Making him wonder what *else* had changed in ten years?

Later she started to smile, lying in his arms naked. With her leg looped over his. And then she started to laugh. Because she had done it without really giving it too much thought. She wasn't worried that she was falling back in love with him or anything like that. She didn't think so. All that mattered was that he was a man, somebody different than Nicky, who looked like he wanted her. She wondered, if he knew, what would Nicky say? Almost wanting him to know. The son of a bitch, let him see what it was like to get hurt.

She moved in Jimmy's arms so that she was looking right at him, conscious of her hair, the way it was spread out on the couch underneath her, the way it must look to him.

He asked her, "What are you thinking?"

And she said, "I can't think of a nicer thing to do than to lie here today and make love to you." She sounded happy. She could hear it in her own voice.

Jimmy said, "Yeah?"

She asked, "Do you know what you're doing?"

"What do you mean?"

"Getting involved with me. Did you give it any thought?"

"Did I plan it? Something like that?"

"I don't think either one of us planned anything. But did you ever think it would happen?"

"No."

She raised herself up on her elbow. Staring out across the room—but still smiling—letting him know she was kidding around and telling him, "You're probably making a mistake. I'm a drunk. A drunk with a lousy marriage."

"And you're being blackmailed. Don't forget that."

"Yeah."

He said, "Let me ask you something. Why, if you don't like your husband—"

"Which I don't."

"Right. So, if you don't like him, why don't you just divorce him?"

"Leave?"

"Well, you already did *that*. But if you're unhappy there, then you could get out."

"Just take off. Get a divorce."

He said, "I'm wondering, is all."

"I could do that. I was at the point, a while back, when I almost did. I was thinking about it when I got the pictures in the mail."

"So?"

"So, the thing is, what would I do? Where would I go? If I

divorce Nicky, what do I have? You think I could walk away and he'd give me anything to live on? A couple of times, I almost begged him to give me a divorce. You know what he did?"

"What?"

"He laughed. Asked me, 'What are you going to do if you divorce me? Don't even think about it or you'll be sorry.' Made it pretty clear that I wasn't gonna get any of his money, and that he was gonna make a lot of trouble for me if I tried."

"Oh."

"Yeah, 'oh.'"

It hadn't occurred to Jimmy that Nicky controlled all of the money.

He asked her, "So, if you divorced him, you'd have to support yourself?"

"Pretty much. And that's if all he does is refuse to give me anything to live on, no alimony." She added, "Even if he doesn't make trouble for me, what am I gonna do? Get a job? Doing what?"

"Go back to modeling."

She smiled. "See, now you're being sweet."

"No, seriously, why not?"

"God, pick up a magazine. Look at the swimsuit issue of *Sports Illustrated*. Something like that. Tell me how old the models are. Twenty, maybe twenty-two. Tops."

"Well . . ." He didn't know what to say. To him, she was beautiful. Her body was great. He couldn't think of her as being too old to model. He figured, you put her next to a twenty-year-old, what was gonna be the difference?

Katherine said, "So what I'm looking at, realistically, I'm looking at being pretty much stuck."

"You can still divorce him."

"If I file for divorce now, say somehow he gets those pictures in his hands. What'll happen then?"

He sat up on the couch. "Well, I was thinking about that. What we could do, we could get ahold of Ellis Bowers."

"What for?"

"See, here's this guy, Ellis. What's he doing? He's got pictures of you and he's asking you for five hundred, a thousand dollars."

"So?"

"He's got you where he wants you. Nice woman, married to a rich man. So why doesn't he ask for more?"

"I'm not sure what you're talking about."

He said it again, "How come he's not asking for more?"

"I don't know."

The guy in the driveway taking a couple of shots at him, Jimmy was pretty sure now, was Bowers. Would they even be able to talk to the guy? He said, "Either he doesn't think you can get more—which doesn't make a lot of sense—or else he's small time. Doesn't know how to think big."

"But I don't want him to ask for any more."

"Yeah, we don't want him asking. But what if we offered?"

She said, "But I can't really get any more. The only way I can get money is from Nicky."

"But Ellis doesn't know that."

He was running it over in his head, the idea that he'd had the day before. Trying to decide if he could make it work. "What if we got ahold of him? Offered him a whole lot of money. More than he was asking. But we make sure it works out. Set it up where he gives us the pictures, the negatives. Everything."

She looked confused. "But how are we gonna do that? I don't have that kind of money."

Jimmy didn't even let himself wonder was he doing it to be a knight in shining armor? Was that all there was to it? Instead he just grinned and said, "I do."

He pulled his jeans on and said, "Look, you have any idea what it's been like? I'm single, I spent ten years in the Marine Corps. My housing, most of my meals, it was all taken care of. And they still paid me. Not a lot. But what were my expenses?" She was quiet so he told her, "I've got money. Enough so that it would seem like a lot to Ellis Bowers. We offer him, say, ten grand. Make him sit up and smell it. But then he's got to give us everything."

"What if he doesn't go for it?"

"Why shouldn't he? It's easy. He doesn't have to work for it. It'll be right there. We hand it to him."

"But what if he tries to cheat us?"

"We'll just have to make sure he doesn't."

He saw the scared look on her face. She said, "If that was him last night, he's crazy. Taking shots at you. How're you gonna talk to somebody like that?"

"Look, maybe I'm wrong. Maybe the man's a nut. We talk to him and maybe he won't go for it. But it's not like we have a whole lot of choice—a bunch of options. What we should do, we should try this. Get Ellis Bowers to stop bothering you. And then maybe you can deal with your husband."

She nodded her head after a minute. "It's worth a try, I guess."

"Sure." Trying to sound more optimistic than he felt. Remembering the night before, diving under the car with a crazy man shooting at him. He said, "Of course it is."

# CHAPTER
# ELEVEN

═══════════════

Susie was having trouble making Nicky pay attention. They were in his den, out of the sun, because Nicky thought maybe he was getting a burn. She had put her clothes back on over her bathing suit because she didn't want Nicky staring at her body, thinking about sex. She wanted him to concentrate on Wesley.

Nicky was watching Orson Welles in *Citizen Kane* on videotape. He had a library full of old movies. Shelves of them lining one whole wall of the den. She'd come over one time, when Katherine was out of town, and looked through them. Maybe four hundred videos. It was like the man owned a video store. They were all new, not taped off cable. And none of them made within the last ten years. Classics, Nicky called them, saying, "Hey, the new movies are nothing but special effects. Trick photography. Nobody has to act today." He'd shown her his collection, opening the doors to the shelves and making her read the titles. Telling her, like it was an original thought, "They don't make them like they used to." Jesus.

Along the other side he had what he called his entertainment center. It had a CD player, a couple of big speakers, and also a forty-two-inch Mitsubishi TV that Nicky usually left on all day long whether he was watching it or not.

What Susie was trying to do, which was turning out to be a lot of work, was get him to turn off the TV and talk about Wesley. She'd mention his name, tell Nicky that she didn't think Wesley was honest, and he wouldn't answer. He kept watching TV like he couldn't be bothered. She walked over finally and turned it off. Stood there until he looked up at her and said, "Hey . . ."

"Nicky, would you listen to me, for Christ sakes. Listen to me for just a couple of minutes." She wanted to shout at him, ask him did he even know how hard it was for her to keep this up? Ask him, Hey, you think you've got problems, how would you like to be in *my* shoes, have to put up with people like you all the time?

He glanced back at the TV and told her, "This is maybe the best movie ever made. You know that? You want to talk, we can talk, but don't go turning the TV off." He grabbed the remote and turned the movie back on. "Do you think I look like him? Orson Welles?"

"What?"

He was looking from her to the TV. A little excited. "Come on. Do I look like him? He's darker than me, a little different build, but still . . ." Touching his face as he spoke, like he could feel the similarities.

She started to laugh. "Do I think you look like Orson Welles, is that what you want to know?"

"The fuck're you *laughing* at?"

"Nicky, hey, I didn't expect a question like that. That's all." She walked over and sat down, being serious about it now. Looking at the movie like she cared and then turning to him and saying, "Yeah, I can see a resemblance."

"You can?"

"The hair is different—yours is lighter and longer. But yeah"— acting interested, like Nicky was on to something important—"I can see it."

"Well, see, the hair—I mean if that's the biggest difference, that kinda thing, it could just be styles, you know. Back then they wore their hair different."

She faced him now and said, "Nicky . . . I can tell . . . it's important to you. But why don't you let it go. Let's talk . . . get things straightened out. And then, I've got to go anyway. You can watch the end of the movie." She reached over and took the remote. "Okay?" She shut the set off. "See, back at the pool, when those men were there, and I showed up—"

"Yeah?"

"Well, it looks bad, you act like I'm not supposed to be there. How's that make me look?"

"I was just thinking, back then, I got a business meeting going on"—he grinned—"and I don't think of you as something that goes with business."

She still had a sweet tone to her voice. She had to act nice but find out everything that was going on at the same time. Push Nicky in the right direction. She told him, "That's a problem right there, if you're thinking something like that. Where's that going to get us?"

"What do you mean?"

She was wondering, did the man maybe do prescription drugs? Was he locked into some kind of Valium haze that she didn't know about? Did he maintain it while he was talking business but then come on in here and fall apart—get into some kind of fantasy world where he thought he was Orson Welles? He had the attention span of a toddler when he was like this. "Nicky, you want to stop thinking of me as some kind of toy, just there when you get horny."

He got a little red in the face. "Hey . . . I don't like talk like that." Nearly making her laugh again because she knew the way he liked to talk when she rolled around on the rug with almost no clothes on.

"Don't let it bother you, are we talking a certain way. This is just you and me getting things organized."

"I *got* things organized."

"Nicky, you don't have things organized. You have a wife that's run off, you got a business deal that's halfway done. If you don't concentrate on it, it's gonna get away from you."

"It's in the bag. Those guys're drooling. And how hard is it going to be to keep Wesley in line?"

"Yeah?" Like she didn't believe it at all.

He stared at her, with a look on his face that she hadn't seen before. She told herself, *Whoa*, because Nicky was letting her see the side of him that did business.

"Hey, I don't mean . . . it's not like I'm saying anything like you don't know what you're doing."

He smiled, but with the look still in his eyes. "Maybe that's exactly what you're implying. See, maybe *you* don't understand what's happening. You see me out there, what am I doing? I'm selling. I may not look like it, I may appear out of it even, but that's the look they want to see so they can think they know more than I do. I let them see it. I get a bunch of people, potential investors, I bring 'em together, and then I sit back, make sure their drinks are full, let 'em talk to each other. And then you know what I do, I make sure I'm the one, out of everybody, I make sure it's me that comes out on top."

Susie couldn't help asking, "How?"

"Let me worry about that."

"But what about me?"

"What about you?"

"Well . . . the way you were looking at me."

"How was I looking at you?"

"I'm your girlfriend. I come over and you act like I'm butting in."

"But you were."

"Nicky, let me ask you something. You got any idea why I came over?"

"To see me."

"Uh-huh, to see you. But more than that, what I wanted to do, I wanted to make sure you were all right. You got all this other stuff happening, you're trying to put together a deal. And what happens? Your wife makes a big scene, starts shooting a gun off when you got a guest over. What you have to do, from now on, is concentrate on what you're supposed to be doing. Let me worry about your wife." She had Nicky's attention now. "Let me worry about Katherine. I told you before that I'd take care of her."

"Uh-huh."

"So I will. It's under control. I don't even want you to think about it." She said very slowly, "I told you one time I worked for an insurance agency."

"I thought you said it was real estate?"

"No, insurance. This guy ran an office, All State, out of Atlanta. The important thing is, he was going under. I mean, he was way over his head. In debt to everybody."

"Yeah?"

"Well, the point I'm trying to make . . . the point is . . . nobody knew it. This guy didn't talk to anybody . . ."

Nicky grinned at her. "You banging him?"

She had to stop, get her thoughts back together, because it was such a stupid thing to ask. "Jesus, Nicky, give it a rest. I'm trying to tell you something here."

He shrugged. "Yeah?"

"The point is, this guy down in Atlanta, he didn't trust anybody. So while he's going under—his whole business collapsing—nobody knew it. He didn't have anybody there he could ask for help."

"I'm not going under."

"Yes, I know that. But we have to be careful. Make sure we take care of everything. The most important thing"—starting to stroke his shoulders now, putting a little effort into it—"you have to trust somebody. You have to trust me."

"I can handle it."

Susie made herself sound really worried. "But are you sure? I don't know what you got in mind exactly with Wesley. But you have to do it the right way. How do you know what kind of person Wesley is?"

Nicky said, "What's the difference? He's got a bag full of cash. You think maybe I should quit? You think I got all the money I need? I can lay my hands on a couple of grand cash, maximum, before I'd have to start selling things. I have people breathing down my neck, wanting to take my *house*, for Christ's sake."

"I know you do. And you have a wife who spends all your money."

"Tell me about it."

"So, no, I'm not saying you should stop what you're doing. I just want you to be careful, is all."

"Jesus, it's under control."

She kissed his forehead, leaning past him to turn the TV back on, seeing the black-and-white image start to flicker on the screen. Turning the volume down low she told him, "I just worry about you. I can't help it." Hoping it was working. He heard it enough, maybe Nicky'd start to believe it.

He gave her a blank look for a second but then smiled. "Yeah, look, it's in the bag."

She sat back, watching his face as he looked at the TV. He knew the lines by heart, saying half of them before the actors spoke. Nicky Kramer, the financial wizard, watching an old movie for maybe the five hundredth time, when there was work to be done. She couldn't believe it.

———

Jimmy drove by Ellis's house twice before he stopped. It was a little frame house that faced the bay, raised up on cinderblock platforms in case the bay ever flooded. There were some overgrown bushes out front, what looked like a pretty big wasp nest in the tree by the side of the house, and the place needed a new roof. Jimmy figured it had a kitchen, a head, and maybe two bedrooms if they were pretty small. The kind of place Ellis Bowers would feel comfortable in, not worry about keeping it clean or having people over for supper.

If Ellis was home he probably already knew Jimmy was there. He thought of Katherine and that was what made him open the door and climb out into the sunlight.

He walked up to the front door, trying to make it seem natural. He caught himself whistling and that almost made him laugh.

He banged on the door pretty hard, heard a shout from inside and then somebody undoing the chain.

Ellis, wearing jeans and a sweatshirt, opened the door, peered out at Jimmy from inside the screen, and said, "What the fuck're you doing here?" His eyes slid past Jimmy like he expected there to be more people with him. Maybe cops or somebody else Jimmy had brought along to help.

Jimmy told him, "Hey, you and I, we keep meeting. I thought I'd come on over. Introduce myself. See if we can talk."

Ellis said, "I got nothing to say."

Jimmy smiled. "I'm Jimmy Decker, just got home from the Corps. You don't think maybe you should hear what I've got to say first? You might be missing something, turns out it could make you a happier man."

Ellis looked at him for a long time and then stepped past him and walked out towards Jimmy's car. He said, "I'll tell you one thing. You got nerve coming here. You kick a man in the nuts, you do something like that, and the next thing you know, you're over at the man's house trying to talk to him." He paused to spit and then said, "Shit."

Jimmy, a step behind Ellis, caught up to him by the car and leaned against the Ford. "Yeah, well, the thing is, a lot of times, people do things like that." Thinking maybe Ellis forgot that *he* was the one who pulled the knife but not saying anything about it. "They try to get over on somebody, maybe they end up hurtin' somebody. The next thing you know, they realize maybe the other person and them, they can work things out." He was watching Ellis carefully, wondering did the man have something under that sweatshirt? Maybe he was carrying the same piece he'd had the night before.

"See, last night, I'm not doing anything, minding my own

business. And somebody drives by and takes a couple of shots at me." He pointed at the rear window. "You see that? I don't know, was somebody trying to tell me something or were they just a pretty bad shot?"

Ellis looked at the window and then back at Jimmy, grinning. "I'd say whoever did that, they were sending you a message. Seems to me if they'd meant to hit you they wouldda." Waiting a second and then saying, "If it was me, what you'd be, you'd still be in that driveway of yours. Else that or the morgue."

Jimmy acted like he had to think about it. "You maybe have a point. Or maybe it was kids. Nothing personal, a bunch of kids playing around with their daddy's gun. But see, the thing is, I probably won't ever even know. I mean, how am I gonna figure something like that out?"

Ellis said, "Even if you could, where would it get you?"

Jimmy nodded. "Exactly."

Ellis turned to look at his house. Jimmy could see now that he did have the gun on him. It looked like a Colt tucked into the back of his pants underneath the sweatshirt, but not far enough down that it wasn't showing a little bit. Ellis was talking to him, though, so it didn't really matter was he the one who took those shots, although he was sure of it now. Still, there wasn't anybody looking to do anything stupid here.

Jimmy cleared his throat. "The reason I'm here is we have a problem. You got something I want."

"Well, I might. I don't know what it is, though."

"Sure you do. You probably take them out at night, look through them so you can get to sleep that much better."

Ellis acted like he just got it. "Oh, the pictures. I talked to the lady two nights ago, told her, Hey, I think the fire sale is over. Told her the price just went up."

"Yeah, she mentioned that."

"You talked to her too, huh?"

Jimmy ignored the question. He said, "The thing is, and I kinda agree, what good is it doing her? She pays you. And I know she already has. And then, you call her up again and ask for more."

Ellis said, "Well, I was thinking, number one, you got this woman, she's got a nice house out there near Gardens Corner. I drove by it. Just to see, you know." He ran his hand through his hair and said, "God*damn*, some people got ever'thing. House like that. Jesus. The other thing, I figured, she got cute, got you to help her out. It's the kind of thing I don't like."

"Yeah, but you could have given her the pictures back even before I came along. And you didn't."

Ellis held his hands out. "What can I say?"

"Hey, I'm not telling you how to do things. I'm just explaining what I think. Where I see the situation going."

"Uh-huh . . . and where's that?"

"Well, you got two choices. No, three. You can keep bothering the woman, call her up every time you need a couple of hundred bucks . . ."

Ellis laughed. "Or when I want to get a peek at her."

"I wasn't gonna say anything about that." He took a deep breath because he knew what Ellis was doing—he was trying to make Jimmy mad. "The other thing you could do, you could give it up. Get out before the thing gets out of hand. Before somebody does something that can't be undone."

"Like me giving the pictures to the lady's husband. Which she knows I'd do. Shit, *that's* my second choice? Just give it up. Why would I want to do that? I'm the one with the pictures. I'm the one that's in the position to tell you what to do."

Jimmy nodded. "Uh-huh. Well, I'm not surprised. I figured I'd say it. Let you know it was an option."

"Well, it ain't one that's gonna take place."

"Yeah. The third thing, which maybe you'll find is something you could agree to, you give me everything—pictures, negatives. Everything."

"I just give them to you? See, that doesn't sound any different than telling me to give it up."

"No, that's not the deal. You give them to me and I give you a lump sum. Make it worth your while."

"What are you talking about—a lump sum—how much money are we talking about here?"

Jimmy looked up into the air and then back down at Ellis. "I'm thinking, I give you five grand. Cash. You don't even have to work for it. I hand it to you, no hassles, and you give me the pictures."

Ellis burst out laughing. "Jesus. Five grand. You know how much I could get for those pictures?"

"I know how much you *think* you can get. But let me ask you a question. Who're you gonna get it *from?* You keep talking about this rich woman—Katherine Kramer. She's got a nice house out there. Swimming pool and all. Sure. But whose money is that? You think she has money?"

"I think, if I wanted to, I could make her get it."

"How? She's gonna go to her husband and say, Hey, I need money, cash, because some guy has pictures of me and I don't want you to see them? I don't think you're being realistic about this. You can try to bleed this woman, get as much cash out of her as you can. But what are you talking about. Maybe, over a period of time, if you keep hitting on her for five hundred, a thousand dollars, *maybe* you'll make five grand. But it'd be a hassle. If you do it my way it's a one-shot deal, over and done with. You go on back to other things. Go find somebody else to take pictures of."

Ellis was working the thing out. Thinking about it. And then he smiled and said, "You got a point."

Jimmy said, "Yeah, we work it out, it's a business deal, that's all."

Ellis nodded. "I can see it. But not for five grand." When Jimmy didn't respond, Ellis told him, "You give me *ten* thousand. No bullshit. You hand me the money and I give you the pictures. Plus which I got to work it out with my partner."

Jimmy let Ellis think he was disappointed, like he'd been hoping to make it five. But ten grand was okay. If everything went smoothly then Jimmy thought it would be money spent for a good cause. He nodded finally and said, "Ten grand. You work it out with your partner, whatever. This is between you and me, though. You want to split the money with somebody, that's up to you."

"Hey, I'm not looking to cheat anybody," Ellis protested. "I'll tell you what. Just to show you what a nice guy I am, I got something for you." He ran towards the house, saying over his shoulder, "Wait here."

Jimmy didn't have long to wait. He heard the screen door slam and watched Ellis come bounding down the steps with an envelope in his hand.

He trotted up to Jimmy, still smiling, and said, "Here. Since we're gonna do business—we're gonna be partners, more or less—this is for you. Come on. Take a peek."

Jimmy opened the envelope, pretty sure already what he was gonna see inside.

There were two pictures, one of them a little fuzzy. But seeing who was in them wasn't a problem. It was Katherine. With her long brown hair falling over her shoulders. In the first one she was standing in somebody's bedroom—Jimmy could see a bed in the background—leaning against the wall, looking like she'd fall down if you took the wall away. Smiling drunkenly into the camera. With her shirt unbuttoned enough so that her nipples were peeking out. The next one was clear—whoever took it had got the focus just right. Katherine's hair was in sharp focus and you could see the vaccination mark on her shoulder. You couldn't see her face, just the top of her forehead and her hair falling in front of her eyes. With her head framed between Ellis's legs. The top of Ellis's head was cut off but it didn't matter. You take one look and you'd know it wasn't her husband.

Ellis waited until Jimmy had put the photos back in the envelope and then said, "Hey, we're talking about a hot-looking broad here."

It went through Jimmy's head to take a swing at Ellis. Wipe the smile off the man's face and then maybe put him on the ground and take that pistol out of the back of Ellis's pants. Stick it in the man's mouth—let him taste it for a couple of seconds—and then march him back up into the house. Ask him, Hey, whereabouts are the rest of the pictures? Do it that way and get the whole thing over with right now.

Ellis saw the look on Jimmy's face and took a step backwards, saying, "The others, the rest of them, they ain't here. I can get them. But it ain't like I'm gonna take you to where they are."

Jimmy waited until Ellis had stopped grinning and then turned to his car. He was in it, reaching to put the key in the ignition, when Ellis called out, "Hey, when we gonna do this?"

Jimmy started up the car and then looked at Ellis. "You get the pictures, all of them, and then call me."

Ellis said, "What's your phone number?"

"Hey, you know where I live. If you can get yourself over there with your pistol, then I guess you can find out my phone number." He put the car in gear and drove off.

# CHAPTER

# TWELVE

Ellis was on his way over to Susie's apartment. Going through town he was thinking about ten grand and how it would feel to have that much cash in his pocket. Thinking also, the hell with Susie. She had all kinds of plans, that was one thing. If she was serious, honest about it, and she could work her way into Nicky Kramer's confidence—get it all set up so that she and Ellis could walk off with a lot of cash—that was fine. She acted like she had some kind of big deal about to happen, gonna rip Mr. Nicky Kramer off or whatever it was she had in mind. Acting real mysterious about it, like Ellis was too dumb to know all the details. Uh-uh. Ellis could take care of *himself.* He'd take Jimmy Decker's ten grand. That'd be fine. Maybe give him the pictures, maybe not. See how it went and then, if it looked like it was the right thing to do, he'd take out that 9mm and tell the Marine to go fuck himself.

He drove down Highway 21 to Route 281—Ribault Road— following it past the new city jail until he got to Spanish Point, took a left and drove down to Susie's apartment, carrying a brown bag that said Piggly Wiggly on it—a surprise for her. He didn't see her car anywhere and he wondered where she was as he walked across the parking lot. After knocking a couple of times he let himself in. He turned the air conditioner on, walked into the kitchen and opened the fridge, and got himself a plate of cold shrimp. Then he went into the living room to wait for Susie.

She got home about an hour later. Ellis was still eating the shrimp. Taking his time because he was content. Ten grand. And all he had to do was wait for it.

It occurred to him that he was probably fooling a lot of people. They thought he was so goddamn dumb. People like Susie and that smart-ass Jimmy Decker—talking to him like he barely spoke the language. Yeah? All his life people had been acting that way towards him. Let them see him now. He had the thing under control.

Shit, it wasn't so complicated. You have a couple of people, they're trying to figure out what the woman, Katherine, is up to. You got the Marine, it was pretty easy to see what he was doing. Ellis figured he was banging the broad, getting a piece of that in the sack, and now he was trying to impress her. Show her what a nice guy he was by taking over her troubles. And Katherine, she'd run off, moved in with the Marine. Leaving her husband to wonder what happened to her.

Ellis didn't know, was Nicky Kramer mad at his wife or did he want her back. It didn't really seem to matter. Because Ellis, sitting there in that nice chair and eating Susie's food, figured either way, Nicky Kramer would probably pay to know where his wife was. It gave Ellis a good feeling, knowing that he was in the middle of it.

He knew stuff—had information—that everybody seemed to want. Looking down, because the funny thing was, all these things going on—and what was in the Piggly Wiggly bag—had made him horny.

He heard the key in the lock and said, "Hey" when Susie walked in.

She stopped in the doorway and said, "What are you doing here?" and then walked past him into the kitchen. He heard water running. She came back into the living room with a glass in her hand. "What are you doing? I don't want you coming here without me being around."

He pretended to be hurt. "Hell, hun-bun, that's no way to be. You gave me a key just so I could let myself in. Now didn't you do that? You come home and I'm here. I'm trying to surprise you—got a present for you. I know where your friend is holed up. You want me to tell you, you should be nicer than that. Ask me how I'm doing first."

"Ellis, I'm tired. And I've got to go see Katherine"—she peeked at her watch—"right away. Where is she?"

"Uh-huh." He popped another shrimp in his mouth and said, "What are you tired from?"

"Shopping."

He could tell she was lying as soon as she said it. "Yeah? You need help with the bags? Want me to run down and get them out of the car?"

"No. I didn't get anything."

He said, "See, I never figured it out. Maybe women, they like to shop so much, maybe to them it's just the idea of it, you know? They go to the store, it doesn't matter are they gonna buy anything or not." Grinning at her.

She said, "Ellis, what the hell are you talking about?"

"I don't know. If I go shopping, what I do, I know what I want before I ever even get there. I'm in the store and out, I got what I wanted, in, what, ten minutes?"

"I like to shop."

"I can see."

She put her hand to her temple like she was getting a headache and walked past him to the liquor cabinet. He saw her pour some Scotch into her water glass.

"Ellis, honey, I got a headache. You-all want to talk about shopping, if you don't mind, could we do it some other time?" Giving the look that she always gave him when she thought he was being a pain in the ass.

Ellis reached for the Piggly Wiggly bag at his feet. "Hey, I don't want to talk about shopping if you don't. Besides, I got something for you."

He walked over to her, the bag in his hand. She started to say something. Ellis didn't even want to know what it was so he put his hand over her mouth and leaned forward until he was almost touching her ear with his lips. Whispering to her, "Hey, you got a headache. Maybe you shouldn't have gone shopping. Walking around the mall, it'll do that to you." He reached into the bag and pulled out a brown wig. "Look what I got."

She was still mad. "Ellis . . ."

He gave her his country-boy grin. "Hell, hun-bun, put this one on. It'll be fine. Get out of those clothes and you and me can have some fun."

"Jesus, Ellis, I told you I got a headache."

Now he was pissed off. The hell with this act she was putting on. He grabbed her arm. "See, I don't think it's gonna work. The headache thing." He held her with one hand and put the wig on her head with the other. When he got it fairly straight he stepped back and looked at her. "There. You see that. A little change like that'll make you feel like a whole new person."

He thought she was gonna say something. Take the thing off and throw it at him. He wasn't sure what he would do then. Maybe he'd leave it alone, let her get some rest. But maybe not. Maybe what he'd do, he'd show her that it wasn't a good idea to treat him *too* badly.

He reached out, adjusted the wig, and told her, "See, you do this, we'll have some fun, do it the way I want to for a change, and then you can go see your girlfriend. She's at that Marine's place, down Meridian Road."

He knew all of a sudden Susie was gonna go along with it. She reached up and straightened the wig, tucked her own hair up into it, and then smiled at him.

"This is what you want, you want me to wear this thing so you can fuck me?" Making a face like he'd seen her make when she thought something was pretty amusing. Saying, "Ellis, honey, if I put on this wig, you think you'd actually be able to *do* it?"

He didn't know for sure, but he thought it was possible that she was laughing at him. Making fun of him for wanting her to wear the wig.

She cocked her head, turned to the side, and started to talk. Almost singing it, "You-all want to fuck somebody else, is that it, Ellis, honey?" She *was* laughing now. "Ellis, you wanna tell me something . . . just to satisfy my curiosity . . . you wanna tell me what color hair your *momma* had?" Confusing him a little bit, because what the hell did his momma have to do with it?

He decided he wasn't gonna let what she thought bother him. She started to remove her top. Taking her time with it and then peeling her jeans off. Stripping for him, and the whole time she was telling him what they were gonna do in bed. Ellis took his clothes off too, hard as a rock for the first time in a while because that's all it took, her wearing the wig. He had a lot of images floating through his head—Katherine Kramer with *her* long, shiny hair, and then some girl he knew in high school, a seventeen-year-old that he'd sat behind in class who had a big set of tits. And his momma too, her face floating just inside his eyeballs so that he got a good look at her. Seeing her tired eyes, looking right at him and then turning into Susie's.

He had to shake his head, concentrate. Still mad because the other times, when he'd tried so hard and not always succeeded, all she'd've had to do was put the wig on. He wasn't seeing her anymore, focusing his thoughts finally and seeing somebody else. Just one person this time: Katherine Kramer. Rich bitch. But the whole time thinking Susie had been lying to him. Ain't no shopping trip she was on. The woman, if she wasn't gonna be honest with him, then fuck her. And fuck Katherine Kramer too. Which was what he was about to do.

---

After he left Ellis Bowers's place, Jimmy was going to drive back and see what Katherine was doing. Maybe she needed some company. And she'd want to know what happened with Ellis Bowers. But he decided instead to drive around Beaufort. Then take a couple of hours to just sit in his car and think about things. Decide what he wanted and see if he thought he could make it happen.

Katherine hadn't been up when he'd left. After he'd told her where he was going, she'd gone back to the couch and laid down again. She'd looked at him for a minute and then said, "If you're going to do that, I might take a nap." She'd been asleep even before he left. As he'd walked out to his car it crossed his mind, should he get rid of the booze that he had? It wasn't a lot. A couple of six-packs in the fridge and a bottle of Johnnie Walker on the kitchen counter. If Katherine woke up—she was there alone, maybe getting a little worried—and she saw that Scotch, what would she do? But he'd decided, leave it there. Let her know it was around if she felt that strongly about it, had to have a drink. Besides, maybe it would be a bigger deal if he took it. It would seem like he didn't think she could make up her own mind.

There wasn't much traffic on the road. It was already hot— middle eighties, with the sun shining down like it was gonna get a lot hotter. Jimmy rolled his window down, turned on the radio, and rested his arm on the windowsill. He was still driving aimlessly, finding himself on Highway 21 after a while and thinking, just for the hell of it, he'd drive past Nicky Kramer's house. Take another look at where the man lived. He wasn't gonna pull in. But he'd drive by, look the place over again. Try to figure out why Katherine had ever gotten involved with Nicky.

He took the left on 17 and then the right onto Cotton Hall Road, slowing down when he got to the pillars, looking up the hill to the house. Trying to get it straight in his head why Katherine had ended up there.

When Jimmy left Nicky's place he figured he'd go back home. He could get Katherine and go somewhere. Drive out to the beach and spend some time without having to think about all this other shit. Pack a lunch, a picnic basket. With sandwiches and maybe a bottle of wine. Nothing else to drink, though. But a bottle of wine, that would be nice. They could eat at the beach. Go swimming.

It took him by surprise—pulling onto Meridian Road, almost home, and looking at himself in the rearview mirror—to realize that he was smiling, grinning like an idiot because the thought of going back to his house, knowing that Katherine was there, made him happy.

There was another car at his house. One he didn't recognize. He shut his engine off and got out slowly. He was aware of the insects humming in the air and the sound of a power boat out on the bay. But he didn't see any sign of Katherine. Saying, "Shit" to himself, he reached back into the car and got his .45 out of the glove compartment.

He walked carefully towards the house, went inside and then upstairs quickly. Katherine wasn't there and he was beginning to panic. Then he heard voices from outside.

He went back downstairs and outside, crossed the driveway, and walked around behind the house. Katherine and another woman were out on the dock. They turned as he came up to them and all of a sudden he felt stupid. They were smiling and here he was with a gun in his hand.

He started to speak, stuck the gun in his pants, and tried to come up with something that didn't sound ridiculous.

The woman with Katherine said, "Hey, I don't know. If this is the way you walk around, you carry a gun in your own house, I'd hate to see you mad." But she was calm about it.

Katherine was watching him as she said, "Jimmy, this is the friend I was telling you about. Susie."

He managed to smile at Susie. Nodded and said, "Hey."

Susie held out her hand. "I've been hearing all about you from Katherine." She was wearing a bathing-suit top and a pair of spandex shorts. She was a little taller than Katherine with a great figure. It looked like even if she tried hard not to be, she'd be sexy. Like it was something she carried around with her everywhere she went. You'd end up staring at her in church. She was grinning, like she knew what Jimmy was thinking.

He said, "Katherine's told me about you too." Feeling more comfortable because nobody was making a big deal about the gun anymore. He said to Katherine, "Don't let me interrupt you. I was gonna go inside and take a shower."

But Susie shook her head. "I've got to be going anyway."

Katherine said, "You're sure?"

And Susie nodded. "Yes." She looked at her watch. "I'm late already."

She walked back to the end of the dock and picked up a handbag.

Katherine said to Jimmy, "Why'n't you walk Susie on up? I'll sit here till you get back." She was looking better. Not hung over. Saying, "Go ahead. I'll just sit here."

Walking with Susie, putting one foot in front of the other, thinking about Katherine back there on the dock, he was aware the whole time that Susie was eyeing him as he was trying to think of something to say. Finally, he looked at her. She had red hair, kind of shorter than he would have normally liked, but it looked good on her. She had a small mole under her left ear and just a touch of make up on her eyes. Jimmy asked her, "You two have a nice visit?"

"I don't know, all we talked about, almost the whole time, was you."

Jimmy said, "Yeah?" Not wanting to sound too interested but still, he wanted to know what they'd said.

Susie laughed.

"What?" he asked.

She had nice teeth. He was looking at them, at her smile, while he wondered what else was he supposed to say to her. Thinking she was attractive, and seemed nice enough. She wasn't *tacky*, at least not from what he could tell. But that was Katherine. He remembered back in high school, she'd say things like that about other girls—make some kind of derogatory remark—if they were good looking. The thought popped into his head that if it wasn't for Katherine, if he hadn't run into her when he first came back, he might have wanted to see Susie sometime, get to know her a little better.

She stopped laughing and said, "Well, see, back there, before you got here, Kate's describing you—saying you were a guy that just got out of the Marine Corps, you know—and I got this idea of you. And suddenly here you come, running around the house with a gun."

Jimmy couldn't help it, he smiled. Not embarrassed about it any longer. "Well, I didn't know . . . seeing the car . . . I thought maybe her husband was paying her a visit."

She gave him a strange look, her head to the side, staring up into his face, and then asked, "Hey, you're not bothered, are you? Me saying this?"

"No, I think if I was on your end of it, I could see the humor. Guy like me comes running up. As long as the gun wasn't pointed at anybody. Nobody got hurt."

"Cause I know some people, I don't know, you can't kid them at all. They'd take it the wrong way."

"No, I'm not offended."

She quit walking and put her hand on his arm. They were out of view of the dock now. Susie's hand resting on Jimmy's arm felt warm and dry. She said, "Hey, I think it's kind of nice that Katherine's here, that she's not with Nicky. See, I don't know exactly what happened between them, but I've met Nicky."

Jimmy nodded finally, aware of her hand on his arm and seeing the look she was giving him, locking into him with her eyes so that he didn't feel he could look away.

She started to walk towards her car all of a sudden so that he had to hurry to catch up.

At the car she turned to him and said, "She tells me you just got out. You spent, what, ten years in the Corps?" Saying it like she really was interested. And then making a show of looking over his shoulder, like she wanted to make sure that Katherine wasn't around. "And now you're back." She glanced at the bay behind him and said, "God, it's beautiful here, isn't it?"

He nodded. "It's something else. I've been a lot of places and this is still my favorite."

"Uh-huh. I can see why. Growing up, we moved around a lot. I was never in one place for too long, so I don't have that, a town I think of as home. It must be nice."

"I'm not sure what it is yet."

"Well, that's understandable." She reached down into her purse and pulled out a big key ring, looking through all the keys until she came up with the one to unlock the door of her car. Then she turned back to Jimmy. "You come back here, to the place you grew up. And now what are you going to do—is that the way you feel?"

"Well, it wasn't like I had a lot of things in my mind. Things I was planning to do."

"Except take it easy, huh?"

Jimmy nodded. "Yeah, that was the only one I could come up with."

She laughed. "Hell, that's a good enough start."

"You think so?"

"Yeah, take it easy. Take your time deciding what it is you want to do next. That way you don't rush into anything and then figure out later it wasn't what you wanted to do. My mother, the one thing she always used to tell me was to think things through. Think before you act. You avoid a lot of mistakes that way."

Jimmy decided that she wasn't putting him on, that she was serious, standing there, the door of her car open now, repeating her mother's advice. Not seeming like she was in a hurry to leave; like, if he wanted to, she'd stand here and talk to him for another ten minutes.

He asked her, "You think Katherine'll be all right?"

"I think she'll be okay. It's not easy. You get married to somebody and a few years later you end up leaving them."

"You ever married?"

She shook her head. "No. But I worked one time . . . about three years ago . . . I worked in an office for a psychologist—marriage counselor. I was a receptionist. So I saw a lot of people in the same situation."

"Yeah?"

"I guess, compared to some of them . . . to some of the people I saw . . . I guess she's doing pretty well."

Jimmy asked her, "Anything I should do . . . ?"

"You mean now? For Katherine?"

"Uh-huh."

"I think do just what you are doing. Be nice, is all."

Then she smiled at him again, and whispered, almost making a joke out of it, "I hope it works out for you, mostly just you being here, back home. I hope it's what you thought it was. But if Katherine gets a change of heart, goes back to Nicky, you could look me up." And then she slid into her car, impressing him, because she'd come right out and told him she was interested, without having to be cute about it. Like she knew he might be interested too. And surprising him, because it felt almost like he'd been taken advantage of, like somebody had snapped a photo of him when he wasn't looking. Or maybe like he'd been somewhere, not thinking anybody could see him, he had done something embarrassing. And then he realized someone *was* looking. That was the way she made him feel and he didn't know why.

After she left he walked back to the dock and said, "That's Susie, huh?"

Katherine asked, "What'd you think?"

"I don't know. You don't get much input, meeting somebody and then five minutes later they're gone."

Katherine said, "She likes *you*."

"What do you mean?"

"I can tell, the way she looked at you. I should be jealous."

He laughed, shaking his head, but thinking it was true. Remembering the look Susie had given him but then telling Katherine, "I don't think so."

Katherine said, "Believe me, I know Susie. She's a friend, but I wouldn't trust her around someone like you."

To change the subject, Jimmy asked, "Did you call her up? Invite her over?"

"I was planning to. I was sitting here, I knew you were going to see Ellis Bowers. I got a little worried. So I was thinking maybe I'd call her up, tell her to come on over."

"Uh-huh. So did you?"

Katherine laughed. "I didn't have to. That's the great thing about Susie. It's why we're friends. I was inside, thinking about it, and all of a sudden she's in the driveway."

"Like she read your mind?"

"Exactly."

They walked up from the dock to the house. Going into the kitchen, Katherine was still smiling, happy. Clearheaded, like she hadn't had anything to drink. It made him feel pretty good, that she would wait for him, wouldn't feel the need to get drunk if she knew he was coming back.

When they reached the living room she put her arms around his neck and then kissed him. She kept her arms there and asked him, "What took you so long?"

"I saw Ellis and then I went for a ride." He told her about Ellis. "I think it'll work out. I could see it, he was already spending the money in his head. Maybe he'll do the smart thing."

But Jimmy was thinking about something else, something that was bothering him, not quite putting his finger on it yet. He said, "Hey, this friend of yours, Susie."

She was still kidding around. "The one that couldn't take her eyes off of you?"

"Yeah, that one. She a good friend of yours?"

"Sure. I know she's not the type I would take to the club. But she wouldn't want to go anyway. I wouldn't want to see her every day, but yes, we're good friends. We can talk to each other. Say whatever we want."

Jimmy said, "Uh-huh. I guess that's good. Having a friend like that."

"Uh-huh."

"But let me ask you something . . ."

"What?"

"When you ran away from your husband . . . ?"

"Uh-huh."

"Where did you end up?"

Katherine stopped smiling. "Here, with you. Why?"

"Well," Jimmy asked, "the thing is, if you didn't call her . . ."

"Yeah?"

"How'd she know that?"

# CHAPTER

# THIRTEEN

To Ellis the house looked like one of those mansions you'd see on TV—on *Knotts Landing* or *Dallas*, something like that. Driving through the pillars and up to the house—gonna pay a visit to Nicky Kramer—all he could think about was what a fucking castle the guy lived in. He got a different idea of who Nicky Kramer was all of a sudden.

Before, he'd thought that the man was nothing but a fuckup. Susie had told him about Nicky practically crying because his wife ran away. But now, seeing where the man lived, it gave Ellis a different feeling for him. Made him think that the other stories were true, the ones he'd heard before he and Susie had gotten together. People would tell him what a cold dude Nicky Kramer was, how rich he was and how he got his money in big-dollar land deals. Now, looking at the house, Ellis could believe it.

He parked his car near the front door and walked across the drive and rang the bell. He had to wait long enough to think about ringing it again, stepping back to look up at the second floor and then moving towards the door again.

When there was no answer, Ellis walked around the house, still admiring it, and finally wandered down to the pool. He saw the guy who had to be Nicky Kramer sitting in a lounge chair but he couldn't believe the way the man looked. He was covered with white cream—suntan lotion.

Nicky took one look at Ellis and said, "What the fuck're you doing here?" Looking at him through dark glasses that were huge and made his face look a little bit like a fish's.

Ellis told him, "Nobody answered the door. So I came around here."

Nicky said, "Is that some kind of answer? I ask you what're you doing and you tell me no one was at the door?"

Ellis was thinking, Fuck this guy. He wanted to be rude, act like Ellis was trespassing? To hell with that. Except that Ellis could put up with it to a point because he hoped there was gonna be some money in it for him. He said, "Well, it's a nice day. I thought maybe I'd come on out. Sit by the pool for a while."

Nicky said, "Jesus." He had a disgusted look on his face. He picked up the phone from the table next to him, looking back at Ellis while he dialed a number.

Nicky said into the phone, "I need a cop."

Ellis said quietly, "You calling the po-lice? You think maybe *they* know where your wife is?" He was enjoying himself because the expression on Nicky's face changed.

The man put the phone down like he didn't know he was doing it and said, "What are you talking about?"

Now Ellis was feeling better. He sighed. "I just wondered, cause

*I* know where your wife is. What you *could* do, you could go get back on the phone, call the cops, and have them send somebody out here because I'm bothering you. Or you and I can talk about Mrs. Kramer."

"You know where my wife is?"

Ellis grinned. "Sure."

"And you want, what, you're thinking I should pay you something for the information?"

Ellis said, "Hey, *that's* an idea."

Nicky nodded slowly, got up, and walked to the cabana without saying anything. He came back carrying a long pole with a net on the end of it. He started to scoop some leaves off the top of the pool water, making his way from near the cabana to where Ellis was standing.

When he got close to Ellis he stopped and said, "I pay you for telling me where my fucking wife is." He sounded furious.

Ellis thought he had the situation under control, enjoying himself and not even realizing that Nicky had started to move the pole again until the thing came swinging up into his body and knocked him off his feet. And then he was in the air, Jesus, like he was floating. Coming back down, the only thought in his head was that he had no idea how to swim.

He hit the water, got a mouthful of it, and then went under. Flailing with his arms, not swimming, because he'd never learned how. But feeling the bottom with his feet and pushing off to come out into the air gasping. He was having trouble breathing because he'd swallowed so much water.

Nicky poked Ellis with the pole. Held it against his chest until he went under. Ellis began to think he was gonna drown if the man didn't let him up soon. He couldn't fight Nicky because all his energy was going towards trying not to drown.

When he came back up, Nicky was sitting on the edge of the pool with his legs dangling in the water. Watching Ellis cough. Holding out a hand and waiting until Ellis was almost there before he pulled it away. Then saying quietly, "You want to keep swimming or you want to tell me about my wife?"

Ellis wasn't thinking anymore, could he make a few bucks out of this. Looking at Nicky, all he was wondering was, was he gonna make it out of here? He'd blown it. But the thing was, he was getting a little pissed. He was careful not to show it but it crossed his mind that if he got out of this he was maybe gonna go back and beat the shit out of Susie because somehow it had slipped her mind to tell him that Nicky could be this way, could throw a man in his pool and try to drown him all because he was trying to help.

Nicky said, "You gonna answer?"

"It's why I came out here. I heard you were looking for your wife, is all, and I saw her."

"Where?"

"In town."

Nicky moved the pole again and Ellis yelled, "WAIT." Scrambling for the edge and saying, "I saw her at some guy's house. She was with some guy. I can tell you where."

Ellis was thinking, Shit, because if he told Nicky where Jimmy Decker was, and Nicky did something drastic, how was he gonna get his money for the photos? Because he'd wanted to string it out, get money from both Nicky Kramer *and* the Marine. He was still afraid that Nicky was gonna drown him but he figured he'd better lie. "They aren't there now. They won't be back for a day. Tomorrow at the earliest."

"Where'd they go?"

Ellis said, "I don't know. I swear to God. I heard your wife had left. And then I saw her. I was in town and I saw her drive by with some guy. I followed them and then I came out here."

Ellis watched him think it over. It was like the man was alone. Finally Nicky said, "I think maybe you're telling the truth."

"I am. So is it okay if I get out now?"

"You know the guy's name?"

Ellis didn't say anything and Nicky yelled at him, "YOU THINK I'M ASKING FOR MY FUCKING HEALTH?"

"Decker. Jimmy Decker."

And Nicky looked like he was filing the information away in his head. He stood quietly, thinking it over, and then said, "Get out of here."

Ellis was wary. He moved toward the edge of the pool, wondering whether Nicky was gonna change his mind and push him back in at the last second. But Nicky ignored him.

Ellis scrambled out of the water and started to walk back around the house. He felt like an idiot. When he was almost out of sight he heard Nicky yell, "Hey."

Ellis turned around.

Nicky yelled, "You ever come back here"—he lifted the pole in his hands—"and this'll seem like a goddamn picnic."

———

Katherine didn't know what to think. Jimmy was pretty calm, sitting there in the kitchen with a can of beer. Not saying a whole lot, but thinking. She'd say something and it would be half a minute before he'd answer.

He had put his gun on the table. Left it sitting there, without saying anything about it. But it was right in front of her. Big and ugly looking. Different from Nicky's .38, the one she'd shot the stereo with. It reminded her of Don Johnson in reruns of *Miami Vice*—he'd have something like that in his hand.

When Jimmy opened his second can of beer she stood up and got one for herself. Not looking at him when she popped the top because she thought he might say something. Make a crack about it. But then it crossed her mind that it was more Nicky's style. She couldn't picture Jimmy making a sarcastic remark. She took a big drink. It felt pretty good, sliding down her throat. Not like gin, which always felt to her like it was gonna go off in her stomach like a bomb. But cool and kind of clean. She told herself she'd have the one because she was thirsty and because he was having one too. Just the one and that was it.

When she put the can down she saw he was smiling. It reminded her of high school, years ago, when she and Jimmy would be driving around, drinking warm beers that they'd either stolen from their parents or paid somebody older to buy for them.

She asked him, "What were you trying to say, before, about Susie?" Wanting to get back to it, bring it out in the open.

"I don't know. We're dealing with things, people . . . that I don't know anything about."

"Sure, I can see that. But Susie's a friend of mine."

"Uh-huh. Maybe she is, maybe all she wants is what's best for you."

"I think so."

"Yeah, you got a friend, but what do you really know about her? She work for a living? How's she support herself?"

"I don't know."

"What *do* you know about her?"

"We're *friends*. I don't know that you have to know everything about somebody to be friends." She was being defensive about it, she could hear it in her voice. Trying not to be, because Jimmy wasn't being mean about it. All he was doing, sitting there with a puzzled expression on his face, he was thinking out loud. But she knew she was being touchy about it, sounding like she was a kid who'd gotten caught lying.

She told him, "I met her in class. Night school."

Jimmy asked, "What course?"

She felt a little embarrassed. "Golf." Saying it like it was something to be ashamed of because she'd signed up when she'd thought she and Nicky should do more things together. When she'd thought a lot of their problems were because of her.

"When was that?"

"Maybe two years ago. Susie was living near Parris Island. I met her the second night of class. And we got friendly."

"So what, you've known her for two years or so?"

She nodded. "Yes. I guess so. But she moved away. Moved back home, I think. California. And then, last October, I saw her again in the grocery store."

Jimmy finished his beer and got up to throw the can away. She thought he'd get another one, wondering about it when he didn't because it always surprised her when people stopped drinking after only a couple of beers or drinks. She could never understand it. If it was up to her—if she was back home on a normal night— she'd keep pouring them until it was time to go to bed and then she'd wake up later with her clothes still on. The one on the table in front of her was almost empty. She thought about finishing it, holding it up to her mouth and taking the last couple of swallows and then going for another one. But she didn't.

Jimmy, leaning against the sink, said, "See, I don't want to be the one to say that maybe your friends aren't what they seem to be."

"But you're worried about something."

Jimmy turned away from her to wash his hands in the sink and then came back to the table with a dish towel in his hands and sat down. "Well, we're in a situation where you're being taken advantage of. Blackmailed. The thing you want to be sure of is who's doing the blackmailing."

"But we know that."

"Sure, we got a character, Ellis Bowers. He's up to no good. That's not hard to see. Maybe he's a Rhodes Scholar—it's a possibility—but I'm having a hard time believing that Ellis . . . thought this thing up on his own."

She was quiet for a few seconds, considering, picking up her beer can and playing with it, rolling it around but not taking a sip. She put it down and told him, "I always thought of her as a good friend."

He said quietly, "Maybe she is. The thing is, why don't we make sure?"

———

Nicky was inside his house with a golf club in his hands—a five iron that he'd had custom-made. He was swinging it back and forth while he spoke. Using it like a pointer while he talked to Wesley Hops. He was all dressed up in a tan three-piece gabardine suit and a wide red-and-yellow-patterned tie. Like he was gonna go out to a meeting or something.

Already he'd knocked over the lamp on his desk, not even seeming to notice when it went crashing down and the bulb broke. Looking at Wesley and shaking the club. "We got a multimillion-dollar business deal going down maybe any day. We've got to get people that hardly know us—people who're just social acquaintances—to give us their money. And me, I got tax problems you don't even want to hear about. I've got to string the investors along, keep them convinced, and we're talking guys so cheap—you want to know what they do?"

Wesley asked, "What?"

"They go to the club—which is where everyone does business—and when they play tennis they use old tennis balls. The things look like maybe their dogs got hold of them."

"Yeah?" Wesley wondered where the hell Nicky was going with this.

Nicky said, "Yeah. One of them told me, like it was a big secret. This guy is a doctor for Christ's sake, a plastic surgeon. He's making, what, three hundred grand a year? Anyway, this guy tells me one day when we're playing tennis, takes me aside and says, 'Hey, try putting your old tennis balls in the dryer. Put 'em on high for twenty minutes and they'll be as good as new.'"

Wesley said, "No shit. It work?"

Nicky shook his head. "No, that's not the point. . . ." But then he looked at Wesley and saw that the man was kidding. He said, "Listen, you see my point? These are some cheap sons of bitches we're dealing with. Don't get me wrong, they have the money. We just got to get it away from them."

"Okay." Wesley stood up, stepped across the room, took the golf club away from Nicky, and said, "Why don't you do this—tell me what the problem is. I see things, they seem to be going along okay. All of a sudden you're getting nervous, breaking lamps with your five iron."

Nicky said, "All right." He walked back around the desk and said, "These guys, what we're doing, we're trying to scam them."

"Uh-huh."

"That's okay. It should work. Except . . ."

Wesley said, "Except what?"

"My wife . . . my wife knows their wives from the club. And some of them from before that, from when she was a kid and lived down here. And some of these businessmen, their grandfathers knew my uncle. They all grew up together. They knew my father too, and none of them like him much because he was a drunk, and he left my mother. And then I went up to Wall Street, which most of these guys figure is nothing but a bunch of thieves. So now I come back with a big deal I want to sell these guys on." He shrugged. "They're a little hesitant, that's all."

"They don't trust you?"

"It's not even that. They have to trust me, or I have to make them trust me, one or the other. But see, they know my wife."

Wesley made a show of looking around. "And your wife isn't here."

"Not right now." He looked embarrassed.

"So that conversation we had, the one out by the pool, when Tom Neff was here and the doctor and the other guy. And I asked you what were the investors gonna say when they saw your wife wasn't around. And you told me not to worry. That was bullshit, huh?"

"No, no. It's not that serious. It's just something I want to resolve. So I don't have to give it any more thought. I want to make sure my wife doesn't say anything to the wrong person."

"Does your wife know what we have in mind?"

"Maybe."

"Where's she at now?"

Nicky said, "What?" Like he hadn't heard.

"Your wife, where is she?"

Nicky didn't answer right away. He walked over to the big gun case in the corner of the room and took a shotgun out. Wesley watched while Nicky loaded it. The whole room was quiet as Nicky slid the shells into the breech. His face was scrunched up, with his tongue sticking out, concentrating—making a big show of loading the Ithaca—sliding the shells into the gun carefully.

When the gun was loaded he walked back to the desk and looked at Wesley, getting a grin on his face. Sliding the pump on the Ithaca back so that it was cocked and ready to fire, he said, "I'm going to bring my wife home. It's not a big deal. I'm gonna drive on over, put the bitch in the car, and that'll be that."

Wesley figured Nicky was doing a sell on him, like he sold those investors he was planning to scam. Rev them up, get them going at full speed until they volunteered to do his work for him. But he didn't care. Nicky with a gun was a joke. Wesley realized if he was gonna see the deal go through, make it work out the way *he* wanted it to, he *was* gonna have to help Nicky out.

He said, "Nicky?"

"Yeah?"

"Why don't you cut the crap. Just tell me where she is."

Nicky said, "I'm not sure." He waited a second and then said softly, "She's shacked up with some guy."

"Where, in town?"

"Yeah. It's the same one she supposedly had the accident with. She knew him from before. From high school or something."

"Tell me more about him."

Nicky snorted, "What's to tell? The guy's banging my wife. He's a Marine, or just got out."

"The guy from the other day."

"Yeah."

"How do you know all this?"

Nicky said, "Susie told me."

"Oh." The word hung in the air for a minute and then Wesley

stepped towards Nicky and took the shotgun out of his hands. He reached over to the golf club, handed it to Nicky, and said, "Here, why don't you stick to golf. Let me worry about what your wife is up to." He was thinking that Nicky needed to relax, to concentrate on pulling off the deal.

He said, "If the time comes when we have to do something about your wife, let me handle it."

"You sure?"

Wesley smiled. "No problem. I'll look around, find out exactly where she is." Thinking, why not? It was ridiculous, Nicky standing there and telling *Wesley* what he was gonna do to some goddamn ex-Marine.

He watched Nicky drop a golf ball on the carpet, take the five iron, and stand over the ball like he was Freddy Couples lining up a putt.

Wesley waited until he hit the ball and watched it roll across the carpet.

He had Nicky where he wanted him and the man didn't even know it. Nicky was worried about his wife, was she gonna wreck his business deal. But there was something else there, something maybe Wesley could use. Even though he might not admit it, Nicky missed his wife.

He had brought his hot-looking girlfriend around, but it didn't look like he was ready to divorce his wife and marry her. A lot of guys were like that. They had something on the side but when push came to shove they wanted their wives. It was interesting, knowing that about Nicky.

He said again, "Let me worry about that end of it."

Nicky had a different expression on his face already. Like he was content. He said, "Hey, I can do that."

Wesley was thinking, Of course you can, because no woman is

gonna fuck up my plans. But all he said to Nicky was, "Sure. It'll *all* work out."

━━━━━

When the phone rang Nicky was upstairs in his room, drinking his second Scotch of the afternoon, thinking maybe what he'd do, he'd go for a dip in the pool.

It was almost time for the kill. He was nearly there. He had the plans, the plats, ready to flourish. He had Wesley—and his cash— ready to show, and he'd hooked a good-sized bunch of fish, all of them loaded and all of them greedy *and* just a little scared. Nicky had the idea all of a sudden that it was gonna go pretty well. Just a feeling that had hit him when he was halfway through his second drink, a glow that somebody might've tried to say was the Scotch, but Nicky knew different. He'd had them before and he believed in them. It made him less jumpy, thinking that things were gonna work out.

Besides, he had an order to the things now. Things he wanted to get done. Get the business deal finished up and get his wife back, teach her a lesson, and then take care of the asshole she was staying with. It was easy when he said it like that—said it out loud—sitting there up in his room. It didn't sound like such a big deal.

It was the way he liked to feel, confident, having a couple of Scotches. Relaxed, so that when the phone rang he knew in his bones it was gonna be good news.

It was Tom Neff. Nicky looked at his watch and then said into the phone, "Tom, you tell your friends to make up their minds." He waited for a moment and then said, loudly, "I don't care if they haven't decided. They have to be ready by tomorrow afternoon."

He laughed and said, just before he hung up, "Tom, you ready to be rich?"

He was feeling great as he hung up the phone. Tom Neff was breathing so hard Nicky knew he could taste it. Neff had said he wasn't sure about the others, but he was bullshitting. Nicky could hear it in the man's voice.

He finished his drink and reached for the phone. When it was answered, he said, "Susie, hun-bun, what're you wearing?" Then, "Uh-huh, uh-huh, do me a favor, huh, take it off and unlock your door."

# CHAPTER
# FOURTEEN

Jimmy took a walk around his yard, scanning the neighborhood. He didn't want to be stupid about it. He went out to the dock. Stood there, staring at the water, remembering what it had been like as a kid. There weren't any problems back then, at least not the kind he and Katherine were looking at now.

He remembered sitting out here with Katherine, high school kids who could spend hours holding hands or talking about anything when they first started going out. Things that weren't really that important but made them pretty happy all the same. Sitting there now, with the tide coming in, he wondered, where had those times gone?

When he went back inside Katherine had a drink in her hand. Sitting in the living room on the couch, making a show of sipping whatever was in the glass. Lifting her head up, with her eyes maybe one quarter of the way shut. A sexy look. Raising the glass once more, slowly, holding it to her mouth like she was trying to be nonchalant about it. But it seemed to him that she'd already had a couple of quick ones. He'd been outside for, what, twenty minutes? She wanted to take a couple of slugs, take the edge off, it could've happened.

He didn't know what to say. Was it something that he should make a big deal out of? Say something to her? Or else maybe take the booze away. Because it wasn't like she was making any kind of big effort not to drink. The last two times he'd left her alone she'd had at least a couple of drinks. He was opening his mouth, not sure what was gonna come out, when she said, like she was reading his mind, "I need it. I'm sitting here, watching you walk around out there. I know what you're doing. You're on a patrol. Making sure the . . . whatever you call it . . . the perimeter . . . making sure it's okay."

"I was looking around, that's all."

She said, "Yeah?" Tired sounding, or else maybe slightly drunk, Jimmy couldn't tell.

She took a drink, held the glass up to her mouth until he heard the ice cubes clink. She stood up and walked into the kitchen. He let her go, heard the sound of the bottle being opened, and then she was back. Walking over to the couch and sitting down.

She said, "Maybe to you, this kind of thing is nothing."

Her eyes were swimmy in her head, like she was already having some trouble concentrating. He wanted to yank the glass out of her hand now, tell her she didn't need it. He thought she was beautiful. All he wanted to do was protect her, get her to stop drinking. Make sure she was all right and then go take care of everybody who was hurting her. Nicky especially. Make him pay a little.

But the thing was, and he knew it just by observing her, she was too used to getting away from it, getting drunk and making the thing fade from her head. It was all she knew how to do.

She took another swallow and then laughed. "I see you sitting there, I can tell, it's killing you. Where were you six months ago? You were in a war, for Christ's sake. Over there, what would you have done if something like this happened? Jesus, you're used to it, fighting, whatever. It's something you were trained to do."

He nodded. "Yeah, they trained me." He rubbed his face with his hands because he wasn't sure he wanted to get into this. He didn't want to have to explain it, put it into words, and wasn't sure that she would understand anyway. He took a deep breath and said, "You know what they taught me to do? The reason they picked me in the first place is cause I got a special talent. They put me in a squad. We were called LRTRS." Pronouncing it "lurters" and then telling her, "Long Range Target Reduction Specialists. Jesus, what a stupid way to put it."

He could tell she was staring at him. "I was a sniper. You give me a rifle, it doesn't matter what it is. Give me a rifle and I can shoot anything with it. It doesn't matter whether it's a target or what. A person? You give me the rifle, send me over to a place like the Gulf and point him out, I could be a half a mile away. I'll drop him."

She looked shocked. "Is that what you did?"

"They pulled me out right after basic. Put me in a squad. That was our job."

"I didn't know."

"The thing is, they got all this high-tech stuff. Patriot missiles, chemical weapons—all the weaponry that the newspapers love to write about. Smart bombs. And still . . . sometimes . . . what it comes down to is a couple of guys like me, one on each side, shooting the hell out of each other." He paused for a second to look at her, see if she was following what he was saying, and then he said, "What you do, you shoot at so many targets, it's all you do. Practice. So when it comes time, maybe there's a person out there, you do the same thing. Make him into a target. It's what you do in your head. To make it all right."

She asked, "What are you telling me?"

"I don't know, I could end the whole thing. Go out there, I got my 30.06 upstairs. I could go out there right now and settle this thing. Take out Ellis Bowers, Nicky. Whatever it takes to get this thing over with. But where would that leave us?"

He stood up. "You have to say to yourself, I can't keep on like this. Whatever happens, *you* have to make some kind of a change. You tell me, 'I want to leave my husband.' You want to change things. You got to *do* it. You can't let things stay the way they are. Your husband, he treats you like shit. And you got some guy out there, he's got pictures of you. You want people to see them? It doesn't matter whether you were drunk or not. The point is, you don't want this guy to have something like that. Holding it over your head."

She stood up too, and banged her shin on the coffee table as she stepped out into the middle of the room. A little mad. Like she didn't care for what he was saying. Maybe trying to be dramatic, he wasn't sure. She said, "Hey, it's easy for you to say. You just got into town. If this thing doesn't work out, you're not the one that's gonna be stuck."

He was mad now himself. Maybe he'd tell her that it wasn't his first choice of a thing to do, getting involved in this.

But she said, "I hope the bastard does send them to Nicky. I hope he sees them. And I wish I could see his face when he does."

He told her, "Yeah, but that's your emotions talking." Trying to calm her down, saying, "It's good that you're getting mad. But you don't want to be dumb about it."

She walked across the room and then back again. Finally, she told him, "You know what I want?"

"What?"

"I want another drink. Half a dozen goddamn drinks. Just forget about all of it."

"Hey, you want a drink, you can have one."

She said, in a dry tone, "Yeah, another drink would probably be good. Say I had two more of them. Strong ones. But the problem is, for every one I had, I'd want another."

Jimmy put his arm around her shoulder and said, "We don't want to do that."

"*You* don't."

"Listen, we work this out, get things straightened out, maybe you won't feel the need."

"You believe that?"

He told her, "I don't know."

She was quiet for a minute. And then she said, "The hell with it. You know what I should do? I should give it up. Go back to that bastard. He wants to ruin my life and maybe I should let him."

"No. You shouldn't."

"Yeah. Why not?" Taking a slug from her glass and spilling some of it so that it ran down her chin. She reached up and wiped it off with her hand, sticking her fingers, one at a time, into her mouth and licking the Scotch off them. Jimmy was thinking, any other time, if they were in bed, something like that, and she did that, licked her fingers one by one, it would've been sexy. But now, knowing she did it out of habit because she didn't want to waste the booze, it was pretty sad.

He stepped around her. Went through the kitchen and out the

side door to his car. Reaching into the glove compartment, to where the envelope with the two pictures in it was. Not really sure what he was gonna say to her, just walking back inside and throwing the envelope on the coffee table. She was still where he'd left her, standing in the middle of the room watching him.

He said, "Why don't you look at it? You want to give up, want to go back to your husband, back to that life? Why don't you see what that life got you?"

She said, "I know what that life got me. But you don't understand how it used to be. It was fun, cause Nicky adored me. It was like a party that never ended, back in New York. I was a model, I had Nicky. Together we did a lot of things. Enjoyed ourselves. Maybe you don't understand it. Maybe you think that kind of life is a bunch of crap. I guess I should be happy here, huh? My life's not that hard. Is that it?"

Jimmy pointed at the envelope.

She asked, "What's that?"

"I think you know what it is. I want you to see it, though, maybe remind yourself. Ask yourself, before you go making any decisions, before you think of going back to Nicky, ask yourself do you really want anyone else seeing those pictures, because if Ellis thinks you don't care if Nicky sees them, he'll threaten to show them to somebody else who you *do* care about."

She put the glass down and reached for the envelope slowly, like she wasn't really paying attention to what she was doing. Being so nonchalant that Jimmy knew it was an act. Maybe she didn't know what was in the envelope—he'd never told her he had them—but she could figure it out.

She slid the two pictures out carefully, looking at them for a long time before she said, "I'm a beautiful person. A goddamn Girl Scout, huh?" Not as mad now.

"Hey . . ." Not finishing the sentence because he wasn't sure what to say. She wasn't acting now. There was a lot of pain in her voice, in her eyes. It hurt her to look at the things.

She asked him, "Where'd you get them?"

"Ellis Bowers gave them to me, the day I went to talk to him. He thought he was being funny."

"I look like a whore."

"No, you don't. You think about it, what do you look like? You look like anyone else that ever had sex. But the thing is, these things, the pictures, we don't want any of them around, we want to get rid of all of them."

She said, "Jesus, what am I going to do?"

"We're gonna figure out a way to get them back." He was watching her stare at the photos, not really sure if she was listening to him.

She had a different expression all of a sudden, leaning forward until her face was only inches from the photo. He thought maybe she was gonna start to cry—wouldn't have been surprised if she did. Maybe she'd burst into tears and rip the things up.

He squeezed her hand. "Hey, we can handle it. Work this thing out." But she wasn't paying any attention to him.

She turned her head towards him in slow motion, staring at him for a second, and then turning, just as slowly, back to the photographs. He could picture that look on the cover of a magazine—sleepy, a couple of strands of her hair falling in front of her face. She'd get it just right, the beautiful hair tousled, the bedroom look of a gorgeous woman the camera had caught by surprise. He could see why she'd probably been a good model, because she had a look, a combination of innocence maybe, and sex.

He started to tell her to quit staring at them, but she interrupted him, speaking so softly that he barely heard her. Like she was talking to herself, or thinking, and it just happened to come out as a whisper. She said, "This isn't me."

He thought at first that he hadn't heard her correctly. Maybe she had said it wasn't fair, something like that. But she said it again, getting excited and speaking louder. "This isn't me."

He wasn't sure what she was getting at. He said, "Hey, I know it's upsetting. . . ."

"No . . ." She was talking quickly now. "I mean it. Jesus, I can't believe it." The words were coming out so fast that he was having trouble keeping up. "I never really looked at them before. When they came, the other day . . . God . . . I got them in the mail and I opened the envelope and took one look. I thought I was gonna be sick. I saw the photos, there were five of them, and I looked at them for a total of maybe fifteen seconds before I tore them up."

"I know you *wish* it wasn't you," Jimmy said.

She pushed her drink away and moved closer to where he sat. He could smell her perfume as she held the picture up—the one where she was between Ellis Bowers's legs with his prick in her mouth—and a touch of booze on her breath too.

He felt embarrassed, looking at the picture she had in her hand. How was he supposed to act? Like the thing didn't bother him? Like it didn't make him want to kill Ellis Bowers?

"Don't you see it? Look . . . my arm." She slapped at the picture with her fingers. "My arm. The vaccination mark."

"What about it?"

"I don't have one, *that's* what about it."

"Maybe your other arm. Maybe the negative got turned around when they developed it." He didn't know if that could happen but he thought it was possible.

"No. I don't have one on either arm. Jesus, I don't believe it."

She took her shirt off, tearing at it, she was so excited. Throwing it on the ground and then turning to Jimmy. Showing him first one shoulder and then the other. Turning like a model—striking a couple of poses like she was in front of a camera, having fun—while he looked from her to the picture on the table, realizing she was right.

Jesus Christ. It had been right in front of him. He'd noticed the vaccination mark the other day, looking at the pictures, when Ellis Bowers had given them to him. But it hadn't meant anything.

She said, "I'm right, aren't I?"

He nodded. "I don't know what to say." He looked at the picture again and then up at Katherine. Seeing her, standing in the middle of the room now, without her shirt, not wearing a bra. He wondered for a second, did she ever wear one? Letting his thoughts wander because he couldn't help it, they were having a serious talk here, discussing something that was very important, and he still couldn't help it, seeing her without her shirt on got him horny.

She said, "Stop it." But she was smiling, not mad at him.

It didn't bother him anymore, looking at the pictures with her standing right there. If it wasn't her, then he had a whole different feeling about the photos. It was like he was looking at a magazine.

She was telling him, "The whole time, for a week now, I've been thinking it over, trying to remember that night. And I couldn't. I figured it was because I got so drunk. I remember getting in a car, but that's it. I looked at the pictures the first day, just a glance. And since then I've been trying to recreate it in my head. Did *I* really do that?

"Maybe I would have. I was so pissed off, trying to do something, get even with Nicky. And maybe I even posed for the one— they got me to stand there, propped me up, with my shirt partly undone. But not the other. Not the one where I'm . . . whatever. I wouldn't have done something like that, knowing they were taking pictures."

Jimmy smiled. "And you didn't."

She smiled back. "I didn't, did I?"

He could tell how she felt. So relieved. She wasn't even paying attention to the glass of booze on the table, letting it sit there like she had forgotten about it. But then he asked her, knowing it was something she was gonna have to think about, "Hey, the thing is, if it's not you, in the pictures, I mean . . ."

She was interested. "Yes . . . ?"

He wanted to let her get used to the idea because he didn't think she had considered it yet. Picking up the photo of the woman with the cock in her mouth and handing it to her. Letting her hold it for a couple of seconds and then asking, "If it isn't you . . . who is it?"

It caught her by surprise, because she hadn't gotten past being relieved. He could see her mull it over, looking at the picture and then up at him. Saying, "Oh my God." Letting the words hang in the air for a minute. "It's Susie, isn't it?"

"I don't know why," Jimmy said, "but who else could it be?"

She put the picture down quickly, like it was too hot to hold, and then said, "Wearing a wig so she'd look like me?"

Jimmy nodded. "Yeah."

"Oh my God."

# CHAPTER

# FIFTEEN

Nicky got even hornier, driving to Susie's apartment. Sitting in the BMW, listening to Cole Porter on the stereo, he wasn't sure, was it because he was on his way to see Susie or was it that everything was working out so nicely. Probably both.

It was a bigger scam than he had ever pulled before. Not that much different in principle from a lot of other things he'd done in years past. But it was huge compared to the money he'd made off anything else he'd been involved in alone. And more dangerous too. The guys from Beaufort—he had Bud Garner, two bankers, a couple of lawyers, and Hills, the plastic surgeon, who was loaded—were all putting up cash. He wasn't worried about them. They'd given him the cash to use for bribes. What were they gonna do, take him to court if he stole their money?

But Susie *was* right, Wesley was an unknown quantity. What was he, a bartender from New Jersey. A guy who had acted impressed when Nicky won ten grand at the casino. That was understandable, except the man had practically drooled over it. And it wasn't as if Nicky had ever really expected to see him again. The man seemed like a typical loser. But six months later, where was he? He was down here with a bag full of money answering Nicky's prayers.

But Nicky didn't have a real good feeling about Wesley, because there was something Nicky could sense, a quality that was becoming more apparent the more time Nicky spent around him.

Nicky knew that when he fucked with Wesley's money, called him up on the phone and said, Hey, I'm sorry, I don't know what to say but the thing is, the deal fell through and I can't get your money back, he knew when he told *Wesley* that, he was gonna have to be careful.

He'd been giving it some serious thought—maybe he ought to take Wesley out. The way it could work, he could get Wesley out to the club again, put a bullet in his brain, make it look like a shooting accident. Nicky could say they were out shooting clay pigeons— which a lot of people knew he did—and he was trying to show Wesley how to do it when there was an accident. Nicky'd never killed anyone, but how hard could it be—how hard would it be to pull that trigger when there was more than a million dollars at stake?

It made sense and would keep Nicky from having to look over his shoulder all the time. Driving along, almost to Susie's now, he got another idea. He could kill Wesley—say he did that, and then got *rid* of the body, took it out in his boat and fed it to the fucking sharks or something. Then he could tell the businessmen from Beaufort, his other investors, that Wesley had ripped them *all* off. Nicky could picture it, he'd throw his hands up in the air and get a hurt look on his face. Fred MacMurray in the last scene of *The Caine Mutiny.* "Hey, fellas, I don't know what to tell you. We've all been taken advantage of."

By the time he got to Susie's, though, he was thinking about something else, looking up to the third floor of the building, wondering could he do a repeat of the other day? Picturing Susie naked and deciding he could do two times easy. Who the hell knew, maybe three.

———

Jimmy tried to talk Katherine out of it at first. He held her in his arms and said, "I don't think you want to go over there. Not yet. What are you gonna do, barge in there, ask Susie what she thought she was doing?"

"I'm going to make her give them to me. Give them all to me."

Jimmy said, "But she doesn't have them all. Ellis Bowers has some."

"Well, I'm not going to sit here, waiting for who knows what, if that's what you're asking. She can get the rest from Ellis." She started putting things in her purse. "Look, I'm not going to do anything stupid. I just want her to know that I know. That bitch."

He got his keys and nodded. "Okay. Let's do it. Go on over for a visit."

Katherine smiled too. "It'll be a surprise, us dropping by."

Jimmy said, "It'll be that, all right."

———

Susie saw Nicky standing in her doorway with a look on his face like he'd just lost his virginity and knew he had good news. He looked like he was about to rape her right there. She'd given it some effort, put a tight little skirt on that ended just below her butt and a halter top, the kind of thing a teenager would wear. Hoping that it wasn't gonna be too long before she was gonna be able to quit all this crap.

He reached out like a kid in a toy store and grabbed one of her tits, gave it a honk. Starting to reach out with his other hand for her skirt, maybe he was gonna rip it off right there, not even seeming to care that they were in the hallway almost.

She said, "Hey, wait a minute, let me close the door at least." He didn't answer her but he did let her step back inside.

It was as far as they got. Nicky pulled at her shirt, tearing it over her head, and saying, "Hun-bun, I got about ten seconds before I explode."

She said, "What's the rush?" Teasing a little. "Nicky, honey, answer me, what's the rush?"

He stopped pawing at her and looked into her eyes. "Hey, what's the matter? Don't you want to fuck a guy who's about to clear one point five million dollars? Cash?"

It took a moment for it to sink in. Susie had been waiting for this for almost three months now but she still couldn't quite believe it. Hearing the words in her head again, running them over to herself just like Nicky had said them. *One point five million cash.* Jesus. She wanted to reach out and pat him on the head, maybe kiss him on the forehead like you would a kid. Tell him, "Good boy" and give him a little gold star.

But she didn't. Instead, she put a big smile on her face and talked to him like she was a kid, saying, "Nicky, you are the *best*." And then she reached down to stroke him inside his pants, letting him push her down to the floor and tear at her skirt. Hearing him say, "Jesus, yes," while she kept adding it up in her head. One point five million dollars. Cash. God, what she could do with that.

Katherine walked three steps past the car before she turned around and said, "Jesus Christ," walked back to the BMW and looked inside, making sure. Jimmy didn't know what she was doing at first. He'd been ahead of her, talking to her, trying to make sure she didn't go into Susie's apartment and start screaming. Telling her to try to remember to stay calm. Then he realized that she was no longer with him.

He walked back and asked, "What's the matter?"

She had a weird look on her face as she stepped back from the car and looked up at the apartment building.

He said it again. "What's the matter?"

"I keep getting surprised. Keep turning around, something new happens, and it catches me off guard. You'd think by now . . . you'd think I might be getting used to it."

"What are you talking about?"

"This is Nicky's. Nicky's goddamned BMW."

"You're kidding me." Hearing his own voice and thinking it sounded like a dumb comment to make.

"What a fool I am," she said.

Jimmy didn't know what to tell her. He was thinking it was a hell of a coincidence. He turned to Katherine and said, "Why don't we go up and say hello."

She tossed her hair back and said, "Jesus." But started walking.

Nicky was standing in the shower singing as loud as he could, some Sinatra thing that he knew by heart. Getting the words right was important. Some people, they would listen to music, act like they appreciated it, but you say to them, Yeah, what are the lyrics? What's the song really about? And they'd look at you like they had sawdust between their ears. Nicky thought if you were gonna listen to music, take the trouble, you should learn what the song was about.

He knew what Susie was doing. Cooking him something to eat. If he stuck his head out of the shower he could smell it—a steak. What he'd do, he'd finish with the shower, put on his robe, which he always kept here, and then he'd go on out to the living room and have Susie serve him dinner.

He got out and dried himself off. Looked in her medicine chest for some deodorant and smeared some under his arms, thinking he'd brush his teeth but then deciding, the hell with it, he'd wait until after dinner.

He heard voices coming from the other room. Susie was watching television. He reached for the robe, a black silk thing hanging from a hook on the back of the bathroom door, and then decided, why bother?

He strutted past Susie's bedroom and down the hall like a rooster, hearing the TV still going. He looked around for Susie, thinking she might be in the kitchen. Then he realized that the voices he heard were coming from the front door. He was trying to decide whether he ought to go back and put the bathrobe on when he heard Susie yell. It was a sound he'd never heard from her, like she wasn't in control of what was happening. He took a step further into the living room, not sure what he was gonna do but mad enough to walk on over bare-ass naked and tell whoever it was to get the hell outta there. See what happened then.

He was getting a picture of it in his head and seeing how funny it would be—almost laughing—when Katherine stepped into the room. She was the last person he expected to see. Susie and a man, the Marine, were right behind her. Nobody moving for a couple of seconds while Nicky started to get red in the face. Started to get embarrassed, moving his hand down now to cover up his pecker. It seemed to Nicky that everything froze. Until Katherine, the bitch, started laughing. Shaking her head at him and laughing like he was the funniest goddamn thing in the world.

Katherine couldn't believe it, her reaction. But she couldn't help it. It was funny. Not in the long run maybe. But right now, seeing Nicky without a stitch of clothing on, it was funny as hell. Her husband looked at her like he was furious, as if it were the other way—he'd caught *her* fooling around—and then he turned and walked back down the hallway.

.He appeared a minute later, wearing a robe, looking from Katherine to Jimmy. Saying, angrily, "What the fuck gives you the idea you can come in here?"

It was all she needed to hear. A trigger. The sound of his voice reached her ears and she lost it. "You son of a bitch. You *fat* son of a bitch."

Behind her she heard Susie ask Jimmy, "You think maybe you and I should get out of here, let these two have a couple of minutes?" Like it was the most natural thing in the world. And Jimmy, sounding surprised, but not upset with the woman, answered, "No, I think I'll stick around."

She knew what was going through Nicky's mind. He was caught, but still, she could tell, he was busy trying to come up with something that he could say. Some way of getting out of it.

Nicky stood on his tiptoes practically. Ignoring Katherine, he said, "Susie, hon, why'n't you go get me a drink?"

When Katherine saw Susie start to move, she said, "Don't.

Don't you leave this room. I'll be out of here in twenty seconds and then Nicky can have all the drinks he wants." She looked at Nicky and said, "You may as well stay here. You and your whore."

Susie moved over to Nicky. Katherine couldn't believe it, the nerve of the woman—the bitch—reaching out and touching Nicky on the shoulder, right in front of her, for God's sake. Saying, "Katherine, you should probably just go. Settle this thing later." Not upset at all, like they were still friends and she was just giving Katherine a little advice.

"What about you and your damn pictures?" she accused Susie.

Susie didn't change her expression. It almost made Katherine think that she was wrong for a second, that she'd made a mistake and Susie hadn't had anything to do with the pictures. But then Nicky began to giggle. Katherine looked from him to Susie, and all of a sudden she knew. It felt like she'd been hit in the stomach. Like maybe she was gonna throw up right there.

"You *knew?*" she said to Nicky. "You *knew?*"

"I told her to do something to keep you from shooting off your mouth."

Katherine was staring at him like she'd never seen him before. Saying, "You *let* them do this to me. Set it up to look like I was cheating on you. Got your girlfriend to put her wig on and pretend she was me." She took a step towards him and yelled, "Why?" And suddenly there were tears in her eyes because she couldn't believe how dumb she felt. Asking herself was it possible that Nicky *hated* her? Wanted to make her suffer this much? It made her feel stupid.

She felt Jimmy's arms come around her and then he led her away while Nicky shouted, "This'll teach you to threaten me. Tell *me* that you're gonna fuck up a business deal of mine!"

She knew Jimmy was going to go back in there and beat the shit out of Nicky. Half of her wanted him to do it. But she said, "Please don't. Just get me out of here."

The last thing she heard, before the door slammed shut, was her husband in there with her best friend, laughing.

# CHAPTER
# SIXTEEN

K atherine sat on her side of the car, staring out the window, watching the buildings go by. And then, when they'd crossed the bridge, she stared out at the salt marsh and the tourist boats on the bay. She was trying to figure it out, how people—maybe somebody out on one of those boats—how was it that they could be having a normal day, going about their business, having fun, while her whole world was falling apart. It didn't make sense.

She wasn't crying now. That had stopped when they were a mile away from Susie's apartment. Jimmy sat quietly next to her while they went through Beaufort and then over the bridge to Lady's Island. It was like he read her mind, cruising right by the turnoff for his house and driving down Highway 21 until she figured out the only other place left to go was the beach.

He drove into the state park, taking the left to the entrance gate and then following the road past the alligator pond and the public beach and on down to where most of the state cabins were. Pulling off finally where the road ended and the lagoon that cut the island almost in half began. They sat without moving for a few minutes and then Katherine, thinking sooner or later she was gonna have to start breathing again, said, "God, it's too hot to just sit here." She got out of the car on her side and waited for Jimmy to walk around.

It was almost nice, walking with him, crossing the dunes to the beach. Halfway there she took his hand, slid hers into his and felt him squeeze it. It had been such a horrible day but still she felt better just because she was with him.

She said, "You remember coming out here after school?"

"I remember a couple of times, coming here when we were supposed to be *in* school."

She smiled. "Yeah." Still holding onto his hand, wanting to squeeze it harder because it felt like they *were* back in high school. She knew it was kind of absurd, to feel like that. Maybe some other time, on a different day, the memory wouldn't be so strong. But it didn't really bother her, pretending for a couple of minutes that that's what this was, a couple of high school kids cutting class. It seemed like it was all right to do that for a little while.

She said, "I come out here sometimes if I want to get away from things. Or if I have something I really want to think about, something that I have to get straight in my head."

"Yeah, well, this is the place . . . you can get away from it here."

There was nobody else around. She saw a couple of people about half a mile away, down towards the public beach, but nobody where they were. They came to a place where the water almost touched the dunes and they had to walk around, climb through the clumps of sea oats to get back to where the beach was clear. Jimmy, reaching down to take her hand again, helped her up onto the dunes, and then stood next to her while they looked out at the water.

He'd been thinking about something for a few minutes. They'd left the dunes and walked all the way down the island on the south point, where the beach curved around and you could see the houses on Fripp Island maybe a half-mile away. Standing with her, with about fifty seagulls huddled by the water and a group of pelicans on a sandbar further out, if Jimmy turned, made a move to his right, he'd see the fishing pier, the little store right next to it, and further on, the bridge over to Fripp.

He wasn't sure if it was something he should bring up. Katherine was holding his hand now and seemed a lot calmer. But, still, he didn't know if she was ready to talk about what to do next.

He gave it a try finally. When he turned she did too, smiling up at him and saying, "You've got something on your mind."

It surprised him because it was what she used to do a lot. He'd be thinking about something—it didn't really matter if it was anything important—and she'd ask him what was on his mind before he was even sure he wanted to tell her. It used to be a joke. They were sitting in his parents' living room watching the TV the first time they saw that show *M*A*S*H* and the guy Radar, the one who always knew when the choppers were coming in with the wounded before anyone else, and he'd told her, "That's you."

Now he said, "It's not something I got figured out completely."

"You want to tell me about it?"

"The thing is, I don't even know is it something we could do. And also, which is the more important thing at this point, is it something that you're gonna want to hear."

Katherine bent down to pick up a shell and then tossed it towards the waves. "Why don't you just tell me? That way, if it's something I'm not comfortable with, I'll let you know."

"Okay." He wanted to get it right. He felt easy standing there with her, just the two of them, talking about things. It didn't matter, right then, what it was they were discussing, like it could've been anything and they would be calm about it. He realized that what she thought was important to him. He wanted her to tell him that what he had in mind was the right thing to do. Not like in the corps—somebody decides that you're gonna do something, it doesn't matter if you're thinking it's stupid.

So he waited for another couple of seconds, and then he said, "Well, we're in the middle of something. It's not doing you a lot of good, going through it, finding out about your husband and your best friend, and I'm not sure how you're feeling. I'm trying to put myself in your shoes. What would I feel like doing? You know, would I want to cry? Or would I just be furious, want to go back over there and do something?"

"I can't see you breaking into tears."

He shrugged. "I don't know. It could happen, I guess. But the point is, I want to try to figure out what's going on inside your head."

"What I'm feeling now?"

"Uh-huh."

After a few seconds she told him, "I didn't get it at first, why he did it. Nicky, I mean. Why would he do something like that—set it up so it looked like I was doing those things in the pictures? I mean, I wasn't even doing it, it just *looked* like I was. The pictures were . . . fake." Pausing for a minute and then saying, "I couldn't figure it out, driving out here, what he was getting out of it. Then I realized, he thinks he's protecting himself."

"From what?"

"From me. From what I was going to do. He thought I was going to ruin his deal. Mess up his 'last chance.' But also, I think in a weird way that was his method of protecting himself so I wouldn't try to divorce him, or try to get money out of him." She sighed. "Hell, maybe he thought it was a way to keep me, save the marriage. He always has so many angles. You never know with Nicky."

"So, how *do* you feel?" he asked.

"I guess what I feel . . . I guess I feel mad."

"I think that's probably the right way to feel. This afternoon, before, when you were at my house and we were looking at the pictures, you looked defeated."

"Uh-huh."

Jimmy said, "But later, when we walked into Susie's place and your husband was standing there . . ."

"Naked."

"I guess a lot of women would have reacted differently."

"Started screaming?"

"Yeah."

"But that's what I did."

Jimmy shook his head. "The first thing you did was laugh at him. Before you started to yell."

"So?"

"So, it's okay. You saw the humor in it, you were able to laugh because by then, over the past couple of months, you'd already seen what he was like. What a jerk he is."

"But . . . we did have something. I mean, the house, that property, our position. There're a lot of people out there who would have done anything to live in a place like that. Have that kind of money. Live the way we did."

"Yeah, but the money wasn't doing you a whole lot of good."

"It's easier, though. It makes things seem better if you do have money."

"You think so?" He hadn't heard her talk like this before. Hadn't seen this side of her.

She smiled. "It doesn't hurt."

"No, I guess not."

He was getting ready to tell her what he'd been thinking. Not sure if it was what she wanted from him. Because if she went along with it, heard what he had in mind and agreed to try it, it was something that they weren't gonna be able to back away from.

He said, "My point is this—the man treated you like shit. Jesus, he's been having an affair. That's one thing. I guess it happens. But the other thing, with Susie, setting up the pictures—"

"Yeah?"

"Well," he said it slowly, "if somebody did something like that to me, made me feel that bad, I'd want to do something."

"What would you want to do?"

He looked out at the water, wondering how to put it. Deciding finally to say it calmly and see what her reaction was. He said, "I'd want to get even."

It took about ten seconds, and then her eyes lit up. She surprised him by standing on her toes and giving him a big kiss. And then she said, "Hey, isn't that a nice thought. Nicky, the son of a bitch, why don't we see if we can ruin *his* day."

Walking back to the car they discussed a lot of different ways to do it. Jimmy asked questions while Katherine tried to tell him about Nicky. But it wasn't there yet; he didn't have the feeling that anything she was telling him was something they could use. Nicky sold real estate, Nicky dabbled in the stock market, Nicky knew some shady people, Nicky liked to gamble. She'd told him all that. And she said she wasn't sure, but she thought at one point he'd even tried smuggling dope in from down south. Hiring people to bring bales of pot up from the Florida coast by boat. She told him finally, "See, that's the thing, for a while, I didn't pay any attention. Nicky would say something, tell me he had people coming over, business—things happening in the middle of the night—or else he'd disappear, say he was going to Savannah, or Atlantic City. And I didn't give it much thought at all."

"Well, you were out of modeling, done with it. Maybe you were tired of worrying about where the money was coming from."

She said, "You know, it's an easy thing to do—forget about money if you think you have more than enough. Nicky would hand me cash. I'd say I had to go shopping, buy some things, and he'd give me hundred-dollar bills." She said quietly, "Nicky wasn't always like he is now."

Jimmy heard her but didn't answer. He didn't know what to say to that because here they were talking about getting even with him.

Katherine shaded her eyes from the sun as she spoke. "I used to be proud of what I was doing. Making a living. There was a time when I was making more than most of the guys I knew. And it's important, to feel secure like that. To know that you can afford to live the way you want." She laughed. "Before I met Nicky, I'd go out with someone and if the guy was a jerk, trying to impress me, trying to let me know he was worth a bundle, I'd end up, a lot of times, figuring out that I was worth more."

"You ever tell any of them that?"

"Yes, one time. The guy was a real jerk. Money was all he talked about. So, yes, finally I said something. He's telling me about a business deal he had coming up. It was gonna make him, I don't know, fifty grand. And I told him, he was trying so hard to show me what a big shot he was, I told him, if it didn't work out I could lend him the fifty thousand."

"What happened?"

"It was almost funny. He got mad and gave me a look like I should've kept my mouth shut. But you know what? I had the feeling, looking at him, that he was giving it some serious thought, should he go for the loan or not?"

"And then you met Nicky?"

"Yeah." She waited a moment and then said, "I know maybe it doesn't make sense to you now. But he was different back then."

"Well, maybe you were different back then too."

"Maybe a little of both."

Jimmy could just see the parking lot where his car was. He asked her, "What about now? He's got this guy Wesley hanging around. What are they doing?"

"I think they're going to buy an island."

It wasn't what Jimmy had expected. It wasn't even something he knew you could do. He said, "You mean, just go out and buy the thing?"

"I know. It sounds strange at first. But yes, they've got a property they're looking at, I think. I heard Nicky talk about it. The idea is to turn the place into another Fripp Island. Or Hilton Head."

"Jesus. He's got that kind of money?"

She shook her head. "No. Hardly. See, I think it's a scam. That's what he was scared of . . . that I knew enough to spoil his deal."

"Maybe you do."

"I don't know. We'd get in an argument, and I'd throw it out. Tell him I was going to warn his investors to back off. I don't know if I would've ever gone that far, though. I don't even know what I would've said to them anyway."

"So all you know, basically, is he gets these other people to invest and then, somehow, he takes their money. And he gets away with it."

"Yes."

"But right now *he's* broke?"

"He's pretty close. He's got, what do you call it, a cash flow problem? He looks like he's got money, lives like he does, but he doesn't really have it. The other thing—which, from what I understand, is bigger—is he's got tax problems."

"The IRS is after him?"

"I guess so. He's got lawyers working on it. But he can't touch most of what he has in the meantime. They've got a . . . a something . . . I forget what it's called."

"A lien?"

"Yeah, that's it. I got tired of hearing about it all the time."

Jimmy thought about Nicky, the big businessman—the whole time, he was fighting to stay out of the poorhouse or the penitentiary. And scared to death that maybe his wife was gonna spill the beans. He said, "So he's scamming these other guys. Gonna take their money."

"They put up the cash. Nicky, all he does is *act* like he's gonna make them rich."

Jimmy thought she just meant money at first—Nicky was gonna take their money. But after running it over in his head again, he said, "Tell me that again."

"What?"

"These people put up cash?"

"That's what Nicky said. He was laughing about it. Saying how easy it was going to be because everybody was using cash."

Jimmy said, "Jesus." Thinking Nicky was gonna have all that money lying around and telling her, "Jesus, it's a beautiful thing."

"What is?"

He smiled. "Cash."

He could see her eyes growing bigger while she thought it over. "Hey, we could make it work for us. Take his plan and use it ourselves," she said.

"I don't know about that. But we could mess up his plans."

She grinned, "Yes. We could do *that*."

———

Nicky called Wesley on the telephone, saying it quietly at first, like if he didn't make a big deal out of it maybe the other man would think it was okay. Being polite at first, a little small talk— bullshit—and then coming right out with it. "Wesley, we're almost there. One more day. But the one thing is . . ."

Wesley was patient, waiting to see what Nicky was up to. Because if the man was gonna make a move, start a scam on him, then it was gonna have to happen soon. "Yeah . . . ?"

Nicky finally just came out with it. "The one thing is . . . you're gonna have to leave that cash with me."

Wesley had been expecting it, would've been surprised even if Nicky hadn't suggested it. He was sitting in his rented house, out on St. Helena Island, with the TV on. Watching a program, CNN news, which he always watched. Hearing it in Nicky's voice, the scam starting to happen.

Nicky said, "See, it's gotta be this way. You've got to act just like the other investors. They see you hand over the money, lay that bag in my lap, with all that cash in it, that'll make it a whole lot easier for them to do the same thing."

Wesley said, "Uh-uh. I let everyone see that money, show 'em I'm one of the boys. I let them *see* it. But I ain't leaving that fucking money with you."

Nicky said, "Hey . . ."

"Don't 'hey' me. I bring the money, I leave with the money. And tomorrow morning you and I divide up what the others give us."

There was a pause while Wesley listened to Nicky breathe. And then Nicky said, quickly, "All right, that sounds fine to me." He started to sound excited. "Day after tomorrow, you and I will be feeling like a couple of kings."

But Wesley wasn't listening. He was staring at the television. Forgetting about Nicky Kramer for the time being because he was seeing a newsman, a guy on location, dressed in a nice suit walking along the boardwalk in Atlantic City while the camera followed him.

Wesley leaned forward and turned the volume up because the picture on the screen was familiar. The newscaster, with an earphone in his ear, and plastic-looking hair, was holding a microphone in one hand, talking about an IBM executive, a married man with a wife and two children who'd been kidnapped a couple of months before and whose body had just been found. The scene on the TV shifted from in front of Resorts International Casino to the swampland outside of Brigantine, and the newscaster's voice droned on, saying police had found a body, a kidnap victim. Talking about ransom, and how it had been paid but the body had never been returned. And some fucking detective, standing in the swamp muck while they loaded the body into the back of an ambulance, telling the newscaster, "We've got a pretty good idea of what happened, got a suspect in mind, but that's all I can say." Wesley, probably the most interested viewer in the country, watching all that and thinking, Holy shit, because he'd never expected the police to find any remains.

He could hear Nicky again. "Wesley . . . you there?" Speaking loudly now, bringing Wesley's attention back from the screen.

"Yeah, I'm here." The police were already talking about a suspect—maybe they knew it was him. He might have left behind some kind of evidence he didn't even know about. So if he wanted to convert his money—switch it to something he could use—he'd better do it pretty fast. He reached over to turn the TV off and then said into the phone, "I'll act like I'm giving my money to you. But it never leaves my sight."

Nicky reassured him. "Well, that's fine, that's okay with me."

Wesley hung up. He was getting the idea that it was gonna be pretty close and he wondered who else had seen the same TV show.

It worried him a little. What was he gonna do if the police or maybe the FBI started to get close to him? And the other thing, what was Nicky gonna do? Cause he surely was gonna try something, it was in his voice. Wesley sat there and thought about it, Mr. Nicky Kramer—hotshot. The man probably thought Wesley was going to be a cakewalk. Nicky'd got himself so excited about the deal he'd forgotten everything else. Forgotten his wife. But that was okay.

Wesley hadn't. He knew where Katherine was, her and her Marine Corps lover boy. He'd followed them. And no one knew it.

# CHAPTER
# SEVENTEEN

J immy was sweating his balls off. He was sitting in a clump of palmettos, with the mosquitos buzzing around his head, and looking up at Nicky's house from maybe two hundred yards away with his binoculars—Nikons, 7 × 50s—which gave him a good view of the front and side of the house. He could see just see the tennis courts and the pool, and then, if he moved them a little to his right, the front door. Tell who came and went.

He'd been there for three hours already. He'd driven down 21 and then taken the turnoff just before he got to Cotton Hall Road, parked the car about a half mile away, and then made his way through the brush to where he now sat. He and Katherine had each driven to the Ramada Inn. He'd told her to stay there until he came and got her. Having to explain it to her, go over it slowly, because at first she was acting like it was a game. He had to tell her that if they were gonna give this a try, it wasn't like they could afford to fool around, do something stupid.

He'd said, "I've got to be able to think about what I'm doing. I'm gonna sit where I can see the house, watch what's going on up there. I know it sounds like it isn't a big deal, but I can't get distracted."

Katherine had asked him, "What do you think is going to happen?"

And Jimmy had taken his time answering. "I got a feeling nothing's gonna happen. Maybe I'll end up sitting in the woods for the next three days, step on a rattlesnake or something, and meanwhile Nicky won't do a thing."

Katherine said, "But see, that's my point, wouldn't it be better if you had company?"

He'd told her, "No."

He'd packed a couple of sandwiches and one of those plastic cups of juice that had the straw built right into the top, thinking it would be enough but forgetting what it was like to sit in the heat for most of an afternoon.

He didn't even know was Nicky's deal gonna happen soon? Or was it still a long way off? He was trying not to swat at the bugs because somebody might see the movement. Then realizing that for all he knew it could've *already* happened. Nicky might already have the cash, he could be way further along than Katherine had thought.

He saw Susie drive up after a while. Didn't know who it was at first, just somebody pulling up in a hatchback, a Mazda RX-7. He put the binoculars to his eyes and watched as Susie climbed out, her skirt riding up around her thighs and taking her time about brushing it back down. Giving somebody a show. Maybe Nicky, up in the house.

A little later she came out to the pool, wearing a bathing suit.

Nicky was with her in tropical-colored long shorts—Jams. He had the string tied under his belly, and his legs were pasty looking. He started making a drink, talking to Susie from twenty feet away and pouring Scotch into a glass. Sitting down at the table while Susie dove in the pool and swam laps.

When she got out, she walked over to Nicky and kissed him on the top of his head, backing away and laughing when Nicky made a grab for her.

Jimmy tried to figure her out. He thought he had an idea what kind of girl she was—beautiful—but she didn't seem like she had much of a conscience.

Every once in a while, if the wind turned, he'd hear a bit of their conversation. Not enough to understand it, but if they got animated, he'd hear their voices. The sounds of their laughter drifted over to where he was sitting. It made him wonder, what the fuck was he doing sitting in the goddamn woods feeding the bugs? Maybe he *would* step on a rattlesnake—a diamondback, which would probably kill him, or else one of those pygmy rattlers, they were so small you never even saw them, just felt a sting on your ankle and then your leg swelled up and maybe fell the fuck off. It was over ninety degrees out and thoughts like that kept going through his head because it wasn't like he knew what he was waiting for.

When it happened he nearly didn't get it. The sun was almost directly overhead. But he was growing lazy, not concentrating that well. He'd watch the house for a while, say ten minutes, and then his mind would start to wander. He knew it was happening but, still, it would take him a couple of minutes to think about the house again. It had happened to him back in the Gulf. You sit around for long enough, try to think about one thing, and your mind starts to tell you to go screw yourself. Jimmy had forgotten how boring it could be watching other people have fun. Jesus, how long were they gonna just sit there while he got hotter and hotter out here? He was beginning to think maybe he was wasting his time. Maybe what he'd do, he'd go back and see Katherine, talk to her about it, and see if she had a better idea. So he wasn't really paying much attention when a car pulled into Nicky's driveway.

Two men got out of the car and walked around to the trunk. It took Jimmy about ten seconds to understand what was happening. There was something about them, the way they were acting, standing by the car and looking around. Each of them carried a suitcase. Instead of going to the front door they walked around to the pool.

Jimmy had an idea now what he was looking at. He hoped he was right. One of the men put his case on the ground and opened it. Stepped back and left it there. Jimmy was no longer tired. The bugs weren't bothering him anymore—they could have disappeared for all he knew—because now he knew for sure what was in the case. He held the binoculars to his eyes, pressed them tightly, and thought, Yes, that's right, open the goddamn thing up, everybody take a look. What was in that suitcase was money. He knew that for a fact.

It happened two more times. The same as before. A car pulled up and a couple of guys got out. One was carrying an attaché case, maybe he had bigger bills, something like that. Jimmy didn't know. The third time it was Wesley, jumping into focus in Jimmy's binoculars. He got out of his car, gazing around calmly, with black wraparound sunglasses on. And then he walked around the side of the house carrying a gym bag.

He didn't open his bag right away and then he just gave everybody a quick peek. He stayed for about an hour and then got up to leave. Jimmy saw Nicky pick up the gym bag and walk

Wesley through the French doors of the house. Five minutes later Nicky came back carrying the gym bag and Wesley walked out the front door with a grocery sack.

When Wesley got to his car he looked in Jimmy's direction. He opened the door and then, taking his sunglasses off, turned, staring like he'd seen him. Jimmy, lying down in the bushes now, because his knees had started to kill him, knew it wasn't possible. But it was a weird feeling, seeing the man's face up close through the binoculars, with his one good eye pointed right towards where Jimmy was. Wesley stared right at him and then got in his car and drove away.

Jimmy was getting restless now, because he'd seen what he'd come for. He watched the others, with Nicky in the middle of the group. They were having drinks and passing folders around, placing papers in them. Acting like it was a business meeting that was ending. He crawled backwards out of the bushes and made his way back to his car, thinking he'd have to figure out what he was going to do fairly quickly. It wasn't like Nicky was gonna leave that cash lying around forever.

———

Katherine asked, "How much?" And Jimmy said, "How much what?" She pushed him, put her hand on his arm and gave him a shove. "The money, dummy. How much do you think it was?"

He said, "I don't know. I couldn't really tell."

She was quiet for a minute and then said, "But you think it was a lot?"

Jimmy wondered if she'd been drinking. He said, "Everybody was walking around like they had half of Fort Knox in those cases. So, yeah, I'd say we're talking about a fair amount of money."

"What are you going to do? You can't just walk into the house and take it."

"See, if you say it like that, no, it doesn't sound like something I could do."

"Well?"

"I'm not gonna just walk in. I'm either gonna go in at night, sneak in, or wait until they go somewhere, get in there then and see if I can find it."

She asked him, "What happens . . . you're in there . . . and somebody finds you? Nicky's got guns in there. He catches you and he points a shotgun at you. I know him, he'll get off on it."

"Well, as of right now, the only thing I can say is, what else am I gonna do? I've got to do something awfully quick."

She nodded. "As soon as he can, he's gonna put it in a bank, take it overseas, Europe, or else down to the Cayman Islands. Someplace like that. It'll be gone before anyone knows it."

"That's my point. It's not like we have a lot of time to decide."

She stared at him. He could see something in her eyes that might not have been there a couple of days before. She seemed determined. "Hey, if you think it could work, maybe it's the last thing Nicky would ever think of. Somebody coming in there and taking it right out of his house."

Jimmy said, "We could surprise him, huh?"

———

Now he was sitting in his car at two-thirty in the morning, staring across the road at Nicky's house. Most of the lights were off and no one had moved since midnight. Jimmy was asking himself what in the world had he been thinking of? It was weird being out here to begin with, with the moon out, making crazy shadows on the ground, the big oak trees with their Spanish moss starting to look like some kind of sleeping dinosaurs. The thought of breaking into a house he didn't know much about was starting to seem pretty dumb.

He was still there, fifteen minutes later, looking at his watch. Deciding, finally, that he'd at least go on over to the house, take a look around, and see if it was possible to get in. He was reaching for the door handle when he saw movement over by the house, somebody coming out.

It was Susie. He thought she might have left something in her car and now she was out here getting it. She walked to her Mazda, stood there for a second, and then glanced back at the darkened house. After a moment she unlocked the door to her car and walked around to do the same thing with the trunk.

She went back into the house. He watched her disappear inside the front door. She came out almost at once. She was having trouble walking, staggering backwards, glancing over her shoulder towards her car every couple of feet. She was putting a lot of effort into it because she was dragging a suitcase. It looked heavier than hell. Jimmy figured the thing must weigh a ton for her to be having this much trouble.

She got to her Mazda and paused, tilting her head like a dog listening. Staring up at the house with her head cocked. Jimmy glanced up at the house too, thinking, Be careful now, girl.

Susie, moving again, struggled to get the case into the trunk of the car. She went back into the house and came out again a minute later with another case smaller than the first one and lighter. The thing didn't seem to be any trouble for her to carry. It was a lot like a big attaché case.

Jimmy started to understand. It fascinated him, seeing Susie doing this, stuffing the second case into the car and then walking around to the driver's door, sliding inside the Mazda while Jimmy was thinking that he couldn't believe it. It was taking place right in front of his eyes, but he had trouble believing that the woman had so much guts. Jimmy'd thought she was just getting Katherine out of the picture, planning to move in on Nicky and maybe help him spend that money. But the thing was—he heard Susie's car start up and he started his car because he was gonna follow her—he hadn't thought she was gonna do *this*. The first night all that money shows up, what does Susie do? She waits maybe six whole hours, and then she steals the cash. Walks right out of there with it while Nicky gets his beauty sleep. Jesus.

Susie wanted to laugh out loud, maybe start singing at the top of her lungs. All that money sitting in the back of her car, while she cruised down Ribault Road towards her apartment. It felt like she was having sex. Sex with somebody besides Nicky Kramer or Ellis Bowers for a change. Like her whole body was wired up, every nerve tingling. If she kept thinking about it she was gonna have an orgasm right there in the front seat of her car.

It had been so easy. Sitting up in Nicky's bedroom, having a couple with him, but being careful not to drink too much. Telling Nicky a lot of jokes because she was in a good mood. Making him laugh and then watching an old movie on the VCR, *The Philadelphia Story*, with Nicky pausing the tape every couple of minutes so he could tell her what Cary Grant, Jimmy Stewart, or Katharine Hepburn was about to say.

She almost told him to shut up, almost said, Nicky, you got *any* idea how much of a jerk you are? But it was all right. One more time was all she was looking at. She could put up with the man's bullshit for another couple of hours. Let Nicky get drunk and watch his movie, stare at the black-and-white images on the TV screen. It was what she wanted.

When Nicky had asked for what was probably his seventh drink, she'd told him she needed more ice. When she was down in the kitchen, she'd crushed up three Valiums, popping the pills out onto the counter. Thought about it and added two more. Then she'd gone back up to the bedroom and told Nicky, "Hey, why'n't we look at that money again?"

He'd said, "No, I got it in a safe place."

She'd pouted. "Nicky, come on, just a peek." She crawled onto the bed and inched her way to where he was sitting. "You know what I want to do?" she asked.

"What?"

"I want to bring that money up here, spread it all around, and then fuck you on it."

"You do?"

She licked her lips. "Uh-huh."

And it was all he needed to hear. He'd gone down and gotten the suitcases and brought them back up. When she asked, "Is that all of it?", he nodded.

Once he finished the drink it took about twenty minutes for his head to start to droop.

Then she waited, staring at his fat butt, thinking, no more, she wasn't ever gonna have to touch him again. She waited until he'd curled up in a ball and started to snore and then gave it another twenty minutes, barely able to control her excitement. To make sure, she held Nicky's nostrils closed for a few seconds to see if he was gonna wake up. All he did was give a snort and roll over onto his back. So she'd packed all that money into a suitcase and a black vinyl briefcase and gotten the hell out of there.

She had it all figured. Take the cash, stop at her apartment for a couple of things, her passport and some clothes, and then grab a flight out of Savannah by 6 A.M. The hell with Ellis Bowers and the hell with Nicky Kramer.

She had an idea that she might go down to the Caribbean. Island hop for a while. Play the rich American woman for a year or two until she decided what she wanted to do next. It crossed her mind that Nicky was gonna come looking for her when he woke up. Maybe even get Wesley involved—if he was able to convince the man that it wasn't his fault. But it wasn't a big deal. She could go to the Caribbean, or maybe Europe, change her name, dye her hair again, whatever it took. She'd stay out of sight for a couple of years. And then it would all blow over. Except for the money. Minus what Wesley had taken back with him when he and Nicky had switched the money to the grocery bag, it was *still* close to a million dollars.

Thinking about it, the way she felt, knowing what was in the back of her car, she decided it was even better than sex. Because there wasn't any man in the world could make her feel like this.

Halfway there Jimmy figured out where Susie was headed. He'd thought at first if it *was* the money she had put in the back of the car, she might just scoot down to Savannah and head for the airport.

But when she went back into town, drove the Mazda down 21 past the air station and then turned onto Ribault Road, he knew she was heading for her apartment. He thought she was taking a chance, staying in town for even an extra half an hour.

He followed her car all the way to her apartment. Saw her pull in and then get out and stand there for a moment. She didn't see him because he'd parked down the block. She did glance around but it seemed as if all she was doing was trying to make sure nobody was watching.

He waited until she locked up the Mazda and went inside her building. Then he walked slowly over to where her car was parked and peeked through the rear hatch window. The trunk was locked, but the suitcases were still there.

He could play it a couple of ways. He could run back to his car, get the tire iron out of the trunk, and then come on back here. Bang, bang, and he's got both the cases. Except what if somebody heard it, either the glass breaking or if the car was wired—had an alarm—the siren. Somebody calls the cops and what if there was one right around the corner? Or say he did get the cases. Susie's still inside tinkling or whatever it was she was doing. Jimmy grabs those cases and tries to hoof it back to his car. What if he gets halfway to his car and drops one of them? It opens up, just like in a bad movie, and he's got twenty-dollar bills, hundreds—whatever—flying all over the goddamned parking lot.

So he decided to wait and then be there to surprise her when she came down. He'd talk to her a little bit, tell her thanks, maybe. Take the suitcases off her hands. Be polite about it.

It took ten minutes. Jimmy was crouched between her car and the one next to it, staring up at the front door of her building, but also turning every once in a while to look at the street, keeping an eye out for anybody driving by. He heard her before he saw her, as he was looking at a car going by. It wasn't a cop—just somebody out late, driving by without even turning to look in Jimmy's direction. The front door of the apartment building closed, and he heard the sound of her heels on the pavement.

He saw Susie, carrying another suitcase, heading for the back of the car. He waited until he heard the key in the lock and then stood up. He didn't want to scare her, do anything quickly, and maybe make her scream. He just stood up slowly, naturally, like you would if you were watching TV and decided to go get a snack. For a few seconds Susie wasn't even aware of him. He watched the way she moved, maneuvering the suitcase into the trunk but being graceful about it at the same time. Seeing the moonlight—or maybe it was the streetlight—on her hair. Making it shine.

For a second all he wanted to do was watch her because there was something very appealing about her. But he made himself take a step forward, with Susie still oblivious, move around behind her, and tap her on the shoulder.

She was pretty impressive, he had to give her that. He'd come up behind her, three o'clock in the morning now, ready to put his hand over her mouth if he sensed she was gonna scream. Not be too rough but just stop her from making a commotion. But she didn't even act scared. He touched her on the shoulder and felt her jump. But not much. She just tensed her muscles a little and stopped trying to close the trunk. By the time she turned there was no expression on her face. Maybe she'd seen his reflection in the car window, he didn't know, but she sure didn't seem frightened.

It took her maybe three seconds, he could almost see the effort it involved, before she broke out in a smile. Looking at him and grinning for Christ's sakes, like she had been waiting for him, and saying, "Hey, it's you."

Jimmy thought maybe if they gave out Academy Awards not just for movies, but if they had a special category for people who acted really well in real situations that had nothing to do with the movies, she oughtta get one. Here she was trying to get out of town with a ton of stolen cash. He comes up and surprises her, does something that would have scared the hell out of most people, and the woman acts glad to see him. She was something.

At first it threw him off, though. Was he wrong? Maybe she

didn't have anything to hide. He remembered when Katherine and he had been in Susie's apartment, with Nicky, bare-assed naked, and Susie had turned to him and said, "Maybe we should get out of here." Acting like it was the two of them together. Like they belonged with each other and Nicky and Katherine were the intruders.

And now she stood relaxed, moving closer to him, swinging her shoulder bag around in front of her. Reaching into it so casually that it didn't get his attention at first. Starting to talk at the same instant. Still smiling, looking at his eyes and saying, "Jesus, I can't believe it. I would've said you were the last person I'd run into." Glancing down to where her hand was fishing around inside her bag, almost frowning for a second, but when she glanced back up at Jimmy she seemed happy again.

She told him, "But maybe it's a good thing you're here. I was gonna call you. Try to straighten this thing out." She had put her hand on his chest, and he could feel the warmth of it through his shirt. Saying, "Cause the truth of the matter is, I was disappointed with what happened the other day in my apartment. All that ugliness, when you and I didn't really have that much to do with it." She was talking quickly. "You know what my mother told me one time? She said the worst thing you could do, the worst way to leave somebody, is when there're bad feelings in the air." Smiling again, she told Jimmy, "Two people like us, we got off on the wrong foot is all."

She had almost convinced him until he saw a little drop of sweat pop up on her temple. He watched it run down her face and it hit him. He'd been right, the woman was bullshitting him, stalling, working under a lot of pressure until she could do . . . what?

He had to tell himself, Hey, look at this, what's happening here? Wondering what he'd do, if he were in her shoes, a load of money three feet in back of her and now he's here and maybe gonna screw up the whole thing. Seeing it from her point of view, how much time and effort she'd put into it. Realizing, as her hand was coming out of her purse, there was no way she was gonna let anybody mess things up for her now.

It seemed like it took a long time, getting it clear in his head what was gonna be in her hand, knowing he had about two seconds to do something about it. But then, moving in what seemed like slow motion to him, he knocked her other hand off his chest and reached for the purse at the same time. Thinking, Shit, because it looked like he was gonna be too late. He was still moving for the purse when her hand popped out and he got the first glimpse of stainless steel. Not a good look because the gun was covered by her hand. Just an image of the metal glinting in the moonlight and of her face changing. All the angles in it becoming hard, like she was gritting her teeth, getting ready to shoot him. It crossed his mind, in the last second before he moved, what was he gonna do, get ahold of the gun and wrestle it away from her? Give her a chance to scream, and wake the whole goddamned neighborhood? Or else get off a shot or two?

He didn't consciously decide to forget about the pistol and just hit her. It was something that he saw himself do as he was actually doing it. Seeing her face, her eyes looking halfway between him and the gun. And taking a step towards her with his fist coming up from somewhere down around his waist. Watching her chin get bigger, like *she* was moving towards *him,* and then feeling his fist connect with her face, stinging his knuckle and hurting like hell for a couple of seconds because he'd hit her that hard.

She crumpled. Didn't go flying backwards or slam into the car. Nothing like that. Her head snapped back, Jimmy watched that happen. But then she just seemed to sag, falling forward into his arms. She was heavier than he'd thought and almost took Jimmy with her. He caught her, though, holding onto her shoulders and easing her to the ground.

Five minutes later he decided he couldn't leave her like that. That was how long it took him to drag the two cases over to his car and lock them in the trunk. He came back and checked the third one, the one she'd carried down from her apartment. But all it had in it was clothes. He put it in the back of her Mazda and then turned around. Susie was still lying unconscious on the ground. What was he supposed to do now?

He could drag her over to her apartment. Carry her upstairs. But then he decided no way. It'd look pretty bad if somebody came out right when he was carrying her in.

In the end he decided to put her in the car. Sit her in the front seat so that when she woke up, had time to think things over and decide that whether she still had the money or not she'd better get out of town—at least she could leave in a hurry.

Even though she didn't weigh much it was harder than he thought. Moving her was a pain in the ass. Her body, completely limp, kept sliding out of his arms. Finally he just dragged her along the pavement until he got to the front door of the Mazda and then, half pushing her and half lifting her, he got her into the driver's seat.

He put the keys in the ignition and then thought what was she gonna do when she woke up? Did he really want her to be there, with no money, if Nicky showed up looking for her? Finally he went back to his own car and got a stack of bills out of one of the suitcases, thumbing through it while he was walking back. He decided it was about ten grand. Not what she'd expected but maybe better than she deserved.

He stuffed the money under her fanny, slid it up high enough that it wasn't in plain sight but so she would feel it when she woke up. It would be interesting. Would she do the smart thing? He could see the bruise already forming on her jaw and he said softly, "See, if it was me, if I was the one gonna wake up tomorrow morning with a headache and ten grand, after taking all that money, it's what I'd do. I'd get the fuck out of town."

# CHAPTER
# EIGHTEEN

K atherine could hardly contain herself. She was alone, waiting for Jimmy to get back. But, Jesus, it had been hours. Sitting there on the bed in a dreary little motel room with stupid wallpaper she tried to picture what it would look like—all that money. How much room would it take up?

She spent the first hour thinking of what a great time they could have, she and Jimmy. They could take that money, go somewhere, and forget all about what had happened here in Beaufort. It sounded terrific to her. It would be like it was when she first met Nicky maybe. She could show Jimmy what fun was like. Open his eyes. The way she had with Nicky.

But then she got antsy. The room seemed like it was closing in on her and even when she turned on the television she hadn't been able to concentrate for more than a couple of minutes at a time.

She'd started to pace back and forth, waiting for Jimmy to return. Waiting to see all that money.

She finally decided to go get a drink. She got in her car and drove down to the Hopscotch Lounge, knowing it was too late to find an open liquor store. At first the bartender wasn't going to serve her. He told her, "Lady, we mix drinks here, we don't sell bottles."

But she said, "I've got people over and I ran out." Smiling at him and holding up two twenty-dollar bills, saying, "Can't you make an exception?"

So here she was. She'd taken the paper off the glasses by the sink and poured herself a drink. And it'd helped. But she needed another one before she was able to sit back down and get her thoughts straight.

Now that she wasn't as confused, didn't have thoughts racing through her head, she could consider her choices. Jimmy was going to come through that door fairly soon, probably bringing a lot of money with him. Where did that leave her?

What she realized was that, in a way, it left her in the same position as she'd been stuck in with Nicky. It left her dependent on a man. Jimmy was nice, he was a great guy. But she had spent, what, a couple of days with him. She hadn't seen him for almost eleven years and now she was thinking of spending a lot more time with him? It didn't quite make sense.

With Nicky, at least she'd seen potential. He was on his way up when she met him. He'd had the image she was searching for. Too fast paced, maybe, in a business sense; he didn't know how to lighten up. But she'd changed that, shown him that there was more to life than back-room business deals.

So what was she going to do with Jimmy? His idea of fun was to go for a walk on the beach. Or spend a day catching blue-claw crabs. She didn't mind eating them but she didn't want to have to catch the goddamn things. Jimmy didn't fit very well in her world at all. She couldn't see him in her kind of house, out by the pool or at the club. He'd never grown up past the way he'd been in high school. Never matured. Never gotten to the point where he could appreciate things, realize that there were better ways to live, better ways to enjoy yourself.

She poured another drink. As she took a swallow, felt the gin burn its way into her stomach, she was seeing a different scenario. What if, and it was just a thought, what if she considered *just* herself? She hadn't done that in a while. What she could do, she could thank Jimmy, split that money up with him. And then she could go somewhere by herself, get a new life.

Jimmy would be upset, naturally. Maybe he wouldn't even understand it. But she couldn't worry about that. She *would* give him some money, maybe not half of it. No, because, the truth was, he had no real claim to any of it anyway. It was basically hers. It had *been* Nicky's and after what *he'd* done, she felt like she deserved it.

She could give Jimmy a little. Say ten thousand dollars. Thank him for his time, for his help. And then wish him luck. Jesus, it would be great. It would be just like when she used to model and made her own money.

She got up and went into the bathroom, washed her face, and then spent ten minutes brushing her hair. Combing it until it was perfect. She was looking at herself in the mirror, swinging her head back and forth so that her hair caught the light. It was like she was back in front of the cameras again, with a photographer telling her, Yeah, that's it, let me see your hair shine. And then she heard a car pull up outside the room.

She shut the light off in the bathroom and walked to the door of the motel room. A little unsteady on her feet but that was okay. She was going to give Jimmy a night he'd never forget. Treat him like a king. It was the least she could do. And then she was going to take that money.

She opened the door with a big smile on her face. Striking a pose, modeling for him, saying, "Hey, I was really worried . . ."

But then she lost her train of thought because what she was doing—just outside the door of the motel room, posing for the cover of *Glamour*—she was talking to Wesley.

He didn't have to do much explaining. He told her that Jimmy was in trouble and that he had sent Wesley to pick her up. She said, "Hold on," walked back inside, and returned with a bottle of gin. He hustled her out to her car before she had time to give it any more thought.

Halfway out to the state park she said, "Hey, wait a minute. . . ."

He could smell the booze on her and figured she was having trouble thinking it through. Now she was probably wondering why, if they were going to see Jimmy, they were headed in the wrong direction.

By the time she did get it, it was way too late. They were almost there. She said it again. "Hey, wait, where're we going?"

And then she started to yell, "Let me out. You're not taking me to Jimmy."

The sound of her voice coming at him from so close was irritating as hell. He let her say a few more things, let her accuse him of taking her to Nicky, and then he put a stop to it. He pulled his pistol out and stuck the barrel of it against her ear.

He said, "Hey, I got an idea. Why'n't you shut the fuck up?"

He took her out to the state park, pulling off the road and driving around the gate so that he could get to the south end where the cabins right on the beach were.

When he stopped the car Katherine got out and started to run. She took off past the cabins and headed across the dunes towards the beach. It was dark out there and he let her get all the way down to the water before he caught up to her. She was standing in the surf, yelling as loudly as she could but Wesley didn't think that anyone would hear her because the wind carried the sound out over the water. When he was ten feet away she threw the bottle of gin at him.

He caught it and said, "No, see, I think you're gonna want this later." And then he walked up to her and grabbed her by the hair, starting to drag her back towards the cabin. "If it were up to me, you could stay in the water all night. Drown for all I care. But instead, I got to get my ass soaked because you decided to go for a swim."

She stumbled and fell to the sand, yelling, "You're pulling it out for God's sake. My *hair* . . ."

But he didn't let go. He kept walking and she had to scramble to her feet and go with him.

He was furious because now he was cold. He was talking to himself, muttering, "I got a reason to keep her alive. Gotta keep her alive until we see what her husband does."

When they got to the cabin he kicked the back door open, pushed her inside and turned on the light. They were in a kitchen, a countertop along one side and a table with four chairs on the other.

He picked up one of the chairs, put it in the center of the room, grabbed her by the hair again, and shoved her down.

She started to scream and he told her, "Hey, one word, one

more word out of you and I'm gonna knock you the fuck out. Okay?" Then he pulled out his roll of duct tape.

When he was finished tying her to the chair he grabbed another chair and set it down so that it was facing her. And then he walked over to her.

He reached out and grabbed her cheeks between his fingers. Hard. And then he put his face down until it was an inch away from hers, so he could smell the gin on her breath. He grinned at her and said, "Hey, little girl, you and I are gonna talk. We're gonna chat, find out what you and the Marine are up to. Okay?"

Katherine tried to twist away but he only held her face tighter. She hissed, "Fuck you."

Wesley smiled more broadly. He said, "Hey, it ain't like any-body's gonna come through that door and rescue you, bitch." He acted like he had to think about it and then he said, "So, no. Fuck *you*."

And then he took a straight razor out of his pocket and held it up so that she could see it.

He touched the side of her face with it. "Hey, Kath-er-rine . . . ever seen what one of these things can do?"

———

Jimmy couldn't believe it, walking in and finding Katherine gone. He thought maybe she was in the bathroom or she'd gone out to get something to eat. Then he realized that her car was gone. He figured what she'd done was gotten drunk and wandered off.

Before returning to the motel, he had stopped at an all-night convenience store, getting some crackers and a six-pack of Miller. Feeling strange about it, standing at the counter and looking out at his rented Ford, the one with all the money in the trunk. Standing in line, with an old black guy in front of him who had a bunch of stuff that he was buying, while Jimmy waited patiently, staring at the TV screen above the clerk's head at CNN news.

He wasn't really paying attention until he saw Wesley's face appear on the screen. They must have used an old photo. It took Jimmy a couple of seconds to recognize him. But, Jesus, there he was. Jimmy had to lean forward, bump into the black guy, and ask the clerk, "Hey, you mind turning that up?"

The clerk said, "What?" A pimply-faced kid who was gonna give Jimmy a hard time until he saw the look on Jimmy's face. Rethinking the situation and saying, "Sure." Reaching back to turn the sound up and then waiting on the black guy while Jimmy stared at the screen and listened to what the newscaster had to say.

Now, sitting on the bed, without Katherine, he opened the cases and gazed at the money, all those stacks of crisp bills, and thought, Holy shit, what was he supposed to do now?

———

Wesley waited until dawn and then stuck a piece of cloth in Katherine's mouth. He took one more look at her and said, "Hey, you should see yourself now." He laughed.

She didn't say anything. So he wrapped some duct tape over the cloth in her mouth and then drove over to Nicky's house.

He thought it was a nice place to sit. Come out here to the pool with a beer, and grab a chair. Sit by the water and relax. In front of him, if he looked across the yard, down the driveway, and beyond Highway 21—maybe three hundred yards away—he could see the first light from the rising sun moving across the salt marsh. He could imagine what it would be like if he owned a place like this.

He could invite friends over, maybe a couple of women. Have them over for dinner and a swim. Everybody enjoying themselves.

It didn't make a lot of sense to him, looking up at the house and at the lawn—with the dumb bushes cut to look like animals—why would a man, say he had all this, why would a man be like Nicky? Thinking, all this stuff, nice house and everything, it should make a person content. Not turn him into an arrogant kid who was maybe trying to wreck Wesley's scam. Of course, Wesley had his insurance now, the cute little wife out at the cabin. But even so.

He had a beer and a little box he'd found out at the cabin on the table in front of him. The beer was in a glass, a long-stemmed crystal glass that he'd found next to the refrigerator in Nicky's pool house. He was sitting out at the pool, with his .357 Magnum slipped down the back of his pants, relaxing. Enjoying the beer, even though it was pretty early, and having a nice time until Nicky woke up. Every once in a while he'd pull the Magnum out of his pants and hold it in his hand. He wasn't playing with it, wasn't holding it in the air and pretending to shoot it—looking at things and going POW. All he wanted to do was remember he had it. In case he had to use it. He wasn't doing anything with the little box either. That was just sitting there.

Half an hour later he heard Nicky start to yell. The man was screaming at the top of his lungs. And then he heard Nicky tearing through the living room, headed for the front door of the house. Wesley waited calmly, taking the gun out of his pants and putting it on the table in front of him.

He was patient about it. Didn't get up and wander around looking for Nicky because he figured sooner or later he'd come out here. The sun was starting to feel pretty good now, taking the chill out of the air.

He had to sit there for another two minutes. Taking a couple more sips, finishing the drink, and then just leaning back in the chair. Calm about the whole thing because here he was, in control.

Nicky came out. He didn't see Wesley. He walked all the way over to the table, fifteen feet from where Wesley sat, and picked up the phone. He turned back to the house, away from Wesley, dialed, and then stood there, moving his hand in the air and saying softly, "Come on . . . come on," until Wesley had had enough and said loudly, "So how's it going?"

Nicky jumped about a foot off the ground and almost dropped the phone. "God—damn. You scared the shit out of me, Wesley. What're you doing? You-all come on out for a drink?"

Wesley said, "I think it's time you and I have a chat."

Nicky started to bob his head. Wesley watched him, thinking it was Nicky's way of coping. Come on out unexpectedly and be waiting for him to wake up, surprise the man, and that's what he'd do. Stand there and fidget, move his head like a fucking puppet until he figured out what to do next. A fat little guy with a silly-assed grin on his face. Looking at Wesley and saying, "Hey you wanna talk. That's fine by me."

Wesley said, "Uh-huh. Actually I came out here for the cash."

Nicky said, "It's kind of early." Staring at the gun on the table for the first time and saying, "What's that there?"

"That's a gun. You've seen one before."

Nicky was still trying to be polite, still trying to figure it out. Wesley watched him struggle with it for half a minute while neither of them spoke and then he said, "I'll tell you, the other day, you dragged me out to your club to watch you blasting away with that shotgun of yours. See, that's one way you can do it, play around with a gun like an idiot. The other way"—he leaned forward and picked the .357 up from the table top—"you can use one like you would any kinda tool. You don't need it, then don't even think about it. But when you *do* . . ."

He could see Nicky start to shake, just a little bit at first. And then he glanced up at the house. Wesley shook his head slowly. "No, man, you don't have to act like somebody's in there, gonna come out and save your ass if things get exciting." He was enjoying this, watching Nicky start to get scared. Feeling something in his gut like the time he'd put the pistol in the mouth of the guy he'd killed back there in Atlantic City. Nicky was beginning to look a lot like that guy. And he didn't even know about his wife yet.

For a minute, Wesley had an image of what it would be like to stick that pistol in Nicky's mouth, make the man suck on the thing—have sex with it—and then pull the trigger. But he couldn't do that. Not yet. He couldn't really do anything like that until he had all the cash.

Nicky started to walk towards the table where Wesley sat. Moving slowly. But sitting down finally and looking at Wesley. Trying to smile. Saying, "Hey, you want your share of the money. I can understand that. But, see, it's kind of early."

Wesley decided to go along with it, because he had to find out whether Katherine had told him the truth. But he had to make sure that the Marine had been successful, had gotten what he'd come for the night before.

He said, "Hey, it's never too early. You run on upstairs and get it. I'll tell you what, I'll go with you, help you carry it. How would that be?"

Nicky told Wesley, "It's in the bank. I can't get it yet. I got it in the bank." Gaining momentum, Wesley could see it. "I can have it a little later. Get it out by, say, ten o'clock."

Wesley started to laugh, the sound startling the shit out of Nicky. He said, "Hey, man, see, I know you didn't put that money in the bank. Ain't nobody in their right mind gonna walk into a bank with one point five million cash. Ain't ever gonna happen."

"Hey . . . I swear to God . . ."

Wesley interrupted. "You're lying."

He saw a change come over Nicky, like maybe it was starting to sink in, they were talking about something serious here. He managed to mumble, "Listen . . . I'm telling you the truth. . . ."

"Then go get the money."

Nicky started to cry. Wesley said, "Hey, come on, Nicky. Ain't no need to be cryin'."

Nicky's shoulders were shaking, he had tears coming out of his eyes, his whole body was shuddering. But he wasn't making a lot of noise. It seemed to Wesley like he was watching a movie—or TV—where some guy was sobbing but the sound was turned down real low. He let Nicky sit there while he thought, Enough, get the man back on track.

He leaned forward and said, "Nicky, stop it." He had to put the barrel of the .357 underneath Nicky's chin to get him to quiet down, "Nicky, goddamn, quit bawling, man."

"That bitch. She took the money," Nicky said.

Wesley nodded. "Your wife."

"What?"

"Your wife got the Marine to come in here last night. I made her tell me all about it."

Nicky looked confused. "What are you talking about?"

"What the fuck are *you* talking about?"

"Susie."

"The redhead, the one that liked to show her titties off?"

"Yeah."

"What's *she* got to do with this?"

"She took the money. Last night. All of it." He held his hands up in the air. "She must've done something, put something in my drink. When I woke up it was gone. And she was gone too."

"Jesus." Wesley gazed at Nicky, transfixed. "You got any idea what a *fucked-up* individual you are?"

Nicky ranted, "Hey, I trusted that bitch. Let her stay here, let her see what I was doing. Showed her all that money. . . ."

Wesley said quietly, "Where's the money at now?" Trying to figure it out, did the Marine have the cash or did Susie?

Nicky was still talking about Susie. "I let her stay here . . . with all that cash. First thing she does, the cunt, she rips me off."

Wesley lost patience with listening to the man blame some woman for something he never should have let happen. He let Nicky ramble for another couple of seconds and then yelled at him, "NICKY."

"What?"

"Where's the money? Does your little girlfriend have it?"

"I guess."

The redhead, Wesley thought, worming her way in here. Showing her tits to Nicky, screwing him stupid, and then taking the money. He said, "Where is she?"

"I don't know."

Wesley thought about it. Nicky was scared to death and being honest for a change, still hoping he could talk himself out of the situation. Sitting across the table with an expression on his face like he was five years old, he didn't understand how close he was to dying. Wesley thought, Jesus, you do meet some interesting people working like this.

He was gonna say something else when the phone rang. Nicky jumped and it even startled Wesley.

Neither of them moved until there was a click and the answering machine came on. Wesley relaxed again, feeling the sun, and trying to figure it out. What was he gonna do to get the money? He was thinking about the cash. When he realized that it was the Marine's voice on the answering machine. Jimmy. Jimmy Decker. Yeah. And goddamn if he wasn't talking about the money.

Wesley said, "Hey, I got an idea, why don't you answer that?"

Nicky said, "Me?"

"Nicky, pick up the phone and find out what the fuck he's talking about."

Nicky started to protest so Wesley reached across the table, grabbed the phone, and said to Jimmy, "Hey, son, how you doing?"

"Wesley?"

"Uh-huh."

Jimmy said, "Put Nicky on the phone."

"No, you're talking to who you want to right now."

"What do you mean?"

Wesley asked, "Hey, how's Katherine?" like he was talking about the weather.

"What about her?"

"You want to know where she is?"

Jimmy said, "Where is she?"

"Where's the *money?*"

Jimmy paused for about two seconds. "I have it."

Wesley said, "See that? It's not hard, two guys like us, there's no reason to fuss."

"What do you have in mind?"

"What'd you do, you bump into a cute redhead during the night, help her carry her bags?"

Jimmy said, "I don't think that's important now."

"Maybe you're right."

Jimmy asked, "So whatta you got in mind?"

"Son, a smart ex-jarhead like you . . . you should be able to figure that one out. You have something I want, I got something you want."

Jimmy said, "Where?"

Wesley could hear it in the man's voice. The Marine wanted to come out here and kill him. That was all right, he could deal with that later.

Wesley said, "Hey, I've heard about the beaches down here, heard they're different from up in Atlantic City. Nicer, not as much trash."

"Get to the point."

"All right. The point is this—you wait two hours, then drive out to the beach at the state park. Don't even think about arriving earlier than that. You'll see my car. You give me the cash and I'll get your bitch back to you."

When Wesley hung up the phone Nicky was staring at him. He said, "What's this about my wife?"

Wesley ignored him. He was trying to get it straight in his head what he had to do. Get Nicky out to the cabin he'd broken into. Katherine was already there and she wasn't going anyplace. Get the money, however he had to do it, and then get the fuck outta here, out of the fucking country even, before some cracker watching CNN news recognized his face and called the cops.

Nicky said, "Wesley, where the hell is Katherine?"

Under Wesley's gaze, Nicky seemed to shrink back into his chair. Then Wesley said, "Well, part of her is right there." He pointed at the box and watched as Nicky picked it up and looked inside.

Nicky screamed, "What'd you do? Jesus, what'd you do to my wife?"

"You'll find out soon enough, you fat little son of a bitch." And then Wesley smiled and said, "Hey, you got your suntan cream on?"

Nicky said, "What? No."

Wesley shook his head. "Too bad. Because we're goin' to the beach."

# CHAPTER

# NINETEEN

Ellis Bowers had been trying to get hold of Susie all morning. He'd called a dozen times. Standing in his kitchen and counting the rings, hanging up and getting a little more pissed off every time.

Finally, he'd gone over. When he didn't see her car in the parking lot, he let himself into the apartment. Some things were missing—some of her clothes, and some cash that she didn't know he knew about, and the picture that used to be over the fireplace—and it crossed his mind that maybe she'd gone off without him. He was trying to figure out where she would go. He drove back to his house slowly and then ran inside, fumbling with his keys and then sprinting into the kitchen because he heard the phone ringing.

He picked it up, saying, "Where the hell you been?" expecting to talk to Susie.

But he heard the Marine's voice instead, the man saying, "It ain't like that's too important. Long as I got you on the phone now."

Ellis's first thought was to hang up, because what if Susie *was* trying to call, trying to get in touch with him, and here he was wasting his time talking to the Marine. But then he thought, Hey, wait a minute. What was Jimmy Decker calling for, was it possible the man *still* wanted to buy the pictures?

He made an effort to sound nice, get a little bit of a different tone in his voice. "Hey, I was gonna call. See if we can't work this thing out."

Jimmy said, "Well, now I'm calling you." Sounding friendly to Ellis.

Ellis said, "I guess you still want those pictures, huh?

"No. They're not all that important. I got something else in mind."

Ellis was immediately suspicious. "What?"

"Hey, all it is, I got to run an errand, drive out to the beach and meet some people."

"What do you want me for?"

"Actually . . . see, I don't know these folks too well. Not that there's gonna be a problem. But I could use somebody else."

"You could use somebody to watch your back, right?"

Jimmy laughed. "I thought you'd understand."

"What's in it for me?" Ellis asked.

"Well, before, you and I, we were talking about ten grand. Wasn't that the number you had mentioned?"

"Yeah, ten grand. But that was for the pictures."

"Yeah, I know that. Seeing as how this is a bit more involved— not a big deal, but it might take up a little of your time—why don't we double that?"

Ellis couldn't believe his ears. "Twenty grand?"

"Yeah."

"Cash?"

"Ellis, it isn't like I'm gonna put it on my American Express card."

Ellis had to think it over. He didn't know where Susie was, didn't know what had happened in the last day and a half. It was like he was out of it. Maybe Susie had got what she wanted and then taken off. Left him here on his own. And Jimmy Decker was offering him twenty grand for what might not be a lot of work.

He said, "I want it up front."

Jimmy said, "Hey, you and I, it's not like we trust each other. I'll give you half now, the other half when we're through."

"What do I have to do, kill somebody?"

"No. This thing works out, everybody'll walk away happy. And you'll walk away a lot richer than when you woke up this morning."

Ellis said, "When?"

"Why don't I pick you up in an hour?"

"Have the money ready."

Jimmy said, "Absolutely."

"And listen, I don't care what you say, I'm bringing a gun. So don't try to fuck me over."

"Ellis, this here is a business deal. Nothing more than that." And then Jimmy hung up the phone.


Jimmy was getting a few things together as quickly as possible. He knew that he might not have a lot of time so he wanted to do the thing right. He was gonna go out to the beach, find Wesley, and try to get Katherine out of there. But how? It wasn't like he could come up with a plan until he saw what the situation was like from close up. The last thing he did was run up to the attic, rummage through some crates until he came up with his 30.06, the deer rifle that his old man had bought for his sixteenth birthday. He loaded it and put it in the trunk of the car next to the suitcases with the money in them.

He drove over to pick up Ellis Bowers. The man stalked out of his house and slid into the passenger seat, giving Jimmy a quick peek of the 9mm tucked into his waistband.

Jimmy pointed at the gun. "I told you, there's not gonna be a need for that."

Ellis said, "Fuck you." Adding, "And I ain't going anywhere till I get my money."

Jimmy smiled. "Here it is." He reached underneath the seat and pulled out a plastic garbage bag and handed it over. Ellis looked inside.

Jimmy said, "You can count it while we drive."

"Where's the rest?"

"You get the other ten grand when we're done."

He started the car and pulled out, taking Pigeon Point Road until it hit Carteret Street. Then he took a left and went past the university, past the Lord Carteret Motel and Fordham's Hardware and across the Beaufort River bridge.

Ellis asked, "Hey, where're we goin'?"

Jimmy grinned. "I forget to mention it. We're goin' to the beach."

"What for?"

"Ellis, why don't you do this, why don't you count your money, make sure I didn't shortchange you. When we get to where we're going, I'll let you know."

Wesley had brought Nicky out to the state park, Hunting Island, to the house that he'd stashed Katherine in. It was one of the privately owned cabins down by the southern tip, close to Fripp Island. As far as he could tell, there weren't any other people down here.

Katherine was lying on the floor when the two of them walked into the cabin. Wesley untied her, made her sit in a chair. The first thing out of her mouth when she saw Nicky was, "Nicky, look what he did to me. Do something!"

But Nicky was looking at her, stupefied. He said, "Jesus."

She looked like something out of the Second World War, like one of those pictures of Nazi collaborators that they'd chased out of Paris. Her head wasn't quite bald, but there wasn't much hair there either. If you took a chicken, plucked out most of its feathers, and cut it up a little bit at the same time, that's what Katherine looked like.

Wesley showed them his pistol again and said, "Hey, shut up, we're havin' a party." And then he handed Katherine the gin bottle and stood over her until she took a sip. And another. Saying, "Come on now, woman, you're a little hung over from last night. You know you want it. It'll loosen you up."

He put Nicky in a chair about ten feet in front of Katherine, so that the two of them faced each other, and then he stood where he could see them both.

He said, "Isn't this nice." And then he shot Nicky.

He did it because Nicky was being a pain in the ass. And because it was something he'd wanted to do ever since he met the man up in Atlantic City.

Nicky had been saying, "Hey, come on, there's no need for this. No hard feelings. Her hair'll grow back. I can take a joke."

Wesley had his .357 out and finally, when Nicky started to tell him, "Hey, you're waiting for the money, I know where we can get even more. Let me outta here, let me talk to Tom Neff . . ." Wesley had shaken his head, acted like it was sad that it had to come down to this, and then sighted carefully at Nicky's left arm and pulled the trigger.

The gun, going off so early in the morning, sounded like a bomb. Wesley felt the recoil, but kept his eyes glued to Nicky's face. The bullet tore into Nicky's arm and went straight through the chair, jerking Nicky backwards. Nicky cried out and fell over, grabbing his arm, and then he doubled over and puked all over the floor.

He looked at Wesley with a speck of vomit stuck to his chin and croaked, "Jesus . . . what'd you do . . . ?"

Katherine began to moan, "Oh my God," over and over.

Wesley glanced at her and said, "Take a drink." Pointing the pistol at her until she did.

Nicky was making gagging sounds. Wesley pulled a roll of duct tape out of his jacket pocket. He said, "See, I wasn't gonna put this over your mouth, but now it looks like I'm gonna have to."

When Nicky's mouth was taped, Wesley turned to Katherine and said, "Hey, Mrs. Kramer. Everything okay?" Being polite about it. "You still thirsty?"

Katherine was staring at Nicky, her eyes a little bit glazed over now, looking at the blood seeping through his fingers as he held his arm. For the first time she took a drink without Wesley saying anything.

Wesley grinned at her. "Well, let me know if you need anything."

He turned to Nicky. "Hey, you comfortable too?" And then he shot him in the arm again, waited for the sound to die down, and then asked, "How 'bout now?"

Katherine screamed.

"Shut up, woman," Wesley told her.

"You're *killing* him."

Wesley said, "I feel like killing *someone*. Maybe you'd rather it be you? How about I take my razor out and start on your ears?"

Nicky was saying something, grunting into the tape over his mouth. He'd bitten his lip and there was a trail of blood running down his chin. Wesley made a clucking noise with his tongue and said, "Nicky, you're gonna have to speak up." He tore the duct tape off Nicky's mouth.

"You crazy son of a bitch. What the fuck're you doing?" Nicky screamed.

Wesley nodded. "I thought that's what you said." He put the tape back on and then told Katherine, "We can play this game until I get the money. See what happens—do I get my money before your husband bleeds to death?"

He patted her bald skull. She tried to move away from him but he grabbed her and pulled her back, sticking his face next to hers. "Hey, *Mrs. Kramer,* you got to admit, it's gonna be interesting to find out which way it goes."

He was feeling great. He had Katherine, which was gonna make the Marine bring the money out. And meanwhile, he could play games with Nicky. And then maybe have a little *real* fun with Katherine, hold that straight razor to her throat and make her play some games with him. Make her work for it.

It really didn't matter if Nicky lived long enough to see the money delivered, because it wasn't like he was gonna live *after* that.

He said to Katherine, "I got an idea—why don't I scoop one of his eyeballs out, make him look just like me. I could use a spoon, something like that." He crouched down until his face was even with Katherine's. "How would that be? Nicky and me, we'd be twins."

And then he stood up, glanced at his watch, and told her, "It looks like something we might try. I think we got time for it." He turned to Nicky. "Whatta you say, Mr. Kramer? Would that be okay with you?"

———

Jimmy and Ellis got to the lighthouse on Hunting Island at about nine-thirty, driving past the entrance gate without stopping. There was no one at the public beach, no cars parked in the lot.

They drove around for about ten minutes before Jimmy decided that Wesley wouldn't have brought Katherine here. No, if he wanted privacy, someplace where there wouldn't be a lot of people, he'd take her down to the south end of the island. To where the cabins were. To where the lagoon began.

He stopped and took the rifle and the three cases out of the trunk, put the cases in the back seat, and leaned the 30.06 against the car door.

Ellis asked, "What's that for?"

"In case we see a deer."

Ellis said, "This is a state park. You can't shoot deer here."

Jimmy didn't know if the man was kidding or what.

Now, as they got closer, he told Ellis, "I'm looking for a car. When I see it parked by a house I'm gonna let you out. You're gonna count to two hundred and then you're gonna walk into the house and give a guy a bag. Then you walk back out here and I give you the other ten grand."

"Just walk in and walk out?"

Jimmy nodded. "Pretty simple, huh?" He rounded a bend in the road, saw where the pavement ended and the gravel road began. He slowed down to a crawl. Thirty seconds later he saw Wesley's car parked about two hundred feet down the road and stopped.

"Look at me," he said to Ellis. "Tell me what you're gonna do."

Ellis looked bored. "Shit—I get out, I count to a hundred . . ."

"*Two* hundred."

"Yeah, right. I count to two hundred and then I walk up to the door. Talk to whoever's in there. Give them the bag. And then I come back. Where're you gonna be?"

Jimmy reached into the back seat and pulled one of the cases up to the front.

Ellis said it again. "Where're you gonna be?"

Jimmy grabbed the rifle and stepped out of the car. He leaned back in and stared at Ellis. "I'm gonna be where I can see you every step of the way. So don't fuck it up."

Ellis said, "Hey, don't worry about it. Just have my money ready when I get back."

Jimmy said, "Start counting," and walked off into the brush.

Wesley said, "That's far enough." He was having to talk a little louder than normal because they were so close to the surf that conversation was difficult. Nicky and Katherine stopped. Wesley swung his head from side to side, convincing himself that there was nobody else around. Thinking, fuck, it had started to rain, the weather was shitty enough that the only thing that would get *him* out here was a million dollars. And then saying to himself, What a goddamn coincidence.

He had brought them out to the water because he didn't want anybody sneaking up on him. He wanted to be in a place where he could see for a good distance in every direction. He'd brought his own money too, the grocery bag with the cash, because he didn't want to let it out of his sight.

The two people in front of him looked pathetic. Katherine kept asking Nicky what was going to happen. She was drunk now, stumbling a lot, and every couple of minutes she'd turn to her husband and say, "Nicky, do something."

Nicky was gray with pain. He was holding his arm but trying to talk to Wesley. He'd stare at the pistol in Wesley's hand like he couldn't believe what was happening and mumble, "Hey, come on, hey, we can work this out." Knowing exactly what was going to happen but still acting like he and Wesley were pals.

Wesley finally had to tell them both to be quiet. He said to Nicky, "Hey, you don't shut your little woman up, make her close her mouth, I'm gonna do this the hard way."

But Katherine kept babbling. She had the bottle of gin in her hand and Wesley didn't have to tell her again to drink from it. Every once in a while she'd take a gulp. It made Wesley want to do her right there—shut the cunt up—but he wanted to get closer to the water, get right up there where the bay met the open ocean and the current would be the strongest. Get them both right there, down by the water's edge, and get it over with. Maybe let them beg a little bit first. And then push the bodies into the water and let 'em drift out to sea. Feed the sharks.

He was thinking he was probably gonna be nice and make it quick. Number one, he wanted to get out of here. He wanted the money and he wanted to be on a plane by that afternoon. He had decided to take his own cash too, even though the stuff was marked, because now that he was planning to leave the country he could spend a lot of it before he went. Do that and then bolt. Or maybe take it with him, go somewhere—Europe, Mexico, who the hell knew. Or maybe he could put it in one of those Swiss bank accounts. Leave it there for a couple of years while he lived off Nicky's cash—the legitimate money—until it was okay to start using the other.

So yeah, he was gonna be nice about it. He was gonna take these two assholes, the arrogant little kid and his drunken wife. He was gonna take them down to the water and put a bullet into their heads. And when the Marine showed up he was gonna take care of him too. Get *all* the money and he would be set for life.

It was working out fine.

From where he sat in the dunes Jimmy saw the three of them as little more than specks. He had expected them to be in the cabin so he had to look through the scope of the rifle before he was sure it was them. He saw the three of them, Katherine, Nicky—holding his shoulder—and Wesley, a couple of steps behind them. Wesley had what looked like a pistol in his hand. Katherine had something wrong with her head. Jesus, he realized, she had no hair. It looked like a little boy's head from this far away, as if somebody had stuck a bowl on her head and chopped everything off.

It took two seconds for Jimmy to realize what was gonna happen. The three of them, out there on the beach by themselves, it wasn't like they were looking for seashells.

He started to move towards them.

Down at the water's edge, Katherine asked again, "What are you gonna do?"

Nicky looked over at her and said, "Shut the fuck up." He was still holding his shoulder but he felt a little better. The fresh air had helped. He said to Wesley, "Look, you wanna take the cash? What the fuck do I care? Take it." Turning once more to Katherine, who had started to talk again, saying, "Goddamn, you don't shut the fuck up, I'm gonna *help* him kill you."

Wesley hadn't said anything for a couple of minutes. Nicky had the impression he was enjoying himself. His eyes seemed to close a couple of times, like he was feeling something inside. But the whole time, even though Wesley wasn't talking, that goddamn pistol didn't move an inch.

Nicky tried again. "Look, you win. Hey"—waving his hand in the air to get Wesley's attention—"you hear me? You want the money. Maybe . . . hey . . . maybe I can even get you more. Work something out. I'm serious, I can call Tom Neff and tell him we need more cash. Yeah . . . I'll do that . . . make a phone call. We can double your money. How would that be?"

When Wesley finally did speak it was like he was talking to himself. "You got any idea the shit I've taken? You got any *idea?* You got any idea how *hard* I worked? *They took my goddamn eye.*"

Nicky watched as Wesley began to work himself up to pulling the trigger.

He said, "Hey . . . Wesley . . . come on, man. This is *me*. Nicky. You want to work something out, hell, we can do that."

Wesley said, "Shut up." He was looking at Katherine, smiling now. "Hey, I know what. I'm gonna do him first. Make you watch. How would that be? Let you watch and see what it's gonna be like."

Nicky said, *"No!"* trying to figure out how far away he was from Wesley. Could he make a move, get the gun away from him?

Counting the feet between them and knowing he didn't have a chance in the world.

From where he was hidden Jimmy saw Ellis walk out the back door of the cabin and wander down to the beach. He was surprised Ellis showed so much initiative. The man was a hundred yards away from Wesley, Katherine, and Nicky. When he got a little closer he waved at them. Jesus, he looked like a clown. He had no idea what he was walking into.

Jimmy held the rifle to his shoulder and looked through the scope. He could see Nicky and Wesley too, holding a pistol in one hand and a grocery bag in the other. And then he looked at Katherine. She held a bottle and was swaying back and forth.

It went through his head that what he could do, he could forget about the whole thing. Go back up to the Ford and get out of there. Leave Katherine, Nicky, and Wesley to finish whatever it was. Let it happen. Wesley could take them both out, take care of Ellis too, and then come on back up here and wonder what the fuck had happened to the money.

But it wasn't a thing that he was even close to being able to do. Nicky, yeah, maybe he could leave Nicky with Wesley. That was something he might be able to do and still sleep every once in a while. But, Jesus, Katherine was down there too.

His training was taking over, as if he were on the range, or else back there in the Gulf, looking through the sight at Wesley, Nicky, Katherine, and Ellis like they were four goddamn Iraqis.

It wasn't something that he gave conscious thought to, the wind or the distance. It was just something that went through his mind as he settled the crosshairs on the back of Wesley's skull. Seeing the man through the scope as if he were fifty feet away, not two hundred yards, the back of his head about the size of a tennis ball from this distance. Jimmy told himself to hurry up. He took a deep breath and as he let it out started to squeeze the trigger.

Thinking, a Long Range Target Reduction Specialist. That's what he was. A specialist. Jesus Christ.


When Ellis was twenty feet away, Wesley yelled, "What the fuck're you doing here?"

Ellis grinned. "He told me to go to the cabin, said to give this to whoever was there." He held up the suitcase and said, "I guess that's you, huh?"

Wesley said, "Open it."

"Sure." He crouched down and started to unsnap the locks of the suitcase, then glanced up at Katherine, gaping at her shorn head. He said to her, "Hey, long time no see." Then he opened the suitcase, peeked inside, and looked puzzled. He said, "Hey, I don't know what you got going, but somebody's fucking around with you."

Wesley took a step towards him, the gun in one hand and the grocery bag in the other. He said, "Move."

"What?"

He pushed Ellis with his foot and said, "Get the fuck out of the way."

He put the grocery bag down and reached into the suitcase, felt around for a second and then came up with a handful of cut newspapers.

He whirled towards Ellis. "Is this some kind of joke, asshole?" He didn't give Ellis a chance to speak, just raised the .357 and shot him in the throat.

Ellis was lifted off his feet and thrown down like he was made of rubber.

Wesley picked up his grocery bag and said to Katherine, "You got a real friend, Mrs. Kramer. Motherfucker doesn't really care about you, he pulls a stunt like this."

He pointed the gun at Nicky's head and said, "You sorry little prick, you're dead now."

Katherine saw Wesley's face explode towards her like it had been pumped up with air and then burst. It was like something you'd see in slow motion on one of those nature channels. Wesley's head looked like it was being hit by an unseen bird of prey. The grocery bag went flying up into the air, hit the ground, and broke open.

It didn't make the slightest bit of sense to her. Even when she heard the crack of the rifle, a second after the man's face disintegrated, she still didn't know what had occurred. She'd gone from being very drunk to suddenly realizing that the man had brought them out here to kill them. It had been that quick. One minute she was asking Nicky what was going on and the next minute she knew she was going to die.

Then Wesley's face disappeared.

She looked at Nicky, saw he was stunned too. Jesus, here they were. The two of them. Out here with two dead men at their feet and neither one of them knew what had happened.

Nicky came out of it first. He yelled, "The *money,*" and threw himself down onto the sand. With his good hand he started to pick up the bills that had fallen out of Wesley's grocery bag. He shouted, "Kate, what're you doing? Get the goddamn money."

He looked demented, eyes wide and his hair spiked out at crazy angles, with a wad of cash in his hand. Swaying back and forth like he was on a boat, the whole side of his body covered in blood as if a wave had come up and splashed him with red seawater.

And then it hit her, too. All that cash, flying along the beach. It was getting away. Jesus, it was fluttering in the breeze and she was just standing there, letting Nicky get it. She forgot about Wesley and Ellis, forgot about everything but the bills swirling along the beach. She started to scurry around on her hands and knees almost, grabbing fistfuls of twenty-dollar bills, stuffing her pockets, working her way over to where Nicky was.

She began to count to herself, calculating by hundreds in her head. Grabbing fistfuls of money and trying to estimate as she went along how much she was picking up. When her pockets got full she began to stuff the money in her shirt, getting frustrated because it slowed her down. She had to stand up every couple of seconds and put a handful down her blouse. But then she'd go right back to it.

She got to a spot near Wesley, and tried to work her way around his body without looking at him. Some of the money had blood on it. How was she going to clean it off? Were you supposed to use cold water or something?

When she actually got next to Wesley's body she spit on it. Told the corpse, "You never should have cut my hair." And then she went back to the money.

She and Nicky were close enough to bump heads when a shadow fell across them. Katherine looked up. Jimmy Decker was ten feet away, carrying a rifle. For a second she hadn't realized who it was. She didn't want to lose count and had to squint into the sun to look up at him.

She wanted to run to him and throw herself into his arms, but if she did, some of the cash might fall out of her shirt. Suddenly she remembered her hair, how it must look, and she tried to hide her head with her hand. And then she saw the expression on his face. Like Jimmy had seen something that he hadn't wanted to.

He didn't say a word. She heard Nicky's voice from behind her. She stood up slowly, hearing Nicky yell again, but still looking at Jimmy.

Jimmy stared back and finally said, "It's getting away."

She was confused. "What?"

He pointed with the rifle. "The money, it's blowing into the water."

She saw that he was right. Some of the money had reached the water. Nicky was in the surf, jumping around like a madman, like an osprey plucking fish from the waves. When she turned, Jimmy had already started back into the dunes.

She yelled his name—"JIMMY"—as loudly as she could. He kept walking.

Behind her she heard Nicky shouting. She turned and saw he was on the beach, still grabbing at the money with his one good arm. He called, "Katherine, Jesus, come on."

She watched him dumbly for a few seconds and then bent down and picked up a twenty-dollar bill.

# CHAPTER

# TWENTY

Jimmy crossed the Florida border about four o'clock that afternoon, going through Jacksonville on I-95 and then stopping for gas just before the exit for St. Augustine. It had been in his mind, ever since he'd left Beaufort, that what he'd do, he'd head down to the Keys. Not really caring which one he ended up at. He could buy his own car, find a cheap place to stay, and maybe drink rum punches on the beach for a while. See how that felt.

When he had shot Wesley Hops it felt good. Like he was back in the corps, on the range, and the man's head was nothing more than a target. Something that he was supposed to be shooting at. Jimmy, squatting in the dunes, smelling the salt from the ocean, had let himself go. Let his brain wander until he really was at war. The whole thing—ever since he'd gotten back into town and run into Katherine—becoming nothing more than an extension of the Gulf War, another part of his career as a Marine.

He saw it now—the last few days—what had happened since he'd gotten into town and how he had never given himself a chance to think it through clearly. He had loved Beaufort. Loved growing up in it, fishing, crabbing, whatever. The smell of the ocean and the way you could tell time by what the tide was. It had always given him a sense of well-being, the lazy feel of the summer heat, the way things seemed to move a little bit slower here than a lot of other places he'd been.

But it wasn't a place that he could come back to. He should have known that. It wasn't going to offer him what he was looking for. Spending time with Katherine, trying to retrieve something that was long dead. None of it was really there for him anymore.

He could have done things differently. Told Katherine he wasn't gonna help her. Tried to begin a new life here. But even so, what he'd been attempting to do, attempting to find—ain't no way it was there to start with.

He felt like crying.

Now, pulling into an Exxon station, with his gas gauge on empty, he wasn't thinking about much of anything except making it through Miami before it got dark. The place had pumps out front and a garage with a couple of bays attached to a little convenience store, with a Dairy Queen built off to the side.

He started to walk past the store by the bays and over to the Dairy Queen. He thought he'd get a cone, something cold. He didn't even see the car on the lift at first. Then he took a couple of steps backwards and looked inside the garage to where a mechanic stood underneath a Mazda. A chill ran up his spine because it *couldn't* be. He saw the license plate, a South Carolina tag on a Mazda RX-7, and had to remind himself that there were hundreds of them just like that from South Carolina. He told himself he was tired from spending too much time fighting the traffic on 95 and then he started walking towards the Dairy Queen again.

But when he saw her, he knew right away who it was. Prettier than he remembered, like a girl on a postcard. She was sitting on the other side of the Dairy Queen at a table set up so that she was facing the highway.

The first thought that went through his head was that he should turn around, get back in his car, and go down 95 to the next exit. He didn't know, if he walked up to her—after she got over the shock of his being here—was she maybe gonna reach into that purse of hers and pull that pistol out again? He could see the side of her face where he'd hit her. The bruise showed through even though it looked like she'd put some makeup over it.

He stepped inside the Dairy Queen and moved all the way up to the counter while he made up his mind what to do. She wouldn't see him unless she turned all the way around and twisted her neck to look inside the building. He wondered what was wrong with her car. The girl behind the counter asked him what he wanted and he told her two cones because, all of a sudden, he didn't want to hide.

The girl got his ice cream and then he walked on out the door, hearing the bell jingle over his head as he made his way to her table.

She started to say something to him, seeing his shadow, speaking without looking up. "The table's taken. . . ." But then she glanced up, saw who it was, and said, "Jesus Christ." Much more startled than when he'd sneaked up on her in the parking lot of her apartment house and taken the money from her.

Jimmy tried to be nonchalant but had trouble carrying it off. So he held out one of the ice cream cones to her and then sat down. It took her a couple of seconds, staring at him with a look on her face that Jimmy couldn't read, before she reached over and took it.

She took a lick of the cone and then finally she spoke, asking quietly, "You following me?"

He shook his head. "Unh-uh. I'm driving south is all."

"Getting out of Beaufort, huh? You got what you wanted and now you're leaving?" She didn't sound too mad, though.

He didn't say anything, couldn't think of anything to tell her because it wasn't what he was doing at all.

She must have seen something in his face, maybe he looked like he felt, because all of a sudden she smiled and said, "Jesus. You're running. You're getting out of there because it didn't work out. Whatever you had in mind, it didn't work out at all."

He was a little bit bothered that she could read his mind that easily. Feeling defensive but also not up to lying. "No, I had a different idea of things. A different feeling as to how things were gonna be."

She stared at him and then smiled. "You loved her." Like it had all of a sudden occurred to her and she was having trouble believing it. Saying it again. "God, you *loved* her."

"I don't know what I felt."

She nodded. "Yeah, well, coming into a situation like that . . ." Dismissing it because it wasn't that important to her but sympathizing with him.

"So, you're here. She's where, back in Beaufort?" she asked.

He nodded. "I think she had a change of heart."

"Uh-huh. I think, looking back on it—Nicky being scared that she was going to mess up his deal, his chance to swindle everybody—that wasn't what she had in mind at all."

"What do you mean?"

"I don't know, but maybe all Katherine had in mind was teaching Nicky a lesson. Making him pay attention to her."

"You think that was all it was?"

"Hey, I don't know." She got up and walked over to the trash can and dumped the rest of her cone in it. Then she looked back towards the garage where the mechanic was working on her car.

Jimmy asked, "What's the matter with it?"

"It quit. That's all I know. I was driving along and the damn thing just stopped running." She ran her hand through her hair and took a deep breath. "Hey, it's been a bad day all over."

Jimmy smiled at her now, the first time he remembered grinning at anything since he left the beach. He looked at Susie. "Yeah, it has."

He had a lot of ideas going through his head. He wasn't sure what he was thinking exactly because he couldn't pin any one of them down long enough to examine it carefully. Finally, he cleared his throat. One idea he was getting seemed to be better than anything else he could think of. He told her, "Hey, you know what you *could* do?"

She said, "What?"

He didn't give it any more thought. Wouldn't let himself because if he did, he might decide that it was stupid. Looking at her, with the cars whipping by behind them and his own car, the rented Ford, parked twenty feet away, he said, "You *could* go on over to the garage, tell the mechanic not to worry too much about what's wrong with your car."

She took a step towards him. "Why would I want to do that?"

"See, you do that, tell him . . . I don't know . . . he can keep the thing even."

"What am I going to do without a car?"

"You want a car. We can get you a car. We get down to Miami, we can stop somewhere and pick up an automobile."

There was about ten seconds when all Jimmy could hear was the sound of the traffic and the drone of the insects in the air. Ten seconds while Susie walked slowly back to the table and sat down. Looking at him like she had just met him and maybe there was something wrong with his face—he had a wart on his nose or something. He didn't say anything. Just sat still while she got used to the idea.

She said, "I leave the car here, walk on over and tell the mechanic to forget about it, and then you and I, we head down to Miami?"

"I was gonna go down into the Keys."

She said, "Uh-huh. The Keys are nice." Looking at the garage and then glancing back at Jimmy. "You hit me last night—took that money away from me. And now I'm supposed to just hop in your car and take off with you?"

He shrugged. "If you want. If you want to let that other stuff bother you, that's okay too."

He watched her think about it. And then she was gone, walking over to the bays and talking to someone inside the garage that Jimmy couldn't see.

He was happier now, thinking maybe this could work. She was somebody he could understand. A hardworking girl who knew what she wanted. And had almost gotten it. None of the bullshit that he'd had with Katherine, worrying was he gonna upset her feelings or not. He watched Susie walk back, seeing the way her hips moved, the way her jeans fit her legs. Thinking to himself, give it a little time, maybe—who the hell knew?—maybe they'd end up liking each other.

She smiled at him, her hands on her hips, and then said, "What do you think, you gonna sit there all day?" Starting to laugh as he stood up. Waiting for him to get to her and then sliding her arm through his like it was the most natural thing in the world. He could feel the skin of her arm on his and liked the way it felt. Walking back to his Ford with her and listening to her laugh quietly.

She was kidding around, making her voice sound like somebody's nagging wife. "Don't forget to get gas. We run out of gas like we did the last time you took me to Disney World and you're not going to hear the end of it." But then she stopped him, grabbed his arm hard, and pulled him to a halt. "You *do* have that money?"

"I got most of it."

"Most?"

"I gave about half away." Thinking back to it—Nicky scrambling to pick up the bills on the sand and then Katherine, half-bald, bending down to help him. What was gonna happen when they tried to spend them? How long before the FBI caught up to them? He told Susie, "I gave Wesley's share away."

She said, "Okay." Taking another couple of steps and then squinting up at his face and saying, "Hey, you know something?"

"What?"

She said it seriously, like it wasn't something she was going to kid around about, "My momma would've liked you."

He laughed then, feeling good all of a sudden. "Hey, maybe I would've liked her."

They started to walk towards his car again, with Jimmy wondering for a second what would have happened if he had said he didn't have any of the money. Wondering did he care?

And then deciding, probably not.